DEAD IN TH

Simon McCleave is a million
first book, *The Snowdonia Ki*
ary 2020 and soon became an Amazon bestseller, reaching
No.1 in the UK Chart and selling over 400,000 copies.
His fifteen subsequent novels in the DI Ruth Hunter
Snowdonia series have all ranked in the Amazon top 20
and he has sold over two million books worldwide. *Dead
in the Water* is the fifth book in the Anglesey series.

Before he was an author, Simon worked as a script editor
at the BBC and a producer at Channel 4 before working
as a story analyst in Los Angeles. He then became a script
writer, writing on series such as *Silent Witness*, *Murder In
Suburbia*, *Teachers*, *The Bill*, *EastEnders* and many more.
His Channel 4 film *Out of the Game* was critically ac-
claimed and described as 'an unflinching portrayal of male
friendship' by *Time Out*.

Simon lives in North Wales with his wife and two children.

www.simonmccleave.com

To find out more visit **www.simonmccleave.com**

DEAD IN THE WATER

SIMON McCLEAVE

avon.

Published by AVON
A division of HarperCollins*Publishers*
1 London Bridge Street
London SE1 9GF

www.harpercollins.co.uk

HarperCollins*Publishers*
Macken House, 39/40 Mayor Street Upper
Dublin 1, D01 C9W8
Ireland

A Paperback Original 2024
1
First published in Great Britain by HarperCollins*Publishers* 2024

A catalogue copy of this book is available from the British Library.

ISBN: 978-0-00-862024-0

This novel is entirely a work of fiction. The names, characters and incidents
portrayed in it are the work of the author's imagination. Any resemblance to
actual persons, living or dead, events or localities is entirely coincidental.

Set in Sabon LT Std by HarperCollins*Publishers* India

Printed and bound in the UK using 100% Renewable Electricity at CPI Group (UK) Ltd

MIX
Paper | Supporting
responsible forestry
FSC™ C007454

This book contains FSC™ certified paper and other controlled sources
to ensure responsible forest management.
For more information visit: www.harpercollins.co.uk/green

To Izzy and George

ANGLESEY

There is a word in Welsh that has no exact translation into English – Hiraeth. It is best defined as the bond you feel with a place – a mixture of pride, homesickness and a determination to return. Most people that have visited Anglesey leave with an understanding of Hiraeth.

YNYS LLANDDWYN

The small tidal island of Ynys Llanddwyn, just off the south-west coast of Anglesey, is named after the patron saint of Welsh lovers – Dwynwen. It is believed she lived in the fifth century and was the daughter of King Brychan Brycheiniog. She fell in love with a man called Maelon, whom she was forced by her father to reject. Dwynwen subsequently dedicated herself to helping those unhappy in their love lives, eventually building a home on this remote island.

The ruins of a medieval church dedicated to Dwynwen can still be seen today, and fourteenth-century poet Dafydd ap Gwilym claimed he saw a golden image of her at the site when he visited. Every year on the twenty-fifth of January, Wales celebrates St Dwynwen's Day, similar to St Valentine's Day in many places around the world.

Thomas Pennant's account from the 1770s mentions small ruins nearby being the prebendal house, which housed Richard Kyffyn in the fifteenth century. He worked with Sir Rhys ap Thomas and other Welsh chieftains to plan for Henry Tudor's return from exile in Brittany, using fishing vessels to send intelligence to him.

At St Dwynwen's Well on Ynys Llanddwyn Island, a sacred fish is said to predict the fate of couples in love; while unsettled waters in the well signals good luck and contentment.

Nearby are two beacons: one that looks like a windmill tower but has been abandoned; the other a guide for ships passing through the perilous Menai Strait, with cottages built to house the pilots who boarded them. In December 1852, this lighthouse saved thirty-six people from three shipwrecks within seven days.

Rocks and geology from about 500 million years ago form the foundations of Ynys Llanddwyn Island – where pillow lavas gracing its beaches demonstrate the awesome underwater forces that shaped it, beginning south of New Zealand. The island has been named in the First 100 World Geological Heritage Sites list – key geological sites of international scientific relevance with a substantial contribution to the development of geological sciences through history.

This place also forms part of a National Nature Reserve, which includes Newborough Warren to the south and The Cefni saltmarsh to the north, all managed by Natural Resources Wales.

PROLOGUE

Anglesey, North Wales
April 2022

It had been half an hour since Detective Inspector Laura Hart of the Anglesey Police Force had been taken hostage. She had been forced at gunpoint to drive the sleek black Audi A5 convertible out of her hometown of Beaumaris on the south coast of the island.

Gripping the steering wheel, she hammered south towards the Menai Bridge which would take them across to the Welsh mainland and beyond. She wondered how the hell she'd managed to find herself in this situation.

What made the whole thing terrifyingly surreal was that sitting in the passenger seat, pointing a Glock 17 handgun at her ribs, was Detective Chief Inspector Pete Marsons of the MMP – the Manchester Metropolitan Police.

Laura pressed the brakes and slowed the car as they came up behind a gleaming white caravan that was being towed by an equally gleaming white BMW 4x4.

Pete looked over at her as if to say *Don't do anything stupid.*

1

For a moment, their eyes met, and Laura felt a sharp emotional pain deep inside her gut.

Jesus, Pete. How has it come to this? she thought to herself with overwhelming astonishment.

DCI Pete Marsons.

Pete. Uncle Pete.

Until very recently, Laura had counted Pete as one of her closest friends. In fact, there had been times when she'd thought of him as the brother she never had. Pete had been her late husband's best mate. Laura, Sam and Pete had trained at Hendon Police College together in the nineties and stayed friends ever since. As probationers on the beat in Manchester, they'd shared their stories of first arrests, scrapes and the highs and lows of those first few months as rookie police officers. And at night, they'd partied together in the bars and clubs of Manchester.

After that, they had been on family holidays together to Pembrokeshire as Pete had kids a similar age to Rosie and Jake. He was godfather to both her children.

Pete had been standing next to Laura when Sam had perished in an explosion at Brannings Warehouse nearly four years ago during a police operation.

They'd picked Sam's favourite songs for his funeral, written her eulogy and then held hands as his coffin had been lowered into the ground to the sound of the Manchester Police pipers.

This can't be happening, can it?

Laura stopped the car at some traffic lights. She glanced over at nearby houses and at cars coming the other way. Everyone was going about their day completely oblivious to the shocking events that had unfolded in her life in the past thirty minutes.

Pete waved the Glock 17 from where he was holding it down by his hip.

'Easy does it, Laura,' he said in a low voice.

For a moment, she couldn't quite believe what was happening. It was like a bad anxiety dream that she was going to wake up from any moment. Maybe if she shook her head or pinched herself she would be taken back to a world where something this hideous wasn't taking place.

Then she fixed Pete with a cold glare.

'Jesus, what the hell happened to you?' Laura hissed.

Pete ignored her.

Laura was trying to process everything that had led up to this moment. She and Pete had spent the past three years trying to uncover who had been responsible for her husband Sam's death. Neither of them were convinced by the results of the Independent Office for Police Conduct's (IOPC's) report and investigation into Sam's death that day. In fact, they became increasingly suspicious of the lead officer on the operation, Superintendent Ian Butterfield. The more they investigated Sam's death, the more they had realised that there had been something much darker going on that day.

It became clear that Butterfield was being blackmailed and paid off by the Fallowfield Hill Gang – a powerful organised crime group (OCG) based in Manchester – to provide intel as well as tip-offs about arrests and raids. It was also apparent that this corruption stretched into the upper echelons of the MMP.

Just over a month ago, Butterfield had been found murdered after he had gone walking on Worsaw Hill in Lancashire. And to her shock, Laura had been anonymously sent CCTV that showed that it might have been Pete who killed Butterfield that day.

And now Laura knew that not only was Pete a corrupt officer, but he had been for a long time.

It was devastating.

3

Laura felt a mixture of nervous nausea and utter fury.

'You killed Sam that day?' Laura asked in an accusatory tone.

'No.' Pete shook his head. 'Sam wasn't meant to be there,' he said quietly.

'Bollocks.' Laura virtually spat the word. She knew he was lying to her – again. 'Sam was on to you wasn't he?'

Pete didn't say anything. She had her answer.

'You got someone to make that 999 call that lured him to the warehouse,' Laura growled. 'I know that was you. Jesus, it's pointless lying to me now.'

Pete nodded up to the traffic lights which had now turned green.

'Just drive, will you?' he sighed wearily.

'Where the hell are we going?' she demanded.

He didn't reply. Maybe he just didn't know.

There was a noise from the boot of the car.

Banging and muffled shouting.

Pete had admitted to Laura half an hour earlier that he'd also kidnapped Claudia Wright, an investigative journalist from the *Sunday Times*. She was now lying trapped in the boot of the car.

Laura glanced back anxiously for a second. It was Laura's fault that Claudia was involved in this. Laura had contacted her a few days earlier with her suspicions about corruption in the Manchester Metropolitan Police and specifically Pete's role in it. Claudia had kept Laura in the loop as she started to dig around. However Claudia had inadvertently alerted Pete to the fact that he was being investigated.

And now she was trapped in the boot of Pete's car.

'You can't keep her in there,' Laura snapped angrily.

Pete shrugged. 'I'll do whatever I want.'

Laura shook her head and gave him a withering look.

4

How could the man who had been such a huge part of their lives – the man her children called Uncle Pete, the man they doted on– become this monster?

'What was it, Pete? Money?' she asked with disdain.

Pete didn't answer her.

They drove in silence as Laura tried to fathom how she was ever going to escape. No one knew where she was. And no one in Beaumaris CID was going to notice her absence for several hours. By that time they could be through Wales and across the border into North West England. And the only person on the planet who knew about her suspicions about Pete was her fiancé, DI Gareth Williams. It would take Gareth far too long to connect her disappearance to Pete.

And then there was a far darker question. Was Pete really going to let her or Claudia go? He couldn't. They knew far too much. Which meant that Pete was planning to kill them and somehow dispose of their bodies. Given that she knew Pete was on the payroll of the Fallowfield Hill Gang, she assumed that's where he was taking them. It would be gang members who would do Pete's dirty work for him.

That meant Laura had to do something drastic. And soon. She wasn't going to drive to Manchester to whatever grisly fate was awaiting them. Not without a fight at least.

They drove for another ten minutes. Above them, the sky was empty, a pale, colourless, radiant void.

Laura's mind raced as to how she was going to make sure she and Claudia were going to get away safely.

Glancing at the rear-view mirror, Laura saw something that gave her an idea.

Completely by chance, there was a white BMW 530 marked police car behind them. However, there was no reason to think that the officers inside had any idea that she was being forced to drive at gunpoint. And she couldn't exactly signal to them and risk Pete shooting her.

But she now had an idea.

And unless Pete looked in the wing mirror, he would have no clue that there was a marked police unit behind them.

A red circular 50 mph speed restriction sign went past.

Here goes, she thought.

Pushing slowly down on the accelerator, she gradually moved the Audi from the speed limit of 50 mph up to 60 mph.

Looking out of the corner of her eye, she saw that Pete was deep in thought. She hoped that he didn't feel or notice that they were gradually picking up speed.

Moving her foot down on the accelerator very slowly, she increased their speed up to 65 mph.

She watched the police unit in the rear-view mirror while trying to conceal their presence from Pete.

Then she continued pressing the pedal down, millimetre by careful millimetre.

Up to 70 mph.

Her pulse was now racing as she took a surreptitious look at the BMW in the rear-view mirror.

Come on, come on. What are you waiting for? I'm bloody speeding!

She held her breath for a moment, willing them to notice her speed.

Then the blue lights on top of the BMW burst into life.

Thank God, she thought to herself with an inward sigh.

The plan had started to work.

As she reduced speed a little, she continued to drive as normally as possible. The longer the BMW was behind them, the more likely that officers would start to check their registration and register with their Dispatch that Laura was failing to pull over.

With her heart now thumping against her chest, Laura took another deep breath. Her mind was whirring with all the possible ways this was going to play out.

Suddenly, the noise of the BMW's two-tone siren filled the air.

It startled Laura and made her jump.

Twisting around, Pete spotted the car. 'Shit!'

Then he glared suspiciously at Laura. 'How long have they been there?'

Laura shrugged innocently. 'I've only just seen them,' she protested.

'I don't believe that for a second.' Pete looked at her sceptically and then snapped, 'Speed up.'

'What?' Laura frowned. 'Really?'

'You think we're just going to pull over to see what they want?' Pete snorted. 'Drive faster, now!'

Laura pushed the accelerator slightly.

What the hell are we doing?

70 mph.

Pete's eyes were full of anxiety as he turned around again. Then he looked at her. 'Faster.'

Laura took the car up to 75 mph.

She felt a hard, metallic jab in her ribs and looked down. Pete had pushed the Glock 17 into her side.

'Don't piss me about, Laura. I said faster,' Pete growled at her.

Laura pressed the accelerator down with such force that the car bolted with the sudden burst of speed. She gripped the wheel, trying to control the car. Her knuckles were white with the effort of holding the wheel. Her breathing was quick and shallow.

95 mph.

She felt sick.

Pete raised the Glock 17, leaned across and pushed the barrel against her ribs.

'Understand me, you need to go faster,' he said with menace.

'Jesus, we're going at a hundred, Pete,' Laura said as they overtook a caravan which went past in a blur.

Pete looked at her. 'Let's be very clear here. I'd prefer to die in this car than go to prison for the rest of my life. So, if you don't go faster, I'm going to shoot you. Do you understand?'

'All right, all right, I understand,' she said in a whisper. She tried to keep her breathing under control, but she was terrified.

Pete removed the barrel of the gun from her side as she pushed the accelerator so that it was hard against the floor of the car.

She clasped the steering wheel but the muscles in her hands were now aching with the effort.

One false move, one tiny mistake, and they would all be dead.

Cottages whizzed past them so fast that it was impossible to make out any of their detail.

Glancing at the rear-view mirror, she saw that the police BMW was still directly behind her. She knew they would have called for back-up by now.

For a moment, she thought of her children. Rosie, nineteen years old, and Jake, who was twelve. They'd already had to suffer the pain of losing their father four years ago. She refused to accept that they would have to go through that again. She was going to come out of this alive – she just needed to work out how.

Suddenly, a thunderous mechanical noise seemed to fill the sky.

What the hell is that? she thought, glancing up.

The looming shape of a black and yellow EC145 police helicopter appeared over the horizon and headed their way at high speed.

'Fuck!' Pete yelled.

There was no way they were going to escape now. The helicopter would be with them until they stopped.

And Laura knew what was going to happen if they didn't stop. They would be forcibly brought to a halt by something like a stinger – a long string of metal spikes – which would be pulled across the road to burst the tyres of a car.

If they were brought to a stop, then what? Pete might well shoot her, possibly Claudia and then himself in a murder suicide.

How the hell am I going to get out of this?

Laura felt a helpless desperation unlike any she'd experienced before.

Then she remembered something. A serious road traffic accident (RTA) she had attended about six months ago. The driver had been wearing their seatbelt and survived. The passenger hadn't been wearing theirs… and didn't.

Giving it a surreptitious feel with her right hand, Laura checked that her own seatbelt was firmly in place. Then she glanced down. Pete was wearing his seatbelt too.

It was a long shot, but she had to try something.

As they cornered a long bend at 90 mph, Laura could hear the tyres squealing under the car.

They hit a straight stretch of road.

To their left, the road was flanked by a long, dry-stone wall.

However, she couldn't swerve and drive into it at 90 mph. She and Claudia would never survive that.

She took a nervous gulp.

Laura pushed the brakes to slow the car a little. Her mind was racing with what to do next – and when to do it.

'What are you doing?' Pete yelled angrily. 'Keep driving!'

70 mph.

Laura grimaced. 'I've got a cramp in my foot.'

Pete pushed the gun hard into her temple.

'Bollocks,' he barked loudly. 'Speed up or I'm going to shoot you.'

60 mph.

Laura looked at him. 'I'm being serious. Just give me a second and I'll be all right.'

Pete's hand started to shake as he pushed the gun harder into her skull.

'I'm not fucking joking! I'm going to shoot you!' he screamed.

50 mph.

Laura eased off the brakes as she realised that it was now or never.

Now!

With a violent turn of the steering wheel, Laura spun the car hard left across a large patch of grass.

The car skidded left and then right as they hurtled towards the dry-stone wall.

'What are you doing?' Pete screamed as the car bounced on the uneven ground.

Laura smashed Pete's arm away just as he pulled the trigger to kill her.

CRACK!

The bullet flew up through the roof.

Hitting Pete with her shoulder, Laura leant down and clicked the red button to release his seatbelt.

She looked up and held her breath.

This is it! Please God don't let me die!

The dry-stone wall was about ten yards away.

Pete glanced at her, realising what she'd done and why.

His hand shot down to grab the seatbelt.

He was too late.

CRASH!

There was the thunderous sound of metal collapsing and glass shattering.

The airbags deployed with a loud hiss.

Laura closed her eyes.

Oh God!

As if in slow motion, Laura felt her whole body being thrown forward and then back. Her head cracked against the passenger door.

Shit!

The car came to a rest and for a few seconds there was an eerie silence.

She sat upright in the seat trying to get her breath and blinking to clear her head. There was a throbbing pain in her temple where she'd banged it.

Then she glanced uneasily over at the passenger seat.

It was empty.

The windscreen in front of her was smashed and splattered with blood.

Outside, Pete's body lay twisted where he had been hurled against the wall. His face was shrouded in dark blood and glass.

His eyes were still open.

He was dead.

CHAPTER 1

HMP Tonsgrove, Anglesey
Tuesday, 18 October 2022
09.22 a.m.

HMP Tonsgrove was a women's prison on Anglesey with a current roll of 760 prisoners. It had been built in 2011 with the intention of it being a Category C prison. That meant that female prisoners who were either coming to the end of longer sentences and close to release on probation or had short sentences that didn't involve violence. The prison's philosophy had been focused on rehabilitation, enabling prisoners to develop skills and education so they could resettle back into the community and find employment. However, in 2018, due to cuts in the UK Prison Service, overcrowding and issues retaining prison officers, the prison began to be used to house Category B prisoners who were serving longer sentences for more serious and violent crimes. The mix of new Category B prisoners and the more established Category C prisoners had proved explosive at times and deemed by the local press and media as a disaster.

Sheila Jones was coming to the end of a sentence for possession and intent to supply Class A drugs in various locations along the North Wales coast. Originally from Wrexham, Sheila had started to go out with a Liverpudlian drug dealer, Shane Deakins, who was affiliated to the Croxteth Boyz gang in Merseyside. Deakins was running a county lines drug-dealing operation out of Colwyn Bay. The NCA – the National Crime Agency – which was the UK's leading force against organised crime and drug trafficking, had been running a surveillance operation on Deakins but it had been Sheila who had ended up being caught in possession of the imported heroin and crack cocaine in Llandudno.

As Sheila arrived on G wing she was greeted by the heady mixture of over-cooked vegetables, body odour and cheap deodorant.

Home sweet home, she thought sardonically.

Music was blaring from somewhere, so everyone had to talk louder to be heard. It was a bloody racket. It was the usual mixture of junkies, prostitutes, scammers and thieves.

Because Sheila was affiliated to a Merseyside gang, she had status and respect from the other prisoners. She knew it was because they feared what would happen to them if they crossed her. Not only would they be intimidated or attacked inside Tonsgrove, their families would be targeted on the outside. Sheila knew there was nothing more powerful and persuasive than telling a prisoner that someone was watching their children going to school. Stuff like that worked a dream.

Looking around, Sheila saw a couple of the girls playing table tennis in the recreation area. On the far side, Fay was braiding someone's hair. To look at her, it was hard to believe that Fay had tossed her baby off the sixth floor of a block of council flats in Liverpool. She was blonde, petite

13

and very pretty. Her defence had been that she'd been suffering from post-partem psychosis but that's not how the jury or the judge saw it. They rejected her defence of diminished responsibility and gave her twenty years. Sheila couldn't understand it. Why would a mother throw her own baby off a balcony unless she was seriously insane?

A huge woman with short hair, tattoos and a fierce expression gave her a nod. Jenny, on the other hand, had stabbed her abusive husband fifty times with a screwdriver after a drunken fight. She told Sheila she had counted each stab out loud, all the way to fifty as her other half lay cowering and bleeding to death. Jenny now did yoga and meditation most mornings with a group of women in the main rec room.

Walking up the main central staircase, Sheila made her way along the open balcony. She got a cheery wave from some of the Liverpudlian girls that she'd befriended since being inside. Most of them had ties to Croxteth or Norris Green in Liverpool. That's how it worked inside. You kept to your own for protection.

Except Sheila had broken the golden rule, which meant she now had to watch her back. It was making her feel uneasy. The fact that they had all waved up at her from down on the recreation area reassured her that she was safe. For now.

Drugs were the primary cause of trouble within the prison. Those who dealt them fought each other for control of the market. And the junkies would do anything to get a fix: fight, steal, have sex… anything.

Sheila made her way towards her pad that she shared with a newbie called Hayley, a 21-year-old girl from Welshpool, who had got three years for dealing weed. Hayley was still terrified most of the time but Sheila had taken her under her wing. She felt sorry for her and Hayley reminded her of her own daughter.

14

'You okay?' Sheila asked as she came into their pad.

There were two single beds that were screwed into the floor and the wall. There was an olive green blanket over each bed. Green plastic cutlery, plates and bowls were arranged on a small cabinet. On the walls by both beds were the obligatory photos of friends and family.

Hayley was watching the TV that was fixed to the wall. The first time Sheila had been banged up they'd been lucky to get a bloody radio in the cell, let alone a TV.

Hayley smiled but she looked nervous. 'Yeah. I'm just gonna…' She gestured to the door and scuttled out anxiously.

What's that all about? Sheila wondered.

A few seconds later, as the doorway darkened with a figure, Sheila realised why Hayley had made herself scarce.

'What the fuck are you doing?' Sheila asked with a frown.

The figure closed the door.

They gave her a look which made her feel very uneasy.

She started to back away as she saw that the figure had pulled out a six-inch kitchen knife.

'Whatever it is,' Sheila said, backing into the wall, 'we can talk about it.'

There was a flash of metal.

She felt the blade enter her abdomen and then the delayed red-hot piercing pain of the stab wound.

She gasped.

Clutching at her stomach, she saw that her hands were covered in blood.

Her legs felt unsteady and she began to slide down the wall as the figure came at her again.

There was no doubt about it. She was going to die.

15

CHAPTER 2

Beaumaris Police Station
Tuesday, 18 October 2022
10.12 a.m.

Detective Inspector Gareth Williams sat back at his desk in the DI's office that was attached to CID in Beaumaris Police Station. He ran his hand over his shaved head and felt a couple of tiny scabs where he'd nicked the skin the previous night. He hadn't been concentrating so it was his own fault. Reaching for his coffee, he realised that it was lukewarm and that he'd only had a sip.

Bollocks.

He'd been distracted all morning.

Something was looming. Something that cast a dark shadow not only over Gareth, but the whole CID team.

Six months ago, Detective Sergeant Declan Flaherty, his right-hand man in CID and close friend, had admitted to murdering his biological son, Callum Newell, who had only been eighteen years old, and Callum's mother, Vicky. Today, Declan was going to appear in front of the judge at Mold Crown Court for sentencing. Gareth knew that Declan might well get a whole life sentence. Not only was he a serving police officer and therefore in a position of responsibility, he had deliberately misled and deceived officers during the investigation into both murders while working on the case himself. Gareth knew it was unforgivable. And since Declan's confession, Gareth had tried to fathom how someone he'd known and trusted could have committed such acts. So far, Gareth had drawn no conclusions and was still mystified.

Gareth had attended several days of Declan's trial to give evidence. He had found it incredibly difficult to see his friend and colleague sitting in the defendant's area of the court. Even though Superintendent Warlow had asked Gareth if he wanted to attend the sentencing, Gareth had made his excuses. It wasn't something he felt he could sit through.

Instead, he was trying to distract himself as much as he could.

Gareth's eyes moved over his desk. The obligatory piles of paperwork that needed reading and signing – overtime sheets, witness statements, evidence requests. They'd been told that the North Wales Police was going to be eco-friendly and that everything would become digital and online. The transition had been predictably slow.

To the left of his computer monitor, some framed photos. The nearest was of Laura, Rosie and Jake sitting on Beaumaris Beach. Now that he was officially engaged to marry 'DI Laura Hart', it had finally become common knowledge in the Beaumaris CID. Although a workplace relationship wasn't technically prohibited by the North Wales Police Force, it was frowned upon. It was deemed that anything that could compromise an investigation or have a detrimental effect on the working environment of a CID office should be discouraged. Gareth and Laura knew that in the long run they would have to work in separate stations and that was fine.

Another photo featured his teenage nephew and niece, Charlie and Fran. Gareth's brother, Rob, lived in Hong Kong and made a fortune working for the Bank of America. He was happily married to a Kiwi called Aleida, had two healthy kids and a penthouse that looked over the harbour. Rob was officially a jammy wanker, but he was happy for his brother. They spoke at least once a week, usually about rugby. More recently, Rob had found some old photos which he'd been sending over sporadically. The last one had showed Gareth as a pretentious eighteen year old with a coiffured quiff trying to look like Dr Robert from The Blow Monkeys. When Gareth had showed Laura, Rosie and Jake, they had literally fallen off their seats with laughter.

On the shelves to the right of Gareth's desk, there was the usual senior officer memorabilia. Framed commendations. A couple of newspaper cuttings. And, of course, his pride and joy: a signed photo of the Grand Slam winning Welsh Rugby team from 2012.

Gareth's mobile phone buzzed and rattled on his desk. His stomach tensed when he looked at it. He knew it was a court official updating him on Declan's sentencing. He couldn't help but feel a devastating sadness when he saw the news.

Getting up from his desk, he took a deep breath and walked out into the CID office.

Come on, Gareth, let's get this done.

Normally the office would be lively and noisy with the odd boom of laughter. However, the atmosphere was quiet and tense. The CID team knew that the news about Declan was due and it had created an uneasy atmosphere all morning. There was no belief on anyone's part that

Declan shouldn't receive the full force of the law and that Vicky and Callum's family get the justice they deserved. In fact, there were some officers who were incredibly angry that Declan had deceived them over his crimes and tried to misdirect the investigation. Others felt the same as Gareth. A bewildering and overwhelming sense of confusion and sadness that one of their own had committed such terrible crimes.

'Morning, everyone,' Gareth said in a suitably sombre tone. 'I've just had word from the Crown Court at Mold... Declan has been given a whole life sentence.'

There was a sudden numbed silence in the office as everyone took in the news. The overused saying about silence, 'you could have heard a pin drop', was never more accurate.

Gareth took a moment and cleared his throat as he rubbed his hand uneasily over his scalp again. 'I know this has been hanging over us for the past few weeks. And, if I'm honest, I'm not sure what I feel. Like many of you, I'm confused and very sad. But I think it's now time to draw a line under this dark chapter in Beaumaris CID's history.'

The tense silence was broken by a ringing phone.

Detective Constable Andrea Jones – early thirties, dark curly hair, olive skin – answered it and began to take notes in a low voice.

'Right, guys,' Gareth said, trying to change the atmosphere in the room. 'We have work to do. I'll be in my office if anyone needs me or if you need to get anything off your chest about what's happened this morning.'

Gareth wandered back to his office, sat down and blew out his cheeks. His faith in the integrity of the police force had been seriously challenged recently. It was only eighteen months since the Sarah Everard case in South London. He knew he might have been thinking naively, but he'd put that case down to a tragic, hideous anomaly. However, Laura's kidnap by DCI Pete Marsons, his death and the subsequent investigation into institutional corruption in the MMP had been shocking. And that, combined with all that had happened with Declan, meant that his belief that most coppers were decent, honest, hard-working people who wanted to serve their community and give something back had been called into question. Maybe it was an issue of recruitment, that more rigorous checks needed to be caried out to ensure that the wrong kind of people didn't join the force. Gareth also knew there needed to be zero tolerance to the kind of casual racism and misogyny that was a hangover from the seventies and eighties when the force was often just one big boys' club and prone to abuse.

His train of thought was broken by a knock at the open door to his office.

It was Andrea.

'Boss, that was the governor from HMP Tonsgrove. A prisoner has been murdered in her cell,' she said, explaining the phone call she'd answered. 'They need CID officers down there straight away.'

'Right.' Gareth processed what she had said for a second. Then he got up and grabbed his jacket and car keys. 'Thanks, Andrea.'

Even though a serious crime had been committed, he felt a sense of relief that he could get back to what he and his CID team did best. Investigate major criminal incidents and get justice for the victims and their families.

CHAPTER 3

Tuesday, 18 October
10.15 a.m.

Laura turned restlessly in her sleep. She'd been reading in bed on her day off when she'd drifted off. Even though she felt aware that she was in the middle of the anxiety dream that had plagued her for the past four years, she couldn't seem to escape it.

She was trapped in 20 August 2018.
Again.
Her mouth was dry and her heart racing.
She and DCI Pete Marsons were standing outside the old Brannings Warehouse. The looming four-storey building had crumbling red brickwork, cracked windows and was covered in graffiti. Her husband, PC Sam Hart, was being held hostage inside by members of a drug gang.
And now the warehouse was on fire.
Suddenly, a gang member in a balaclava and holding a handgun rushed from the warehouse. Before she'd had

time to react, the man grabbed and spun Laura around and put her in a choke hold. He then jammed the handgun hard into the side of her head.

'Get back or I'll shoot her!' the man shouted at Pete.

Laura tried to get her breath.

Pete put up his hand. 'Hey, take it easy.'

The man dragged Laura back, his forearm hard against her throat. 'Right, me and her are walking out of here, got it? If anyone comes anywhere near us, I'm going to kill her!' he growled in a thick Mancunian accent.

'Fine.' Pete nodded. 'I just need you to calm down.'

Laura looked at Pete in desperation.

He gave her a reassuring look and nod. 'It's all right, Laura,' he said under his breath.

The man continued to drag Laura backwards slowly.

A figure appeared at the double doors – an SAS officer holding his Heckler & Koch assault rifle against his shoulder, ready to fire. He wore a black helmet, Perspex goggles, balaclava and Kevlar bulletproof vest. The SAS officer immediately spun and pointed the machine gun at the man who was holding Laura.

'Take the gun away from her head!' the SAS officer snapped loudly.

'Don't get any stupid ideas, pal,' the man hissed through gritted teeth. 'Otherwise I'm gonna blow her fucking brains out!'

'Drop your weapon now!' the SAS officer barked again.

The man snorted. 'No chance!'

They staggered backwards, away from the warehouse. Laura's head was starting to swim from the lack of oxygen. The gun barrel was jammed so hard against her skull, she thought it was going to crack. She tried to pull his forearm away from her throat.

'You're suffocating me!' she gasped.

'Shut up, bitch!' he growled, pulling her backwards and away from the burning warehouse.

For a second, she thought she was going to lose her balance and fall.

Then something caught her eye. The red laser sight glimmering from the SAS officer's gun. It was still trained in their direction.

Then she remembered something from her Tactical Combat Training.

Making eye contact with the SAS officer, she tried to indicate she was about to make a move that would allow him to have a safe, clean shot.

'Just so you know,' he whispered. 'I had a good time kicking the shit out of your copper mates in there.'

He was talking about her Sam.

GO FUCK YOURSELF!

Raising up her foot, she stamped with all of her strength down onto the gang member's instep.

In that split second, he loosened his grip on her throat and she bit as hard as she could into the flesh of his forearm.

'ARRGGHHH,' he yelled in pain and released her from the choke hold.

In that moment, she dropped to the ground as fast as she could and covered her head.

CRACK! CRACK!

Two bullets hammered into the man's chest and he crumpled into a heap. He was dead before he dropped.

She gasped as she got up.

Pete went to her. 'You okay?'

But she had other things on her mind.

'Where are the police officers who went inside?' she asked frantically as she stumbled towards the SAS officer and pointed to the warehouse.

He shook his head. 'We can't find them.'

Thick black smoke now billowed like an onrushing tidal wave out of the double doors. All Laura could see beyond was the inferno of the warehouse burning inside.

Please God, let Sam be alive!

The SAS officer looked at her and coughed heavily in an effort to expel the soot and smoke from his lungs. 'Don't worry,' he gasped. 'I'm going back in. I'll get them out.'

Suddenly, the air ripped apart with noise and flames as the windows along the front of the warehouse exploded in an eruption of fire and glass.

And Sam was somewhere inside.

Time was suddenly trapped in slow motion. Laura reached out, but slowly, as if she was pushing her hands through sand. Her mouth opened, but any sound was trapped inside her chest. She was frozen.

Then she was picked up and flung backwards by the force of the blast.

She landed heavily on her back and lay there winded.

For a moment, everything became silent. An eerie darkness, as if all the light had been drained from the sky.

She sucked in oxygen, but the air felt hot and thick. She didn't know if she was drowning or suffocating. The silence had now been replaced by a high-pitched ringing in her ears.

She looked up and the sky seemed to be filled with fire, smoke and fragments of brick that began to rain down on her...

Waking with a start, Laura took a deep, terrified breath.

Jesus!

She looked up at her bedroom ceiling. Her pulse was racing and her brow sweaty.

Then she practised the breathing technique she'd been

shown when she'd been diagnosed with PTSD after Sam had died.

Breathe in for five, hold it for five, let it out slowly for eight. Breathe in for five, hold it for five...

As it was explained to her, the holding of the breath allowed CO_2 to build up in the bloodstream. This enhanced the cardio-inhibitory response of the vagus nerve which stimulated your parasympathetic system.

Laura didn't really understand what all this meant. But she did know that it produced a calm and relaxed feeling in her mind and body.

Counselling had also helped her deal with the loss but it had been a long, painful journey to where she was now. And although her anxiety about that day had now become sporadic rather than a daily event, it still took the wind out of her sails and often gave her an emotional hangover the next day.

Looking around the bedroom, Laura waited for her breathing and pulse to steady before moving the pillows and sitting up in bed. She stretched out her legs, pulling back her toes to extend her calves.

God that feels nice.

Most mornings she would trek down to Beaumaris Beach for an early morning swim. It had become a ritual all year round – rain or shine. She'd been swimming when it had been snowing. The sharp intensity of the cold sea cleared her mind and invigorated her to such an extent that it had become incredibly addictive.

Laura reached for her reading glasses and her iPhone.

There was a reminder on the screen that she was on leave today. And that meant she could wander down to the beach for her swim a little later.

Brilliant!

Jake was now on his half-term holiday from school so

25

they had made various plans. And Laura was adamant that Jake wasn't going to spend the whole week playing FIFA on his Xbox.

Glancing over at Gareth's socks and shorts that had been dumped to one side of the chair, she gave a little growl of annoyance. Then she caught herself and reminded herself that they were getting married in two months' time and that she needed to be grateful.

Something on her phone caught her eye. BBC News popped up on the her screen.

Welsh detective, Flaherty, given whole life sentence for double murder on Anglesey.

She felt the pit of her stomach lurch with the news.

CHAPTER 4

Gareth and Detective Constable Ben Corden arrived at HMP Tonsgrove. Blond and handsome, with an athletic build, Ben was a bright young copper whom Gareth had taken under his wing. They shared a love of rugby, especially now that Ben had been selected for the North Wales Police team.

Despite being a copper on Anglesey for over thirty years, this was Gareth's first visit to HMP Tonsgrove. His first impression of the modern prison was that it looked like a secondary school. Just with very high wire mesh fences surrounding it. Each building had its own primary colour – green, red, yellow – for doors, window frames and railings. There was a large Astroturf pitch on the far side. To their right, a large exercise yard with benches, a workout area, and basketball and netball hoops.

'Doesn't look like a prison to me,' Gareth muttered. This was a world away from the old Victorian jails he'd visited such as Walton in Liverpool. Maybe that was a good thing. However, looking at HMP Tonsgrove, he wondered if they'd come too far the other way. The balance between deterrent, punishment and rehabilitation was a fine one. If life was easier and more comfortable inside prison than outside, spending a short sentence locked away would feel like a risk worth taking. However, there were some who had resorted to crime out of sheer desperation. A decent education programme with a particular focus on work-based skills and trades had to be a priority. Locking prisoners in their cells, sometimes for up to twenty-three hours a day, wasn't going to solve the problem of re-offending. Gareth didn't know what the answer was to such a complex problem. What he did know was that more people in England and Wales were being sent to prison every year than anywhere else in Europe. And 70 per cent of those prisons were overcrowded. He wasn't sure that building more prisons was a long-term solution. The priority had to be significantly lowering the incidents of re-offending. That would not only help overcrowding, it would lessen the workload for an already over-stretched UK police force.

'Looks like HMP Rhoswen,' Ben remarked, breaking Gareth's train of thought. Ben was referring the new men's 'super prison' over in North East Wales that housed nearly two thousand prisoners.

'Yeah, and look at the mess they've made of that place,' Gareth said darkly as he parked the car in a visitor's space. Next to them were two marked police units and a Scene of Crime forensics van. Otherwise the car park was relatively empty, which suggested that it was before visiting hours when relatives would arrive in their droves.

The autumnal sun was unusually warm. A rhombus-shaped shadow fell across the main recreation yard and there were rectangles of clear blue sky between the buildings. The scene was still except for a male prison officer patrolling the area over by a long one-storey building. He was walking a huge German Shepherd who gave an almighty bark that seemed to reverberate across the whole prison site.

Ben sniffed the air. 'It's great that we can smell weed and we're not even inside the buildings yet,' he remarked sarcastically.

Gareth rolled his eyes. 'Better than Spice, I guess.'

Synthetic cannabinoids – such as Spice or Black Mamba – were now responsible for over half the deaths in all UK prisons. Their use had become endemic and it was very difficult to stop the drugs coming into prisons. Children's drawings, photographs and specific pages of books could be soaked in Spice, passed onto prisoners during a family visit, and then smoked.

Gareth and Ben made their way across the car park and towards the reception in the visitors' area.

Taking out his warrant card, Gareth looked at the young woman behind the counter.

'DI Williams and DC Corden, Beaumaris CID,' Gareth explained. 'We're here to see Governor Parveen.'

'Of course.' The young woman nodded sombrely. Gareth assumed that she knew why they were there.

'DI Williams?' asked an authoritative voice.

It was Governor Sanam Parveen – forties, tall with intelligent dark eyes and a businesslike manner. She had been the governor for less than twelve months. A trained psychologist, Parveen had spent over twenty years working in the UK Prison Service.

'Yes,' Gareth replied with an affirmative nod. 'This is my colleague, DC Corden.'

'Hi there,' Parveen said with a half-smile, but she was

29

clearly preoccupied by what had happened that morning. 'I'll take you over to G wing now.' She beckoned for them to follow her towards the security gates.

Giving the prison officers behind the glass panel an authoritative wave, Parveen ushered them towards the automatic doors which slid open and then closed again.

They found themselves in a small glass-panelled holding area.

'Mind you don't step behind the yellow lines,' Parveen said, pointing to the floor. 'Otherwise the sensors won't work and we'll be stuck in here.'

A moment later, the next set of automatic doors buzzed open with a clunk.

'You haven't been at Tonsgrove long, have you?' Gareth asked as they made their way along a corridor which had large photos of Anglesey and Snowdonia hanging from the walls. It was more of an attempt to make conversation than anything else.

'Less than a year,' Parveen replied. 'Still early days.'

'What can you tell me about Sheila Jones?' Gareth asked.

'Nothing much really,' Parveen admitted. 'Boyfriend is a drug dealer from Liverpool. She got involved in helping him and got caught. She was serving a sentence for possession with intent to supply.'

'You think that's why she was targeted?' Gareth asked.

'I don't know,' Parveen admitted. 'As far as I know, Sheila had been keeping out of trouble while she was here.'

Ben frowned. 'No fights or arguments recently?'

'Nothing that I or my officers know of,' Parveen explained. 'And they usually know everything that's going on. It's that sort of a prison.'

They came through a heavy steel door and outside into the middle of the prison. It seemed to be hotter than when they'd entered ten minutes earlier. The air smelled of cooked food like that in a school or a hospital. The sunlight strobed through the tall fencing, dappling the ground with patterns and shapes.

The stillness was broken by some angry shouting from somewhere.

'Obviously everyone's upset and disturbed by what's happened to Sheila,' Parveen said as she unlocked a door through the fenced walkway. 'Emotions are running high.'

'Of course,' Gareth said as they stepped through the fence.

They headed left and entered through yet another steel door. There was a green sign that said G Wing. Next to it was a large scenic photo of Snowdon with a quote painted in italics on the wall – *Every moment is a fresh beginning*.

HMP Tonsgrove really was bright, shiny and new. It was as if Google had made a prison, he thought.

Going up the stairs, Gareth saw the white-and-blue evidence tape that had been secured across the top. They ducked underneath it and came out onto the main corridor and recreational area of G Wing. There were half a dozen or so police officers milling around. A few prisoners watched on from a distance.

'The room is down here,' Parveen explained as they headed for a brightly lit corridor which looked more like something you'd find in a hospital.

Room? Not cell then? Very progressive, Gareth thought.

A Scene of Crime Officer (SOCO), in a full white nitrile forensic suit, mask, hat and rubber boots, came out of the second room down on the left. They were holding a small evidence bag which was placed carefully into a plastic container.

'I'll let you take it from here,' Parveen said.

Gareth looked at her. 'We're going to need a room set aside so we can interview witnesses,' he explained.

'No problem,' she replied. 'We've got six meeting rooms on the ground floor. Just grab one of those.'

'Thanks.'

Ben pointed up to the ceiling where there was a camera. 'And if we can get the CCTV footage from this morning as soon as possible, that would be great.'

'Of course. I'll talk to our security team,' Parveen said helpfully. 'Anything else, I'll be in my office, which is also down on the ground floor. As you can imagine, there are a lot people I've got to talk to this morning.'

'No problem.' Gareth nodded. He could see the concern on her face momentarily. If there had been any failures on the part of the prison which had contributed to the murder, then she would be quickly out of a job.

As Parveen walked away, a SOCO approached and handed Gareth and Ben two nitrile forensic suits.

Gareth got the familiar chemically smell as he pulled the suit on, which rustled noisily. He then snapped on the blue latex gloves and slipped on the white rubber boots which felt tight.

Gareth moved slowly down the corridor before arriving at the room where the murder had taken place.

Lying in the far corner was the body of a woman in her forties.

The woman's eyes were still open with the pained expression frozen on her face. Her skin was milky and her lips a dark blue colour.

Despite his years on the force, Gareth felt disturbed as he looked at her face.

Around her body was a huge pool of dark blood that had started to coagulate and become sticky. Her clothes were soaked in blood from the abdomen down and he assumed that she had been stabbed, maybe more than once.

While a SOCO took a series of photographs of the woman and the crime scene, another figure was crouched down, using tweezers to extract evidence from the body.

As they turned and looked at Gareth, he saw it was North Wales' chief pathologist, Professor Helen Lane.

'Morning, Gareth,' she said in a detached tone.

'Helen,' Gareth said and then gestured. 'Bit of a mess. What can you tell us?'

'Whoever attacked your victim wasn't taking any chances,' Lane observed. 'They stabbed her three times.' She gave him a dark look. 'It's a nasty, vicious attack.'

'Any forensics that might help yet?' Ben asked.

Lane shook her head. 'Nothing yet.'

'Boss,' said a young male SOCO, looking over. 'Got something.'

The SOCO approached and held up a black hair scrunchie. Entwined into it were strands of dark red hair. 'I found this by the wall under the bed,' he said, pointing to the location.

Gareth looked at Sheila. Her hair was dyed blonde.

'Well whoever's hair that is,' Gareth said. 'It's not our victim's.'

Gareth looked at Ben. Maybe it was a significant discovery.

CHAPTER 5

Tuesday, 18 October 2022
11.12 a.m.

Laura was pottering in the kitchen. As she stretched up to put some tins away, she felt a piercing pain in her left side. She had cracked three ribs in the car accident in which Pete had been killed. When she thought about it, she had got off relatively lightly with a couple of cracked ribs and concussion. The fact that the *Sunday Times* journalist Claudia Wright had also survived felt like a miracle.

The *Sunday Times'* exposure of corruption in the MMP and the IOPC meant that a full independent public inquiry had been ordered. In fact, Laura knew the inquiry was starting very soon and that she would be called as a witness.

Right, let's not think about any of that. She tried to put those thoughts out of her mind.

Instead, Laura went over to her Spotify playlist, selected 'Like Sugar' by Chaka Khan and turned up the volume. Then she started to dance as she whizzed around, tidying, cleaning and sorting. She couldn't have felt more content at that moment.

Laura sang the chorus at the top of her voice.

'MUM!' Rosie said pulling a face as she entered while texting something on her phone at the same time. 'Cringe. I will never be able to unsee that.'

Laura laughed and gave her the finger. 'That's the problem with Gen Z. You lot have no sense of fun and no sense of humour.'

Rosie rolled her eyes and then smiled. 'Just because we don't find casual racism, misogyny and homophobia funny, doesn't mean we don't have a sense of humour. You Gen X lot just throw the word *woke* around so you can continue to be bigots.'

Laura grinned but she wasn't going to get into it again. She continued to sing and dance as Rosie sat on a chair at the table, glued to her phone. Her afternoon shift at the hair salon didn't start until 2 p.m.

'What time do you need to leave here?' Laura asked. Rosie still hadn't started to learn to drive so Laura was mum's taxi service.

'I'm not going in,' Rosie said with a huff.

Laura frowned. 'What?'

'Seriously. I washed a woman's hair yesterday and I'm sure she had nits or fleas,' Rosie groaned. 'And she stank.' Rosie looked at her with a dry smirk. 'I officially hate my life.'

'Maybe if you learned to drive...' Laura suggested sensitively. Rosie had been through a traumatic time in the past two years and had suffered from panic attacks for a while. Counselling and medication had helped but Laura didn't want to pressure her. 'I was thinking, maybe you could learn to drive on an automatic. And if we could find a female driving instructor, that might help.'

Rosie gave her an unconvincing nod. 'Maybe.'

Jake charged in as if he'd just scored a goal. 'Mum, guess what?'

'What?' she asked with a wry smile.

'I've just packed Messi on FIFA!' Jake yelled triumphantly.

'Oh, well that's good,' Laura said encouragingly, although she didn't know what the word 'packed' actually meant in this case. 'Messi's good isn't he?'

She spotted Jake giving Rosie a withering look. But Rosie seemed to be engrossed in something she was reading on her phone.

'And then on career mode, I just got transferred from the Wrexham Academy to AC Milan,' Jake continued.

'Everything okay, darling?' Laura asked as she noticed Rosie's uneasy expression.

'Can I have waffles?' Jake asked.

'No,' Laura said. 'I'm not buying waffles any more. They're not good for you.'

'But I love waffles,' Jake protested.

As Laura went over to the table, Rosie turned her phone to show her the screen.

There was a photo of Pete.

Underneath there was a headline.

Independent Inquiry Into Police Corruption In Manchester Force Starts Today.

Jake wandered over. 'What is it?'

'Nothing,' Laura and Rosie said in unison as Rosie quickly flicked her screen to something else.

Pete had been both Rosie and Jake's godfather and his death had been incredibly hard to explain to Jake.

CHAPTER 6

HMP Tonsgrove
Tuesday, 18 October 2022
11.53 a.m.

Having changed out of their forensic clothes, Gareth and Ben had gone to the ground floor of the prison and found a spare meeting room they could use to begin interviewing witnesses to Sheila's murder.

The room had been painted a soothing shade of light green. There were plants along a large window that had a wooden slatted blind. At the centre of the room was a large oval table surrounded by about ten padded chairs.

Gareth had arranged for the recording equipment from Interview Room 3 of Beaumaris nick to be brought over. Even though the initial interviews were informal, they needed to record them in case anything their interviewees told them needed to be used as evidence. Gareth had learned his lesson the hard way. He'd interviewed a witness about a murder at Beaumaris without recording it. The witness had given vital evidence to him, only to retract it and claim he'd never said it.

Gareth pulled the file for Hayley Ross, who had been Sheila Jones' cellmate – or in HMP Tonsgrove, *roommate*.

'Hayley Ross,' Gareth read out loud to Ben, '21-year-old girl, from Welshpool. Three-year sentence for possession with intent to supply a class B drug.'

Ben raised an eyebrow. 'Weed?' he asked.

'Weed and ketamine,' Gareth replied. 'Prior convictions for possession, petty theft and credit card fraud.'

'There must be several prisoners in here who know exactly who killed Sheila Jones and why,' Ben stated.

'Yeah, well it's basically impossible to do anything in a place like this without anyone knowing,' Gareth agreed. 'The problem is trying to convince them to talk to us. Not only are we the bastards that put them in here, it's a pretty dangerous environment to grass on anyone.'

Before they could continue, the door opened and a male prison officer with a dark beard led Hayley Ross into the room. She was tall and skinny with blonde hair that was parted in the middle. She was wearing grey trackies, a hoodie and Adidas trainers.

Gareth got up from his seat. 'Are you Hayley?' he asked politely.

Hayley nodded but didn't say anything. Her body language and face showed that she was nervous.

'I'll let you take it from here, gents,' the prison officer said as he gestured to the door.

'Thanks,' Gareth said and pointed to a chair further down the table. 'Do you want to come and sit down, Hayley?'

She nodded, sat down timidly and then began to bite at what was left of her nails.

Gareth pointed to the recording equipment. 'Just so that you're aware, even though this is an informal interview, we will be recording it in case anything you say needs to be used as evidence in court. Do you understand that, Hayley?'

'Yes,' she replied in a virtual whisper.

'Okay,' Gareth said as he leaned over and pressed the red record button. There was a long electronic beep. 'Interview conducted with Hayley Ross. HMP Tonsgrove. Tuesday, eighteenth of October. Present are Hayley Ross, Detective Constable Ben Corden and myself, Detective Inspector Gareth Williams.'

Ben shifted in his chair and looked across the table. 'How long had you been sharing a room with Sheila, Hayley?' he asked in a gentle tone.

Hayley gave a little shrug. 'About a year I think.'

'Oh right,' Ben said. 'Would you say that you and Sheila were close then?'

Hayley nodded but didn't say anything. She visibly took a deep breath and then tears welled in her eyes. She seemed embarrassed as she reached up and dried them with the cuff of her hoodie. 'Sorry...'

'You don't need to apologise.' Gareth gave her a kind smile. 'What happened to Sheila was horrible and you're bound to be upset.'

Silence.

'Can you tell us where you were when Sheila was attacked?' Ben asked.

I was talking to Jamilia on the other side of the wing,' she explained.

'Jamilia?'

'Jamilia Cole,' she said defensively. 'I'm not lying. Ask her.'

Ben took a moment. 'But it was you who discovered Sheila when you went back to your room, is that right?'

Hayley nodded as she wiped more tears away. Her hand was visibly shaking.

'That must have been very upsetting for you,' Gareth said in an empathetic tone.

There was another brief silence.

Gareth looked over at Hayley and managed to catch her eye. 'Did you know that Sheila was going to be attacked this morning?'

Hayley immediately shook her head adamantly as she looked away from Gareth's gaze.

He watched her for a few seconds.

She seems to be hiding something, he thought.

'For the purposes of the tape, Hayley has shaken her head to indicate that she didn't know that Sheila was going to be attacked this morning,' Ben stated.

'Hayley,' Gareth said, attempting to get her to look in his direction. She didn't and instead looked down at the floor. 'Did you know that Sheila was going to be attacked at some point today or in the future?'

'No,' Hayley said unconvincingly. She was definitely lying to them.

Another silence.

'Listen, Hayley, if you do know something, you can tell us. Whatever it is,' Gareth said quietly.

Hayley gave him a scornful look. 'Yeah, I won't be doing that,' she snorted under her breath.

'Can you tell me why you can't talk to us?' Ben asked.

They could both predict what she was going to say but it was a question that needed answering.

Hayley shook her head as if they were moronic. 'Why d'you think?' she said under her breath. 'I haven't got a death wish, have I?'

'If you think someone would try to intimidate you or harm you if you talk to us—'

'I don't *think* they would…' Hayley said interrupting as she sat more upright in her chair. 'I *know* that if I talk to you, I'll be leaving this prison in a box. No one is gonna talk to you or tell you anything. Cos there are girls in here who can get to you wherever you are.'

Gareth gave Ben a frustrated look.

CHAPTER 7

CID, Beaumaris Police Station
Tuesday, 18 October 2022
12.10 p.m.

Andrea looked at her computer screen with frustration. She was running a couple of checks through the Home Office Large Major Enquiry System (HOLMES), a powerful database used by the UK police for the investigation of major incidents. The HOLMES app was usually restricted for use on computers within police stations or courts. Of course, it was no coincidence that the acronym matched the surname of Britain's most famous fictional detective. Andrea thought this was a little ironic because, as far as she could see, Sherlock Holmes was a narcissistic heroin addict with Asperger's.

'Come on,' Andrea muttered under the breath in annoyance. HOLMES was so slow and unresponsive that sometimes she just gave up.

Sitting back at her desk, she grabbed her coffee and took a long swig.

God, that's better, she thought at the strong taste of coffee in her mouth.

Her eyes moved over to Laura's desk, which was empty. She was on leave. Andrea didn't like to admit it, but she already missed her.

Andrea's parents had both been killed in a car accident when she was only six. It had turned her world upside down. Her maternal grandmother lived in Trinidad but social services decided that it wasn't appropriate for Andrea to go and live there. Instead she was moved between care homes and foster families until she was eighteen.

Since arriving at Beaumaris nick, Laura and Andrea had formed a close bond. Andrea saw Laura as the mother she'd never had. In fact, Laura was born the same year as her late mother – so they would have been the same age.

'Andrea?' said a voice.

She looked up and saw Detective Constable Charlie Heaton approaching. In his early twenties, he had coal-black hair, a short beard and a slightly rounded baby face that made him look younger. Charlie had moved upstairs from uniform only three months ago so he was still finding his feet in CID. But from what Andrea had seen so far, he was diligent and hard-working. She also thought he was cute but she hadn't yet shared that with anyone.

'Yes,' Andrea said looking up from her desk.

Charlie gestured to a print-out that he was holding. 'Uniform have brought up a missing person.'

'What is it?' Andrea asked. They didn't usually get involved in missing persons cases unless there were suspicious circumstances.

'Abby White,' Charlie explained. 'Her aunt called in to report it. She's been missing since last night.'

Andrea raised an eyebrow. 'Why aren't uniform dealing with it?'

'She's only seventeen,' Charlie said. 'And her aunt claims

43

that she just vanished from the family home and it's completely out of character.'

Andrea knew that as a minor, they needed to deal with this as a matter of urgency.

'Have you got an address?' she asked Charlie.

'Yes,' he replied, gesturing to the print-out he was holding.

Andrea got up from her desk and grabbed her jacket. 'We'd better get down there.'

CHAPTER 8

HMP Tonsgrove
Tuesday, 18 October 2022
12.13 p.m.

Gareth and Ben were sitting opposite David Rice, the prison officer responsible for the section of G Wing where Sheila Jones had been murdered. Rice was in his early fifties and thick set, with short grey hair that was thinning on top. He had a sharp nose and jaw which made him look a little pointy.

'Just so you're aware, David,' Gareth said as he gestured to the recording equipment. 'We will be recording this interview today in case you tell us something that we need to use as evidence in court.'

David gave a nonchalant shrug. 'Yeah, of course.'

Gareth pressed the red button and the electronic noise sounded. 'Interview conducted with David Rice. HMP Tonsgrove. 12.13 p.m., Tuesday, eighteenth of October. Present are David Rice, Detective Constable Ben Corden, and myself, Detective Inspector Gareth Williams.'

Gareth then waited for a couple of seconds before

looking over. From the brief conversation when he'd arrived, he had Rice down as a bit of a know-it-all.

Gareth reached over, took a floor plan of G Wing that he'd been provided with and turned it around so that Rice could see it.

'David, can you confirm that you are the officer in charge of this area of G Wing at this prison?' Gareth said.

'That's right,' he replied as he peered over at the floor plan.

Gareth looked at him. 'But you weren't in that area when Sheila Jones was attacked and killed?'

Rice bristled a little. 'No. I was attending to an issue in another area.'

Ben frowned. 'An issue?'

'Just a bit of petty theft. The usual,' he replied casually.

'How well did you know the victim, Sheila Jones?' Gareth enquired.

Rice sat back in his chair indifferently. 'As well as I get to know any of the girls in here.'

Very helpful, Gareth thought sardonically.

Gareth looked at Rice. He was beginning to annoy him. 'How would you describe Sheila Jones?'

'She kept herself to herself really,' Rice said.

'Can you think of anyone who'd want to harm Sheila?' Ben asked.

'You're joking, aren't you?' The question seemed to amuse Rice slightly. 'As far as the girls were concerned, Sheila Jones was untouchable.'

'Why was that?' Gareth asked. He still hadn't had any proper intel on Sheila except for her official police record.

'Her fella is Shane Deakins,' Rice said. 'And Shane is a Scouser and a very naughty boy, if you know what I mean? He's well connected up in Liverpool. He was running county lines in North Wales. All sorts.'

'And that made Sheila untouchable?' Ben asked to clarify.

'Of course,' Rice snorted. 'No one was gonna touch Sheila or all hell would break loose. So God help whoever did this, cos they've got a world of pain heading their way.'

Gareth wondered why Governor Parveen hadn't flagged this up when they'd first arrived.

'Any ideas who might have done it?' Gareth asked.

'Nope,' Rice admitted. 'Like I say, I can't believe someone's had the balls to do that to her.'

'Was Sheila selling drugs?' Gareth asked.

'No idea,' Rice admitted. 'We do our best but there's always drugs here. And that's what causes all the problems.'

Gareth looked at Rice. 'But you don't know if Sheila was involved?'

'No,' Rice said. 'Given who her man is and their connections... But I'm saying nothing. And I didn't see her dealing.'

Ben looked up from the A4 notepad where he was taking notes. 'Had Sheila had any rows or arguments with anyone in the last few days or weeks?'

'No,' Rice said. 'The only person I ever saw Sheila rowing with was the boss.'

Gareth raised an eyebrow. 'The boss? You mean Governor Parveen?'

'Yeah,' Rice replied with a knowing expression.

'Do you know why they were arguing?' Gareth asked.

'Not my business, is it?' Rice said. 'And in this prison, I keep my nose out of stuff like that.'

Gareth picked up on Rice's tone.

'This prison is different to others?' he said with a quizzical expression.

'Oh yeah,' Rice said with a meaningful nod. Then he

pointed up to the CCTV camera. 'Big Brother is watching you, if you get my drift?'

Gareth wasn't actually sure what Rice was getting at. 'I'm not sure I do.'

Rice took a few seconds to think about his answer. He leaned forward as if he was about to tell them something clandestine. 'I've worked in prisons where the governor is virtually invisible. But not here. Nothing gets past her ladyship. And the last officer that challenged her was out of here the following day. So, as I say, I keep out of it.'

Gareth looked over at Ben. It didn't sound as if Governor Parveen was particularly popular with the staff.

CHAPTER 9

Gazing out at the view from her kitchen, Laura took in the stunning vista. A calm strip of water, the Menai Strait, lay in front of Beaumaris. Behind that, the dark blue ribbon of sea, the Welsh mainland coastline only three miles directly across from the town itself. The towering darkness of the Snowdonia mountains, which even in summer were continually shrouded in traversing patches of mist at their dark summit, loomed menacingly over the tableau.

It had been nearly a year since the Snowdonia National Park Authority had backed a motion for Snowdonia to be known by its Welsh name – *Eryri* – in the future, as well as Snowdon being called *Yr Wyddfa*. Laura was proud of her Welsh heritage and felt it was no different to the city of Bombay being changed back to Mumbai in India, or Rhodesia to Zimbabwe.

Above the Snowdonia mountains, the endless, cloudless, azure sky seemed too perfect today. That's what she'd missed when she first moved to Manchester – the Anglesey sky and the feeling of endless space.

She went over the kitchen counter, grabbed her tea and walked out and down the hallway to the living room. The house was unusually quiet and peaceful as she went over to her favourite spot on the sofa, slumped down and placed her tea on the small table beside her.

Stretching out her legs, she arched her back. She had promised herself that she would get down to Beaumaris Beach for a swim. However, her eyelids were heavy as she turned and lay fully reclined on the sofa.

God, I cannot remember the last time I napped on this sofa, she thought as she drifted away and began dreaming vividly of the day that she'd been abducted by DCI Pete Marsons, six months earlier.

The car had just crashed and she was sitting in the driver's seat in a total daze.

Police officers raced across the road towards the crumpled BMW.

Opening the driver's door, Laura swung her legs out and tried to stand. Her feet were unsteady but she didn't care. Then Laura had a horrible thought.

Claudia!

The investigative journalist, Claudia Wright, who had also been abducted by Pete, was trapped in the boot.

Gripping onto the side of the car to keep her balance, Laura moved to the back of the car just as two police officers arrived.

'Are you okay?' the older male police officer with a beard said.

She looked at him as she attempted to open the boot. 'I'm DI Laura Hart from Beaumaris CID. There's a woman inside the boot.'

Both officers looked confused as Laura yanked at the release for the boot. It was stuck.

Claudia was now banging and yelling from inside.

'Come on, you need to help me,' she urged them.

'Let me have a go, ma'am,' the police officer said.

Her head still dizzy, Laura stood to one side as the officer reached under the metal lip, pushed the release button and tried to pull.

Nothing.

'Bugger,' he said under his breath.

Laura leaned close to the boot lid. 'Claudia, it's Laura. Everything's going to be okay. We're going to get you out of there,' she said loudly, trying to reassure herself as much as Claudia.

The female officer had a strange frown on her face. She looked over at Laura. 'Ma'am, there's a strong smell of petrol around here. We need to get her out as quickly as possible.'

Now she mentioned it, Laura noticed the fumes were getting stronger and stronger.

Oh God, this is not good.

The bearded officer shook his head. 'I can't seem to unlock it. The accident must have jarred the automatic central locking.'

Laura smelled the petrol again. If they'd fractured the petrol tank and it was now leaking, the car could go up at any point. Even the tiniest electrical spark in the engine could set it off.

'Hang on in there, Claudia,' Laura yelled again. 'We're going to get you out.'

The female officer was now trying the boot and had reached under to push the button.

Nothing.

'It's not releasing,' the female police officer said in frustration. 'It's jammed.'

Come on, Laura. Think.

'The keys,' Laura said as she moved unsteadily to the driver's door and grabbed the keys from the ignition.

Looking at the electronic fob, she saw a black button with an image of the car with its boot lid up.

She pressed it.

Nothing.

Shit!

She pressed it again.

Nothing.

For fuck's sake!

Then she heard a crackling sound coming from the front of the car, under the bonnet.

She could smell burning.

If the petrol ignited, Claudia was going to be burned alive and they might all die in a ball of flames.

Laura looked at the two officers as her pulse quickened. 'I'm serious, we need to get her out of there. I can smell burning.' She was terrified.

Looking down into the car, Laura saw where the electrical wires had been ripped from the dashboard and were now hanging precariously in mid-air. One spark from them, and they were all going to go up in flames.

The bearded officer gave the boot another frustrated yank. 'Jesus, this is not going to open without some serious brute force.'

Laura looked at him then gestured over to their marked police car. 'Have you got anything that we can use to get it open?'

Without replying, the bearded officer turned, sprinted to the car, opened the boot, grabbed something and ran back to them.

Laura saw that he was carrying a large black steel crowbar.

Suddenly, Laura heard a crackling sound coming from the engine. She turned to see smoke coming from underneath the bonnet.

Oh Jesus...

The bearded officer gestured to them. 'Get away from the car. Both of you.'

Laura shook her head as her heart thundered in her chest. 'It's my fault she's in there. I'm not going anywhere.'

'There's no point in all of us dying,' the officer snapped at her as he shoved the crowbar under the lid of the boot.

'I'm not going anywhere,' Laura said again emphatically as the female officer took a few cautious steps back.

Laura glanced over to the front of the car. There was now thick black smoke pouring from under bonnet.

'The engine's on fire,' she said.

'I know,' the bearded officer said breathlessly as he gave the crowbar another almighty yank down. 'Bloody hell!'

Nothing.

It was stuck.

There were a few seconds of silence.

Then Claudia started to bang on the boot again. Her muffled cries seemed to be getting quieter.

Oh God, is the smoke getting into the boot of the car?

Laura braced herself. She sensed the car was going to explode any second.

There were flames now lapping at the edges of the bonnet.

Placing his foot against the bumper to give himself leverage, the officer wrapped both hands around the crowbar, jumped up and then down so that the whole of his bodyweight wrenched against the boot.

He jerked it with everything he had.

CRACK!

The boot flew open and the officer stumbled backwards, nearly losing his balance.

Moving quickly, Laura grabbed Claudia by the arms and dragged her as she tried to scramble out.

'Oh my God!' Claudia screamed as she fell to her knees on the ground.

'It's okay, I've got you,' Laura reassured her. 'But we need to run now!'

Laura pulled Claudia to her feet.

They all sprinted away from the car and across the grassy verge of the long country road where they had crashed.

They got about thirty yards away.

Laura turned back to look.

BANG!

There was an almighty noise which split the air.

The car erupted into a ball of orange flames.

The force of the explosion knocked Laura backwards.

'Jesus,' Claudia whispered.

Laura looked at the black outline of the back of the car, now engulfed by a ferocious fire where she had been standing only seconds earlier.

The air was filled with thick black smoke.

'That was close,' Laura whispered, her whole body now shaking with emotion. 'Too close.'

Blinking open her eyes, Laura looked up at the living room ceiling. Her heart was still racing from the dream. She took a deep breath, sat up and blew out her cheeks.

CHAPTER 10

Pen-y-garnedd
Tuesday, 18 October 2022
1.09 p.m.

A patrol car, with its distinctive yellow and blue markings and HEDDLU – POLICE lettering, was parked outside the detached house where Abby White lived with her aunt and uncle in Pen-y-garnedd, a tiny village which was about four miles north of the Menai Bridge.

Knowing that there was no time to lose, Andrea marched up the neat stone path. The front garden was immaculate, with a small wooden sign that read ROSE COTTAGE. There were hanging baskets on either side of the door.

A young, male uniformed officer, gawky and dark-haired, stood outside the front door and nodded at her.

Andrea and Charlie showed their warrant cards. 'DC Jones and DC Heaton, Beaumaris CID. What have we got, Constable?'

'The niece, Abby White, went missing from the house last night,' he said. 'She just vanished.'

'And she lives with her aunt and uncle?' Charlie asked.

'Yes.' The constable nodded and looked at his notepad again. 'Zoe and Gavin Spears.'

'And they have no idea where she might have gone or why?' Andrea said.

'No,' the officer said, now looking down at his notebook. 'She's seventeen. Friends and family have been searching the local area for her. We've had a look around and there's no sign of anything suspicious,' the constable explained hastily. Everyone was acutely aware of the time pressure.

Andrea would make sure that she and Charlie checked again.

'Okay, we'll hold off on an FLO until we know more,' Andrea said, thinking out loud. If they believed that a crime had been committed, a police officer would be appointed as the Family Liaison Officer (FLO) to provide an ongoing line of communication between the family and the police.

The constable pushed open the door, and Andrea and Charlie walked in purposefully. The house was tidy and smelled of air freshener and coffee. Coats hung neatly from hooks in the hallway. Boots, shoes and trainers lined up tidily. A small, patterned rug covered the wine-red tiled floor. Instinct told Andrea that there was order and normality to the Spears household as far as first impressions went.

Andrea remembered being told that it was the first ten minutes that normally gave a clue as to whether there was something to worry about. And there was always a slight apprehension before meeting the family in a case like this. How were they going to react to her as a police officer? Some were hostile and overemotional. Some were stunned and quiet. And some simply pretended that it wasn't happening.

As Andrea and Charlie came into the small, neat kitchen, they saw a woman sitting at the table, her fingers pawing at a mug of tea. Zoe Spears.

A female uniformed police officer, tall with dyed-blonde hair in a ponytail, rested against the kitchen counter. She looked over as the detectives came in.

'Ma'am,' the officer said as she instinctively straightened. Probably young, ambitious and keen to impress CID officers. After all, Andrea and Charlie were the same rank as her – Constable – so there was no need to call her 'ma'am'.

Andrea showed her warrant card. 'Thank you, Constable. We can take it from here.'

The officer nodded and left.

Zoe Spears was in her early forties but looked younger. Her hair had been dyed black was straight and shoulder length. She was stick thin and wore a very tight long sleeved top and leggings that seemed to cling to her skin.

Zoe looked up from the table, smiled uncertainly. *She doesn't know what bloody day it is, poor woman,* Andrea thought. Zoe had that horrible vacant look Andrea had seen before. Shock and fear.

'Mrs Spears? I'm Detective Constable Andrea Jones and this is my colleague, Detective Constable Charlie Heaton. Can we sit down?'

Zoe nodded. 'Of course, sorry. Yeah. It's Zoe.' She lifted her mug to take a sip of tea, and Andrea could see that her hands were trembling slightly.

'Is your husband here?' Charlie asked.

'He's gone out with some others to look in the fields at the back...'

'Zoe, I know that this is a very difficult time for you. I can't imagine what you're going through,' Andrea said in a gentle voice. 'We just need as much information as we

57

can get. The more you can tell us, the more likely it is we can get Abby home safely.'

Zoe nodded but Andrea could see the tears welling up in her eyes.

'Shall I make us a cup of tea?' Charlie suggested quietly.

Andrea gave him a knowing smile. 'Yes, thanks. That's a good idea.'

Taking the kettle to the sink, Charlie filled it up as Andrea got out her notebook. She glanced over at the fridge, which was covered in magnets, family photos and drawings. Even in those few seconds, she deduced that the Spears didn't have any children of their own as the photos seemed to only feature a girl in her teens – whom she assumed was Abby.

On the surface, this is a nice family, Andrea thought. And that meant alarm bells were starting to ring.

All families had their secrets.

Charlie took two mugs and popped teabags in them.

'I know you've already told my colleagues, but could you run through what happened last night for us?' Andrea asked, keeping her voice soft.

Zoe shifted awkwardly in her chair. 'Abby was upstairs with Becks. They were watching telly. Becks left just before midnight. Me and Gav went to bed shortly after that. I assumed Abby was asleep. I got up just after six this morning and noticed Abby's door was open.' Zoe took a shaky breath to compose herself. 'I looked in... but she wasn't in there. Her bed hadn't been slept in.'

'And Becks is Abby's friend?' Charlie said as he brought mugs of tea over to the table.

'They're best friends,' Zoe explained.

Andrea frowned. 'Have you spoken to Becks since?'

'Of course,' Zoe said, sounding a little annoyed. 'But Becks is as confused as we are. Abby was in her room when she left.' Zoe's eyes filled with tears. 'I just don't understand what's happened to her,' she said, sounding distraught.

Charlie sat down and then looked over. 'When was the last time you saw Abby?'

Zoe bit her lip for a moment as she wiped the tears from her face. 'When Becks arrived. That was about eight.'

'Okay,' Andrea said. 'Have you checked her room? Are there any missing clothes? Or toiletries, make-up?'

'No. There's nothing missing,' Zoe sighed. 'That's why we're so scared.'

This is not good, Andrea thought. In her experience, teenagers who ran away took stuff with them.

'Could she be at a friend's home?' Andrea enquired.

'No.' Zoe shook her head adamantly. 'We've tried everyone but no one's seen or heard from her.'

Charlie raised an eyebrow. 'What about her phone?'

Zoe shook her head. 'No. We can't find her phone anywhere. We've called it but it's turned off.'

Andrea looked at her. 'We're going to need Abby's number and her mobile provider.'

'Of course,' Zoe said.

'I know this is difficult, but could you let us have a recent photograph of Abby?' Andrea said.

Zoe thought for a moment and then said, 'I've got one on my phone from a few days ago?'

Andrea pulled out her contact card and handed it to Zoe. 'If you can text me that now, I can circulate it.'

Zoe nodded and flicked through her phone.

'Thanks,' Andrea said as her phone buzzed with the photo. She opened the image. There she was. Abby White. Seventeen. Long red hair tied in a high ponytail, a pink Adidas hoodie, black baggy trousers and Converse All Star trainers. She didn't look like she had a care in the world.

'We'll need a description of what she was wearing,' Charlie said.

'The same hoodie, trousers and trainers as in the photo I sent you. And a black Sam Fender T-shirt that's got a Newcastle Brown Ale logo on the front. I don't think I've got a photo of it,' Zoe said.

'That's fine,' Andrea said as she wrote the details down. 'I know what you mean.'

'And Abby is your niece, is that right?' Charlie asked.

Zoe nodded. 'Yes. She's my sister's daughter. But my sister is working abroad for a while and didn't want to take Abby out of school. So, she lives here.'

'How long has Abby been living here?' Andrea said.

'It's been nearly five years,' Zoe replied.

Andrea frowned. 'That's a long time,' she remarked.

'I'm afraid my sister isn't very maternal,' Zoe admitted. 'And Gav and I couldn't have children, so we love having her here.'

'But you have spoken to Abby's mother?' Zoe asked.

'I've left her a message but she's in the middle of nowhere so I haven't managed to speak to her yet,' Zoe explained. She sounded exasperated.

'Does your sister have a home in the UK?' Andrea said.

'She's got a flat in Chester,' Zoe explained. 'But like I said, her work takes her all over the world.'

'What does she do?'

'She's a journalist.'

'What about Abby's father?' Charlie said.

Zoe shook her head. 'No, he left them when she was four. No idea where he is but I think that's for the best. She's not in contact with him.'

'We're going to need his name,' Andrea explained.

'Chris White,' Zoe said. 'The last I heard he was living and working in a studio in Shrewsbury.'

60

'Studio?'

'He's a musician,' Zoe said in a withering tone. 'Guitarist. In some Britpop band in the nineties that had two hit singles, so he thinks he's God's gift.'

'But as far as you know there's no contact?' Charlie asked to clarify.

'No,' Zoe replied.

'Have you noticed anything different about Abby or her behaviour in recent days?' Andrea asked, now refocusing.

'No. She's been the same... Bit moody, but she's a teenager,' Zoe said with a shrug.

'Anything at home that might have upset her or given her a reason to not want to be here?' Charlie asked.

Zoe clearly took slight exception to Charlie's insinuation. 'No. Everything's fine. She's been planning a big Halloween thing with her friends. They all seem to love Halloween. Not like when I was a kid.'

'Anything bothering her at school or college? Friends, bullying, anything like that?' asked Andrea.

'No. She moans about it, but she actually likes going to college. She's doing really well.'

'Relationships of any kind?' Andrea asked. 'Were there any bitter exes who wouldn't take no for an answer?' She had seen insanely jealous teens do all sorts of hideous things to ex-girlfriends and boyfriends.

'No. Not that she's mentioned. A couple of boys at school that she likes, but nothing that I know of,' Zoe said, but then she clearly thought of something.

Andrea looked at her. 'Whatever it is, however small, you need to tell us,' she said in a serious tone.

'There was a boy she mentioned called Edward Davies,' Zoe said now deep in thought. 'Becks said that he'd been bothering Abby. In fact, Becks called him "a stalker" and said he was creepy. But Abby laughed it off and said it was nothing.'

'Edward Davies?' Andrea said to clarify as she wrote the name down in her notebook. 'Is there anything else you can tell us about him?'

'I think he's a bit older than Abby and Becks. They said he lives on his own in a bungalow somewhere in Castellior,' Zoe explained.

Charlie looked over at Andrea and nodded. 'Yeah, I know where that is.'

'Okay,' Andrea said as she put away her notebook. She could feel her pulse start to quicken. Her instinct was that there was now a concern that Abby was genuinely missing. It was a judgement based on her initial impressions of the family and the portrait Zoe Spears had painted of Abby. She wasn't ruling out the possibility that Abby had run away, but she seemed happy and in a stable home.

Andrea shot Charlie a look – she could see that he was thinking the same thing.

They might well be dealing with an abduction.

The first 24 hours in an abduction were critical and they'd already lost valuable time.

CHAPTER 11

HMP Tonsgrove
Tuesday, 18 October 2022
1.24 p.m.

Gareth and Ben were now sitting in the prison's main security office. In front of them was a bank of monitors linked to both the external and internal CCTV cameras. The screens showed prisoners wandering along corridors, at work in the kitchens, the laundry or across in the education block.

The Chief Security Officer (CSO) – fifties, grey beard, plump, thick glasses – was searching through the CCTV footage from that morning.

'Nearly there,' the officer said with a forced smile.

It had taken him ten minutes to locate the correct camera, download the recorded CCTV and get it so that it was now on the screen in front of them. If Gareth was to guess, the officer was new as he seemed to be struggling with the technology.

'Different system to the one I'm used to, you see,' the officer said by way of an explanation as he gave an embarrassed smile.

'That's all right,' Gareth said in a reassuring tone. 'I got a washing machine a year ago and I still have no idea how to use it.'

'Right,' the officer said, laughing rather too hard.

'You're new here?' Ben asked.

'Oh yeah,' the officer replied. 'I've only been here four weeks.'

Gareth frowned. 'Any idea what happened to the last CSO?'

The officer thought for a few seconds as he continued to use the mouse to pinpoint the exact timecode. 'Erm, bit of a difference of opinion... I'm not sure,' he mumbled.

However, Gareth was now interested. 'Oh right. Difference of opinion with Governor Parveen?' he asked, fishing for more information.

The officer nodded. 'Something like that.'

Gareth waited for a second and then asked in a nonchalant tone, 'I assume that you and Governor Parveen get on though?'

'I don't really know her very well yet,' the officer said unconvincingly.

I wonder what that's about?

'Right, this is it,' the officer said, clearly relieved that they could talk about something else.

Gareth looked at the monitor and saw the corridor where Sheila Jones' room was located on G Wing. The timecode read: 09.23 18.10.22.

The officer played the footage. For a few seconds, the corridor was empty. Then a figure appeared walking up the corridor. It was Sheila Jones. As far as Gareth could see, she was relaxed and unflustered as she went into her room.

A few seconds later, another figure moved very quickly up the corridor from the other end towards Sheila Jones' room.

Gareth moved towards the screen. 'Can you freeze that for a second, please?'

The officer paused the image.

The figure coming up the corridor had a black hoodie pulled up and a balaclava concealing their face. It was impossible to see anything.

Gareth shot a frustrated look over at Ben.

'Okay,' Gareth said. 'Can you play it now?'

The officer clicked his mouse and the footage continued.

The masked figure went into the room.

A second later, someone fled the room.

It was Hayley Ross.

Ben glanced over at Gareth. 'So, Hayley lied to us about where she was when Sheila was attacked.'

Gareth nodded as he continued to stare at the monitor.

The timecode continued for about a minute before the masked figure came out of the room and headed in the opposite direction, away from the camera.

'If we can keep this playing,' Gareth said.

After five minutes, Hayley Ross appears back in the corridor. She moves very cautiously down the corridor, before looking into the room and then running away, presumably to raise the alarm that Sheila had been attacked.

Gareth pointed to the bank of screens. 'We can see that the attacker goes down that corridor and turns right. I'm assuming there's another CCTV camera at the end of that corridor too?'

In fact, by Gareth's calculations, the CCTV on the next corridor would be far more useful in terms of evidence as the attacker would be walking towards the camera.

'There is.' The officer pulled a face. 'But it's faulty.'

Gareth raised an eyebrow. 'Faulty?'

Are you joking?

The officer nodded apologetically. 'I can have a look for you, if you like?'

'Please,' Gareth said before looking over at Ben as if to say: *What the hell is going on?*

The officer clicked the mouse until he found the correct file and then clicked again so that it was up on the same monitor.

The screen was black.

'Sorry,' the officer said with a shrug. 'I did flag it up with the governor when I first arrived.'

'What did she say?' Gareth asked in frustration.

'Budget cuts,' he replied. 'She said we could look at replacing it next month.'

Gareth shook his head in disbelief. 'Yeah, well next month is now too late.' The CCTV footage they had was virtually worthless in terms of tracking down whoever had murdered Sheila Jones.

CHAPTER 12

Andrea and Charlie arrived at a small bungalow in Castellior, a tiny hamlet about two miles north of Menai Bridge. It was the address they'd been given via the electoral roll for an Edward Davies, the boy that Zoe mentioned had been pestering Abby.

The outside of the bungalow was tatty and dilapidated. The white paintwork was flaky with dark, damp patches. The front garden was overgrown with knee-high weeds and there was an old fridge propped up against the front window.

'Something tells me Edward Davies isn't house-proud,' Andrea said as they trod carefully up the cracked paving stones to the front door.

Charlie looked around at the other nearby houses that were all neat, tidy with well-tended gardens. 'The neighbours must love having him here.'

Andrea laughed. Then she realised that she'd laughed

a little too much. She wondered if the fact that she found Charlie attractive was getting to her?

Oh God, don't laugh at every little joke he makes, she thought. *Don't be that person.*

Charlie took a step forward and gave a heavy knock on the scruffy door as there didn't seem to be a bell. Andrea noticed that he was wearing a smart-looking silver watch and cufflinks on his shirt.

A few seconds later, the door opened very slowly and a young man peered out at them with bloodshot eyes. He was wearing a baseball cap and a black tracksuit that was slightly stained. He had a patchy beard.

The air was suddenly thick with the smell of weed.

Christ, he's stoned out of his head, Andrea thought immediately.

'Edward Davies?' Charlie asked, holding up his warrant card.

'Yeah,' he grunted. His voice was gravelly. He then put his hand up to his mouth and coughed.

'DC Heaton and DC Jones, Beaumaris CID,' Charlie explained politely. 'Okay if we come in for a minute?'

I'm not actually sure if I want to risk going in there and catching something, Andrea thought dryly to herself.

Davies frowned as if he didn't really understand the question. Then he said, 'Erm, I'm actually in the middle of something so...'

Andrea pushed the door, giving him no choice but to get out of the way. There was a missing teenage girl, so she wasn't going to stand on ceremony. 'Won't take more than a few minutes.'

Davies looked very confused as they came into his hallway. It had a horrible, red patterned carpet and an old mirror up on the wall.

Andrea pointed to the door on the left. 'Okay, if we go in here and talk?'

'Actually, I…' Davies said anxiously.

Andrea entered the filthy, untidy living room and looked for a safe place to sit.

The floor was strewn with pizza boxes, beers cans and takeaway trays. There was a huge television with a video game playing. On the stained coffee table was an ashtray full of spliff ends and to one side there was a small bag of marijuana.

Jesus, people actually live like this.

Davies went over to quickly hide it.

'You understand that possession of a Class B drug is a criminal offence, Edward?' Andrea said as she moved a few things from the sofa so that she and Charlie could sit down.

'Sorry, I…' Davies muttered and then slumped down into the armchair.

Andrea sat forward and looked directly at him. 'At the moment, we're not interested in that,' she said pointing at the bag of marijuana. 'Do you know Abby White?'

Davies nodded and blinked.

'When was the last time you saw her?' Charlie asked as he took out his notepad and pen.

'I dunno,' Davies replied defensively. 'Saturday night.'

Andrea raised an eyebrow. 'Saturday night?'

'She was at a party that I went to in Menai,' Davies explained.

'And you haven't seen her since then?' Charlie enquired.

'No,' Davies said furrowing his brow. 'Has something happened to her?'

Andrea ignored his question and gestured. 'Don't mind if we look around do you, Edward?'

'No,' Davies said with a shrug. 'Is Abby in trouble?'

Andrea and Charlie got up, made their way out into the hallway and then into the kitchen which smelled of sour milk. The sink was full of dirty cups and plates. They then went into what they assumed was Davies' bedroom. The bed was unmade and clothes scattered untidily across the floor.

Andrea squatted to take a quick look under the bed while Charlie opened the doors to the pine wardrobe.

'Anything?' Andrea asked.

'Nope,' Charlie replied.

They took a look in a tiny bedroom that was full of boxes, clothes and general rubbish.

Davies had come out to see what they were doing. 'What are you looking for?'

'How would you describe your relationship with Abby White?' Andrea said sharply.

'Relationship?' Davies said with a furrowed brow.

'Are you friends?'

'Erm, I dunno. Not really.'

'We understand that you've been pestering Abby recently?' Charlie said.

'Pestering? No,' Davies said, sounding concerned. 'I haven't. Who said that?'

'So, if we take a look at Abby's phone, we're not going to see any texts or calls from your phone to hers?'

'No...' Davies said, but Andrea could see he was lying.

'Where were you last night, Edward?' she asked.

'I was here. All night.'

'Can anyone vouch for that? Did you see anyone or speak to anyone on the phone?' Charlie said.

'No.' Davies' breathing was shallow. 'Look, if Abby is missing, it's got nothing to do with me... You should be talking to her uncle.'

Andrea frowned. 'Why do you say that?'

'Cos Abby said her uncle was an old perv and that he scared her,' Davies said hastily.

'Are you talking about Gavin Spears?' Andrea asked to clarify.

'Yeah, Gav,' Davies nodded. 'She said he gives her the creeps the way he looks at her and that.'

'Abby told you that?' Andrea said sceptically.

'Abby told a few of us at a party a few months ago.' Davies shrugged. 'I think she'd drunk too much. She got upset.'

Andrea looked over at Charlie. Davies seemed to all intents and purposes to be telling them the truth. And if what he said to them was true, then Abby going missing from the family home was very concerning.

CHAPTER 13

HMP Tonsgrove
Tuesday, 18 October 2022
2.12 p.m.

'In your interview this morning,' Gareth said as he looked across the table at Hayley Ross, 'you told us that you weren't in your room when Sheila was attacked and you had no idea that she'd been killed until you returned.'

Gareth and Ben were back downstairs in the meeting room at HMP Tonsgrove. Having seen the CCTV, they needed to interview Hayley Ross again as she had clearly lied to them.

'Yeah,' Hayley replied defensively.

Gareth frowned. 'And you stand by that, do you?'

'Eh?' Hayley clearly didn't know quite what Gareth meant. 'Look, I don't understand why you've brought me back down here. I'm meant to be at an NA meeting.'

Gareth reached for his laptop and turned it around so that Hayley could see the screen. 'For the purposes of the tape, I'm showing Hayley Item Reference 893G.' Gareth played the CCTV footage from that morning. 'As you can see, Hayley, this masked person comes into your room at 9.23 a.m. this morning. And then a few seconds later, you come out and run away down the corridor. Is there anything you can tell us about that?'

Hayley shrugged but now looked frightened. 'I didn't see anything.'

Gareth looked at her. 'But you told us that you weren't there, Hayley.'

'Yeah, well I was. But I didn't see anything, I swear down.'

'Can you tell us why you lied to us?' Ben asked.

Hayley gave Ben a withering look and rolled her eyes. 'Why do you think?'

Ben looked at her. 'If you can tell us why you lied to us, please,' he asked in a calm tone.

Gareth knew full well what she was about to say but he needed to hear her say it nonetheless.

'Cos I was scared,' Hayley mumbled as she began to chew at her nails.

'Why were you scared?' Gareth said in a tone that bordered on naive.

'Why d'you think?' she snapped. Her anxiety was clearly getting to her. 'Some psycho came bursting into our pad with a bloody mask. They killed Sheila. Why do you think I'm bloody scared,' she said with an angry brittleness.

Gareth waited for a few seconds. 'How did you know that person had come to attack Sheila and not you?'

Hayley was breathing deeply, trying to compose herself. 'They pointed for me to get out of the room,' she said quietly.

'Did you recognise them?' Ben enquired.

'No.' Hayley replied with a scowl. She then pointed to the laptop screen. 'You can see their face and head are covered. How could I recognise them?'

Gareth sat forward in his seat. 'Maybe you recognised their voice?'

'They didn't speak,' she said as she shook her head.

'Who do you think it was that came into your room, Hayley?' Gareth asked gently.

Hayley pulled a face as if this was a ridiculous question. 'I dunno, do I?'

Gareth arched an eyebrow. 'Come on, Hayley. You must have some idea.'

'No, I don't.' She shook her head adamantly. 'And even if I did, I wouldn't tell you.'

Ben gave her a quizzical look. 'Why not?'

She rolled her eyes again. 'I'm not a grass.'

Gareth waited for a few seconds again. 'You and Sheila were friends, weren't you?'

Hayley nodded uncertainly. 'Yeah,' she replied warily. 'So what?'

'Don't you want the person who did this to Sheila to be brought to justice?' Gareth asked. 'Don't you think Sheila and her family deserve that?'

The question seemed to hit a nerve as Hayley's eyes filled with tears. 'Course I do,' she said, sounding choked. 'Sheila was a nice person. She was good to me and looked after me.'

Gareth narrowed his eyes. 'Then why won't you tell us who you think might have done that to her? Don't you owe it to Sheila to tell us that?'

'I told you,' Hayley whispered as she wiped a tear from her face with the cuff of her top. 'I'm not a grass. Do you know what they do to grasses in a place like this?'

Silence.

'It's bad enough you've brought me down here again,' Hayley said as she sniffed. 'I ain't saying anything else. I wanna go back to the wing.'

Gareth exchanged a frustrated look with Ben. It seemed that no one was willing to talk to them.

CHAPTER 14

Tuesday, 18 October 2022
5.55 p.m.

It had taken Laura all day to finally get down to Beaumaris Beach for her daily swim. She didn't mind one bit. She'd spent a lovely day pottering around the house and hanging out with Jake. They'd started to watch a US comedy television series called *Young Sheldon* which they were now binge-watching. She loved to watch Jake giggle at the jokes as his face lit up with amusement.

Once Rosie had arrived home from work, Laura had packed up her stuff, grabbed Elvis, their beautiful caramel-and-white Bernese mountain dog, and headed down to the beach. It was a relief to have the beach almost to herself after the hectic days of summer when Beaumaris was flooded with tourists. Now the flat, wet sand was only populated by a couple of dog walkers in the distance.

Laura had placed her things beside a tangle of driftwood and then waded into the sea to get that giddy, icy rush once again. Gazing up into the sky, she had seen that a faint outline of the moon had started to appear and in the distance the horizon was showing the lightest touches of indigo as sunset approached.

She just bobbed around in the water as her whole body burned with an icy sting. Her head was clear and any stress had evaporated from her whole being.

This is better than any drugs you could give me, she thought to herself.

Cold-water swimming was so addictive. Lying on her back, she kicked her legs and swam further out. She gazed up at the sky, enjoying how the sea had numbed her head. With her arms outstretched, she floated and bobbed gently. She was a minuscule dot on a tiny planet in an endless universe. And what a relief it was to get a sense of perspective.

After another five minutes, her body was starting to shiver in the water and it was time to get out. For a moment, she gazed across the icy water that now lapped at her shoulders. The darkening, colourless shadows of the Snowdonia mountains on the Welsh mainland cut an uneven line across the horizon. It was only three miles across the narrow strip of sea between Laura and those mountains. Yet, because of there being two tidal pulls, the Strait was a lethal mixture of powerful undercurrents and whirlpools.

As Laura padded over the wet sand, a wave raced over her feet and covered them. Soft ribbons of birch-coloured Oarweed, the local kelp seaweed, gently curled around her toes and then disappeared as the wave receded.

She quickly dried herself, pulled on a thick navy hoodie, trackies and a woollen hat. Grabbing Elvis' lead, she stroked his head. He looked up with his big, doleful chestnut eyes.

'Come on, boy,' Laura said in a cheerful tone. The endorphins were accelerating around her whole body and making her feel happy and energetic.

By the time she got back to her house, Gareth's car was on the drive. She smiled to herself at the thought of seeing him. She couldn't wait for their wedding day. Maybe losing Sam had made her more grateful for the life she had and given her the ability to live for each day and enjoy the small things. She knew only too well how that could all be taken away in the blink of an eye.

Kicking off her trainers, Laura came in through the kitchen door and gave Elvis a bowl of water.

Then she wandered down the hallway to the living room where she assumed Gareth was sitting. Her skin still prickled and glowed from her swim.

'Ah, thought I'd find you skulking here,' she joked as she went over and gave him a kiss.

'Mmm, salty,' Gareth said as he touched his lips.

'I was late swimming today,' Laura explained, pointing to her wet hair that she had now tied back.

'Well, you certainly picked the right day to have off,' Gareth sighed as he sipped his beer. 'A murdered prisoner at Tonsgrove. And a missing teenage girl in Pen-y-garnedd.'

'Yeah, I spoke to Andrea earlier,' Laura said as she flopped down on the sofa next to him and then turned to put her head on his lap and hook her feet over the end of the sofa.

'She rang you on your day off?' Gareth asked.

'No, I rang her,' Laura said.

'Sometimes I think you two are joined at the hip,' he joked with a smile.

Laura frowned. 'But the two aren't linked?'

'Not as far as we know,' Gareth replied.

'You were at Tonsgrove today?' Laura asked.

'Yeah.'

Laura looked at him. 'You met Sanam Parveen?'

'You know her?' Gareth asked sitting forward.

'I'm sure I've crossed paths with her. The name rings a bell.'

'What did you think of her?' Gareth asked, clearly intrigued.

'I can't exactly place her, but Andrea says she's ruthlessly ambitious,' Laura replied. 'Doesn't sound like my cup of tea. She sounds very cold.'

'Yeah, that's the impression I got,' Gareth said.

'Murders in prison are a nightmare to investigate,' Laura said as she thought back to her time in the MMP. 'In fact, we had a murder in Strangeways when she was there. No one would speak to us. Not even the screws.'

'That's the picture I'm getting from our initial enquiries today,' Gareth admitted.

'Luckily for you, I'm back in work tomorrow,' Laura joked.

'That is lucky,' Gareth said sardonically.

There were a few seconds of comfortable silence.

Laura frowned. 'Right, so what's our first dance going to be?'

'At our wedding?' Gareth asked.

'Of course, you muppet,' she said rolling her eyes.

'Muppet? Charming,' Gareth said with a smile. 'We don't really have a song, do we?' he admitted.

'We don't really agree on music,' Laura said, thinking out loud.

Gareth swigged his beer and looked at her. 'We both like the Fleetwood Mac album *Rumours*. Maybe something from that?'

'Really?' Laura snorted. 'An album written on copious amount of cocaine which deals with betrayal, devastation, heartbreak and addiction?'

'And that's not romantic?' Gareth quipped.

Laura gave him a sarcastic smile. 'Stevie Wonder?'

Gareth's face brightened. 'Stevie Wonder. Everyone loves Stevie Wonder.'

'If you say "I Just Called to Say I Love You" though...' Laura warned, 'I will hurt you.'

Gareth raised an eyebrow. '"Ebony and Ivory"?'

'How about "fuck off",' Laura laughed. '"Signed, Sealed, Delivered"?'

'Yes,' Gareth said triumphantly. 'Perfect.'

'Although, doesn't that imply that as a woman I'm being objectified?' Laura asked.

'No, it doesn't,' Gareth groaned. 'And it's a man singing to a woman.'

'Oh yeah,' Laura grinned. 'In that case, let's go for that.'

CHAPTER 15

Laura came into the CID office holding a fresh coffee. She saw that most of the team had already assembled for the morning briefing. She made her way over to her desk, put the coffee down and turned her chair to face the scene boards that had now been set up for Sheila Jones' murder and Abby White's disappearance. Even though she'd only had one day off, she felt refreshed and energised.

Gareth came out of the DI's office and made his way over to the scene boards. He began to roll the sleeves of his cobalt blue shirt as he went. They'd been together for a while, and Laura still found him incredibly attractive.

'Morning, everyone,' Gareth said as he pointed to one of the scene boards which featured a photograph of Abby White at its centre. Written around the photo were the time and date of her disappearance and her date of birth.

Laura gazed at the girl in the photo. Her lovely, innocent smile reminded her of Rosie. For a moment, Laura was taken back to the awful events of the spring of that year. Rosie had been abducted by a man called Henry Marsh. Laura remembered the terrible, sickening, desperate feeling of the moment she knew that Rosie had been taken. She knew that was exactly how Abby White's family would be feeling right now.

'As most of you know, this is Abby White,' Gareth said. 'She's seventeen years old and she went missing from the address that she lives at with her aunt and uncle in Pen-y-garnedd on Monday night. For those of you who don't know, it's a tiny village about four miles north of the Menai Bridge... Andrea, can you bring us up to speed, please?'

Andrea got up and went over to the board. 'At the moment, we don't seem to have any obvious contributing factors to explain Abby's disappearance. Family home seems stable. No criminal record. Nothing out of the ordinary in her life. Abby lives with her aunt and uncle as her mother is working abroad.'

'Has she been contacted?' Gareth enquired.

'Her aunt, Zoe Spears, said she's sent Abby's mother a message and is waiting to hear back. She also said that Abby seemed happy, there was nothing troubling her and there'd been no major issues or arguments. There don't appear to be any belongings missing from her room. All of that makes her disappearance very suspicious and worrying... However, there's no sign of her mobile phone. We've tried the number but it is currently switched off.'

Gareth looked over. 'I assume Digital Forensics are trying to triangulate the phone's GPS?'

'Yes, boss,' Andrea said. 'They should have something later this morning.'

'And no signs of a struggle or anything suspicious in the house?' Laura enquired.

'No.' Andrea shook her head. 'It's as if she vanished into thin air.'

'Relationships?'

'Nothing... Although Zoe did mention an Edward Davies. She seemed to think he'd been hassling her with messages but Abby told her it was nothing. Abby's best friend Becks Maddison described Davies' behaviour as "stalking".'

Laura frowned. She didn't like that sound of that. 'Had it been reported to us?'

'No,' Andrea replied.

'What did he have to say?' Laura said.

'Davies doesn't have an alibi for the Monday night,' Charlie said looking down at the notes in his notepad. 'Claims he was in on his own all night. Didn't see or talk to anyone. We did check the house and there was nothing there that made us suspicious.'

'Let's check Abby's social media and phone records,' Gareth suggested. 'We need an idea of how serious this harassment was. If anything pops up, we can seize Davies' phone and have a decent look at it.'

'There is something else,' Charlie said.

Gareth looked at him. 'Go on.'

'Davies claimed that Abby had told him that Uncle Gavin is an "old perv" and that he "scared" her,' Charlie explained.

Gareth raised an eyebrow. 'Have we spoken to him yet?'

'Not yet.' Andrea shook her head. 'He was out with some locals looking for Abby when we got there.'

'Run a PNC check and look on HOLMES,' Gareth said. 'See if he's got anything on there.'

'Have we searched the family home?' Laura asked.

'Uniform did a preliminary search when they got there,' Andrea explained.

'We need that house and the surrounding area searched thoroughly. Lofts, basements, garden sheds, bins, everything,' Laura said.

Laura remembered the shocking case of Tia Sharp, a twelve-year-old girl, who was reported missing in South London in 2012. She was found murdered, wrapped in a sheet and placed in a bin bag, in the loft of her grandmother's home a week later. Her grandmother's partner, Stuart Hazell, pleaded guilty to her murder.

'Might be worth bringing in the Canine Unit if this doesn't resolve itself quickly,' Gareth suggested. 'Either way, if we haven't found Abby by lunchtime today, I'll hold a press conference.'

'I've distributed the photo of her to all units on Anglesey and North Wales,' Andrea said. 'It should be in everyone's inbox. Let me know if it's not.'

'Good,' Gareth said. 'Any family or friends she might have gone to?'

Charlie looked over. 'Her father is a Chris White who lives in Shrewsbury. Apparently she doesn't have any contact with him.'

'Shrewsbury isn't that far,' Laura stated. 'And she's at an age where she might want to find him and have some kind of relationship. Maybe it wasn't something she thought she could share with her aunt and uncle.'

'Worth checking,' Gareth agreed. Then he moved onto the second scene board which featured a photo of Sheila Jones at its centre. 'Right, this is Sheila Jones. Aged forty-three. She was murdered in her room at HMP Tonsgrove yesterday morning at 9.23 a.m. She was serving a six-year sentence for possession and intent to supply Class A drugs in various places along the North Wales coast. Her partner was Shane Deakins who is affiliated to the Croxteth Boyz gang in Merseyside. Deakins was running a county lines drug-dealing operation out of Colwyn Bay,' Gareth said. 'And according to everyone inside HMP Tonsgrove, that made Sheila untouchable. Or so they thought.'

As Laura looked at the photograph, she realised that she had known Sheila Jones when they were much younger and at primary school. And she remembered that her family had moved over to the Welsh mainland when everyone moved from primary school up to secondary school. It didn't have a bearing on the case itself, but it was sad to see her up there as a victim of murder on the scene board. The last time Laura had seen Sheila, she was a shy ten-year-old who lacked any confidence.

'Do we think Sheila's murder has something to do with what Deakins was doing on the outside?' Andrea asked.

'Possibly. I've seen a drugs turf war on the outside spill over into what happens in a prison,' Gareth said. 'The problem so far is that no one is willing to tell us anything. Her cellmate is too scared to say anything. The prison officer responsible for the area of G Wing where the attack took place wasn't forthcoming either. He wasn't even willing to speculate on who might have attacked Sheila. We've also got a faulty CCTV camera on our killer's route away from the scene of the attack.'

'Do we think that's deliberate?' Laura asked.

'If it is, that would mean that Sheila's murder was an inside job,' Gareth said.

Laura shrugged. 'Wouldn't be the first time I've encountered corrupt prison staff.'

'No, of course not. But at the moment, we're dealing with a culture of silence from the prisoners and the staff at Tonsgrove which makes our investigation almost impossible. We're now relying completely on forensic evidence.' Gareth gave a frustrated sigh and then perched on the edge of the table. 'Ben and I are going to talk to Barry

McDonald, the prison's teacher. He was the last person to talk to Sheila that morning. I need to know who Sheila's next of kin are, asap. Let's get a phone log of all calls into and out of the prison in the days leading up to her murder.'

As Gareth turned back towards his office, Laura could see his frustration. It gave her an idea.

Getting up from the desk, she walked across the CID room and knocked on his open door.

'You okay?' she asked as she watched him smooth his hand over his scalp. Gareth usually did this when he was feeling stressed, so it wasn't a good sign.

'Yeah. I'm worried about Abby White. Girls like that don't usually vanish without a trace and for no apparent reason,' Gareth admitted. 'And I think the investigation into Sheila Jones' murder is going to be problematic if no one is going to tell us anything and everyone is working against us.'

'I've realised that I went to primary school with Sheila Jones,' Laura said. 'I mean, I haven't seen her since she was ten, but it was just very sad to see her photo up there.'

Gareth gave her an empathetic nod. 'Yeah, of course.'

Laura plonked herself down on a nearby chair. 'So, I've got an idea that might solve your ongoing problem.'

Gareth gave her a quizzical look. 'What are you talking about?'

'Put me undercover in HMP Tonsgrove,' Laura said.

'What?' Gareth looked horrified. Then he frowned. 'Are you joking?'

'No.' Laura shook her head. 'I worked most of my career in Manchester. I only just started working as a police officer in Beaumaris. I'm still a virtual stranger.'

'Is this because we watched *Donnie Brasco* last night?' Gareth asked.

'No... Partly,' Laura admitted. 'If no one is going to

talk to you about what happened to Sheila Jones, you need someone on the inside.'

'No way,' Gareth said forcefully. 'It's far too dangerous. What if someone recognises you? Or what if someone finds out you're a copper?'

'You pull me out,' Laura said with a shrug. 'Otherwise you're going to be banging your head against a brick wall in this investigation. Plus you can put one of those tiny phones inside the heel of my shoe for emergencies. I've seen that done before.'

'Was that in a film too?' Gareth said dryly.

'No that was in Strangeways actually.'

Gareth gave her a searching look. 'Why do you want to go into Tonsgrove?'

Laura took a few seconds to respond.

'I suppose I always felt sorry for Sheila when she was at school,' she admitted. 'Her home life was terrible. Her clothes were dirty and sometimes she smelled. The other kids used to tease her and say she was a stinky tramp. I guess I want to find out who did this to her.'

'Warlow would never sanction it,' Gareth said.

He was talking about Superintendent Richard Warlow who was the most senior ranking officer at Beaumaris nick.

'Why don't you just ask him,' Laura suggested.

There were a few seconds silence.

'No. It's a crazy idea. Sorry,' Gareth said adamantly. 'Let's see what this Barry McDonald can tell us before we do anything dramatic like put you in there undercover.'

'He's going to tell you the same as everyone else,' Laura said with a knowing look. 'He doesn't know anything. And even if he did, he wouldn't tell you anyway.'

'Let's see, shall we?' Gareth said with shrug.

CHAPTER 16

HMP Tonsgrove
Wednesday, 19 October 2022
10.37 a.m.

Gareth and Ben were now back inside HMP Tonsgrove and being escorted across the yard towards the education block. They walked along the pathway flanked by an eight-foot wire fence. The icy wind picked up as it blew across the prison site and made a low groaning sound. Gareth regretted not putting on some form of hat as his ears and the top of his head were stinging from the cold.

A woman wolf-whistled at them from a window high up and it reverberated across the whole site. Others cackled with echoey laughter. Ben looked up and the woman mimed giving him a blow job as she stuck her tongue in her cheek.

'Could be your lucky day, Ben,' Gareth quipped.

'Don't worry.' The male prison officer rolled his eyes. 'You get used to it,' he said wearily.

Gareth gave Ben a wry smile before peering up at the miserable grey sky, which had started to fill with soft drizzle. As they approached the education block, the air was filled with the smell of oil, the sound of metallic banging and a tinny radio playing dance music.

There were a couple of prisoners working on an old Fiat car which had its bonnet up. Gareth guessed it was some kind of motor mechanics course. The two women prisoners who had been inspecting the engine, turned to stare at them. Gareth assumed they knew they were coppers – and that essentially made them the enemy.

The officer led them inside and Gareth could feel the warmth beginning to thaw out the tops of his ears. The air was thick with the smell of paint and glue, like the craft room in a school. They made their way along a corridor that was lined with more photos and inspirational quotes: EDUCATION IS THE MOST POWERFUL WEAPON YOU CAN USE TO CHANGE THE WORLD – NELSON MANDELA.

They arrived at an untidy classroom and the officer gestured to a man sitting behind a desk. He was in his late forties, greying goatee and scruffy hair. The man exuded the persona of an old-fashioned teacher – jacket with leather elbow patches, corduroy trousers and thick glasses that had been fixed with a strip of plaster.

'Barry?' the officer called over. 'These are the detectives from Beaumaris.'

Barry nodded, got up and gave them a suspicious look. 'You're here because of what happened to Sheila, aren't you?'

Gareth nodded. 'Mind if we sit down?'

'Suit yourself,' Barry said in an unfriendly tone.

Gareth looked at Ben as they perched on a nearby table.

'You're one of the teachers here, is that right?' Ben asked as he fished out his notebook and pen.

'Yes, that's right,' Barry replied. 'English mainly. Humanities.' Then he looked over at them. 'Listen, I make it a rule not to talk to the police usually. I've seen too many women in here that have been mistreated or let down by the system. But I was very fond of Sheila, so...'

Gareth felt a little frustrated at Barry's attitude but it wasn't uncommon. 'You saw Sheila on Tuesday morning just before she was attacked. Is that right?'

'Yes. She had an assignment that she wanted to give me. It's coursework towards her English GCSE,' Barry explained.

'How did she seem?' Ben asked.

'She was fine,' Barry said and then paused for a moment. 'Actually, she was more than fine. She seemed genuinely happy that morning which makes what happened to her even more tragic.'

Gareth got the feeling that Barry had got to know Sheila pretty well while teaching her. And he might be the only person who would tell them anything about her.

'And how did Sheila seem recently? Was she worried about anything or had she been involved in any arguments?' Gareth asked.

'Not that I know of. I got the feeling that she was in a new relationship within the prison,' Barry said. 'I don't ask about that sort of thing. It's not my business. But I'd overheard a few things in class.'

'Do you know who that relationship was with?' Ben asked.

'No... And I'm not saying any more than that,' Barry snorted. 'I'm not giving you names. It's taken me a long time to get the women's trust in here. Plus, if I give you a name, that makes me vulnerable. There are plenty of women in here that I don't want to get on the wrong side of. And sometimes they're married to some very dangerous men who know where I work.'

'This is a murder enquiry,' Gareth said in a serious tone

even though he understood Barry's concerns. 'So, if you're withholding evidence from us and our investigation, that is a criminal offence.'

Barry gave him a wry smile which Gareth found irritating.

'I know my rights, Detective,' Barry said in a pompous tone. 'Arrest me for obstruction and see where that gets you.' He then sat forward on his seat and looked over at them. 'No one in here is going to talk to you about what happened to Sheila. On the outside, she was involved with some very dangerous people. It doesn't matter if you're a prisoner, a screw, a teacher or a probation worker. Everyone's too scared to say anything. It's like there's a code of silence in here and God help anyone who breaks it.'

'That's not true.' Ben stopped writing and glanced at Barry. 'Governor Parveen told us that she would make sure we got as much help with this investigation as we needed.'

'Governor Parveen!' Barry snorted. 'Jesus, the only thing she's interested in is her next job. She wants to sweep what happened to Sheila under the carpet as fast as she can. And certainly doesn't want your lot poking your noses into how she runs this prison.'

Gareth could feel his frustration growing. 'I think that Sheila and her family deserve some kind of justice for what happened to her, don't you?'

'I completely agree with you,' Barry said with a condescending nod. 'That doesn't change the fact that no one will talk to you and you're wasting your time trying to get them to.'

Gareth was starting to wonder if Laura's idea of going undercover might be the only way of finding out what had happened to Sheila.

CHAPTER 17

Menai
Wednesday, 19 October 2022
10.49 a.m.

Andrea and Charlie arrived at the small café – The Coffee Shop – in Menai where Becks Maddison, Abby White's friend, worked. It was modern and fashionably minimal inside with lights strung across the ceiling, simple tables and chairs and a large blackboard with various coffees, teas, cakes and pastries written in white chalk.

A mixed-race girl, about the same age as Abby, approached. She was pretty, with braided hair and wearing a navy blue apron.

'Table for two is it?' she asked politely with a smile.

Andrea pulled out her warrant card discreetly. 'DC Jones from Beaumaris CID. We're looking for Becks Maddison?' she said in a soft voice.

'That's me,' Becks said, immediately looking concerned. 'Is it Abby? Have you found her? Zoe has been texting me,' she babbled anxiously.

'I'm afraid we haven't found Abby yet,' Andrea said. 'But we do have a few questions we'd like to ask you. Is there somewhere quiet we could go?'

'Erm, we could go out the back,' Becks suggested, pointing to a door that was half open and clearly led to an outside space.

'Thanks,' Charlie said as they followed her across the café and out through the door.

Becks blinked at them nervously. 'I don't understand, what's happened to her...'

'You were with Abby on Monday night, is that correct?' Andrea asked.

'Yes,' Becks said and then her eyes filled with tears. She put her hand to her face to wipe them away. 'Sorry, I...'

'No need to apologise,' Andrea reassured her as she reached into her pocket, pulled out a tissue and handed it to her.

'Thanks,' Becks said as she took the tissue. 'I'm just so scared.'

Andrea gave her an empathetic look. 'Of course.'

Ben looked at her and asked, 'Can you tell us what time you arrived and left her home?'

'I think I arrived about eight,' Becks said with a thoughtful expression. 'And I left just before midnight... I just don't understand where she could have gone.'

'And you were in Abby's bedroom the whole time?' Ben asked.

Becks nodded.

Andrea looked at her. 'What were you doing?'

'We watched an episode of *Made In Chelsea*. I don't really like it but Abby thinks it's hilarious,' Becks explained. 'Then we were just watching stuff on YouTube and TikTok.'

'And you stayed in her bedroom the whole time?' Andrea said.

Becks nodded but she looked overwhelmed again as she took a deep breath.

'How did she seem to you?' Ben said.

'Fine. She was fine.'

'Nothing bothering her? No arguments with anyone?' Andrea asked.

Becks shook her head. 'Not that I know of.'

Ben looked at her. 'Do you know an Edward Davies?'

Becks nodded. 'Yes,' she said. 'Unfortunately.'

'You don't like him?' Andrea enquired.

Becks pulled a face. 'No... He's a total loser.'

Andrea raised an eyebrow. 'We understand that Edward has been harassing Abby?'

Becks frowned and thought for a second. 'Erm, I'm not sure it was harassing. He's been messaging her and asking her to go out and stuff. And she's blocked him.'

'Was Abby scared by any of this?' Ben said.

'Oh no.' Becks shook her head adamantly. 'She thought it was funny. Edward's just a bit of a dick, that's all. Pretty harmless. And Abby can stand up for herself.'

'Is there anyone else that you can think of that would want to harm Abby?' Andrea said.

'No,' Becks replied but the question seemed to upset her again as a tear rolled down her face. 'Abby is lovely. Everyone loves her. She wouldn't hurt anyone. That's why I don't understand why this has happened.'

'How did she get on with her Aunt Zoe?' Ben asked.

'Zoe is a total legend. They get on really well.'

Andrea narrowed her eyes and then asked, 'What about her Uncle Gavin?'

Becks bristled but didn't say anything for a few seconds.

93

'Becks?' Andrea prompted her.

'I dunno,' she said hesitantly.

Andrea looked at her. 'Whatever it is, you need to tell us,' she said gently.

'He's a bit creepy,' Becks admitted. 'And Abby didn't like to be around him on her own.'

'Do you know if anything had happened to make her feel like that?' Andrea said.

'No. I'm not sure. I think it was just the way he looked at her. And sometimes he'd just barge into her bedroom when she was getting dressed,' Becks said. 'You don't think he's got something to do with it?'

Andrea didn't reply as she reached into her pocket, pulled out her contact card and handed it to Becks. 'This is my card. It's got all my numbers on it. If you think of anything else, please call me. However small you think it is, it might help us find Abby.'

Becks nodded as she looked thoughtfully at the card.

Andrea got the feeling that Becks wanted to tell them something but was hesitating.

'Is there anything else you want to tell us?' Andrea asked in a soft voice.

Becks paused for a second, then said, 'We weren't in Abby's bedroom all night. I'm really sorry.'

'Where were you?' Andrea said.

'There's a little summer house in the garden. It's got a sofa and a Bluetooth speaker,' Becks explained. 'We snuck out of Abby's window and went in there.'

'Why didn't you tell us that?' Ben asked.

Becks hesitated.

'Whatever it is, you just need to tell us,' Andrea explained in a kind voice.

'We went out there for a smoke,' Becks admitted.

'Weed?' Andrea asked.

Becks nodded but looked nervous.

'Don't worry about that,' Andrea reassured her. 'Where was Abby when you left to go home?'

Becks looked at them. 'I left her in the summer house listening to music.'

CHAPTER 18

CID, Beaumaris Police Station
Wednesday, 19 October 2022
11.58 a.m.

Gareth knocked at the closed door and heard a 'Come in' from the other side. Opening the door, he walked in and saw Superintendent Richard Warlow, dressed in his police uniform, looking back at him with his usual dour expression. He was tall and wiry, with a mop of grey hair and wore thick rimmed glasses. Gareth had little time for Warlow. He was petty, controlling and lacked any sense of humour. In CID they called him Partridge, after the comedic television character Alan Partridge. Not only was Warlow inept, but he also had an inflated sense of his own importance and spent more time self-promoting than doing his actual job.

Warlow also had a strange sniff, like a nervous tic, which meant you could identify him coming down the corridor before he arrived. Gareth had joked that all Warlow could sniff was his next promotion.

'Come and sit down, Gareth,' Warlow said, gesturing to a chair in front of his long wooden desk.

'Thank you, sir,' Gareth said as he went over and sat down.

'You wanted a word?' Warlow asked as he sat back on his big, black office chair and interlaced his fingers. 'Is this about the murder investigation at HMP Tonsgrove?'

'Yes, sir,' Gareth replied.

'How is it progressing?' he asked as he took off his glasses and began to clean them.

Gareth let out a sigh. 'I'm afraid we've come up against a bit of a brick wall.'

Warlow pulled a face. 'How do you mean?'

'Essentially there seems to be a code of silence in the prison. Both prisoners and staff,' Gareth explained. 'No one wants to talk to us. We have one piece of CCTV that is of no real use. Another CCTV camera wasn't working.'

Warlow put his glasses back on and narrowed his eyes in disbelief. 'Really?'

'We've interviewed prison officers, a prison teacher, and Sheila Jones' cellmate,' Gareth said. 'Everyone is too scared to say anything for fear of reprisals either inside the prison, or against family on the outside.'

Warlow gave Gareth a meaningful look. 'I assume you've met Sanam Parveen?'

'The governor? Yes,' Gareth replied, giving nothing away.

'What did you make of her?' Warlow asked, but there was something about the question that suggested Warlow wasn't telling him everything.

'Businesslike, ambitious,' Gareth said warily. 'I get the feeling she's not popular with the staff.'

'I've had the National Crime Agency on the phone to me this morning,' Warlow explained with a meaningful expression. He then leaned forward and looked at Gareth. 'They're running some kind of covert operation on Parveen.'

What? Why the hell are the NCA involved?

Gareth frowned. 'I don't understand, sir.'

'What I'm about to tell you stays within the confines of this room until we've spoken to the officers from the NCA.'

'Of course.'

'Sanam Parveen's family come from Lahore in Pakistan,' Warlow said. 'Her uncle is Sajit Parveen. The NCA suspect that he runs a drug gang trafficking heroin from Pakistan to the UK. The Parveen family are based in Blackburn.'

Gareth's eyes widened. 'Why are they looking at her?'

'They had a tip-off that Sanam was controlling the sale of drugs inside HMP Tonsgrove,' Warlow said with a dark look. 'At the moment, they've got no more than that tip-off. And she has no criminal record. In fact, her rise up the career ladder in the UK Justice system has been meteoric. So, it might be someone trying to sully her reputation.'

'But if she is involved in the selling of drugs at Tonsgrove, she might also be involved in Sheila Jones' murder,' Gareth said, thinking out loud.

'That is a possibility that I flagged up with the NCA,' Warlow said. 'They're sending over a couple of their chaps from Manchester to talk to us.'

'I do have a suggestion about the investigation into Sheila Jones' murder that I wanted to run past you,' Gareth explained.

'Fire away,' Warlow said.

Gareth looked at him. 'I want to put an undercover officer into Tonsgrove.'

Warlow thought about Gareth's proposal for a few seconds and then gave him a quizzical look. 'Do you think that's the only way to gain intel about her death?'

'I really do,' Gareth replied.

Warlow thought for a few more seconds. 'Who do you suggest?'

Gareth looked at him. 'DI Laura Hart. She hasn't been with us for long. And she spent a lot of time living and working away in Manchester.'

'Yes... That does makes sense, I suppose,' Warlow said as he nodded thoughtfully. 'And she's happy to work undercover?'

'It was her idea, sir,' Gareth said. 'And she has some experience of working undercover.'

However, Gareth could feel his anxiety growing at the thought of Laura going into Tonsgrove.

'There is now a major problem with that type of operation,' Warlow said with a knowing expression.

Gareth raised an eyebrow. He knew what Warlow was going to say. 'How would we put an officer into Tonsgrove to dig around into Sheila's murder, if we think that Sanam Parveen is corrupt?'

'Exactly,' Warlow said. 'I sanctioned an undercover operation a few years ago at HMP Rhoswen on the mainland. But we had the full co-operation of the governor and the prison officers.'

Gareth ran his hand over his scalp thoughtfully. 'I think with the NCA's help, we could put Laura in there without anyone at Tonsgrove knowing who she is. And I'm assuming the NCA would jump at the chance to have an undercover officer in there too?'

'Possibly. If there is a way of getting Laura into Tonsgrove without anyone knowing, then maybe it's a viable proposition,' Warlow said, but then he narrowed his eyes. 'And you're aware that putting her in there without anyone knowing her identity does make her far more vulnerable.'

'Yes, sir,' Gareth replied. 'I am aware of that. We both are.'

Even as he said it, Gareth couldn't help but feel a growing sense of unease.

CHAPTER 19

Pen-y-garnedd
Wednesday, 19 October 2022
12.35 p.m.

Andrea and Charlie drove along the road out of Menai towards Pen-y-garnedd. After a few minutes, they passed a sign on the right that read WEM FARM. Up ahead, there was a small set of temporary traffic lights that had been set up for some roadworks outside a church.

Andrea pulled the car to stop beside the churchyard and looked out to her right. All she could see were the lines of whitish grey headstones. Their tops tapered away into the distance. The perimeter wall of the church was old and covered in ivy and moss.

As she looked over at Charlie, she could see that he was staring over at the churchyard – he was clearly lost in thought.

'You okay?' she asked.

'Yes, sorry,' Charlie said, blinking and looking back over at her.

Andrea frowned. 'Sure?'

Charlie gave an uncertain nod. 'Being here just reminded me of something, that's all.'

Andrea didn't respond but gave him a look as if to say that she was happy to listen.

'Something that happened here when I was a probationer in uniform,' Charlie said with a sad expression. 'We got called to that farm back there. A girl had been out on her bike when she was run over by her brother in a tractor. She was only six.'

'That's horrible,' Andrea said empathetically.

'It was first time I'd ever seen anyone dead,' Charlie remembered and then visibly took a breath. 'And the girl was lying there on the path. Her mother was screaming hysterically. And I just froze. I didn't know what to do or say. Luckily my sarge was really experienced.' Charlie then gestured to the church. 'And we went to her funeral the following week. I just haven't thought about it for a while but it stayed with me.'

'Of course, it did,' Andrea reassured him. 'You wouldn't be human if it didn't.'

'Thanks,' Charlie said with a grateful expression.

Andrea looked up and saw that the traffic light was now green. She put the car into gear as they pulled away.

The next few minutes, they drove in thoughtful silence.

Eventually Charlie gestured to his phone. 'I should be getting that check on Gavin Spears back any second now.'

Charlie had organised a check on Gavin Spears on the Police National Computer (PNC). It would show prior convictions, cautions, warnings or reprimands. It also gave dates and outcomes of any criminal justice proceedings.

Both Edward Davies and Becks Maddison had told them that Abby was uncomfortable around her uncle Gavin. That she might even be scared of him.

It sounded as if his behaviour around Abby was inappropriate.

Then Charlie gave Andrea a significant look as he gestured to his phone. 'Message from the DBS.'

'What is it?'

'Gavin Spears was convicted of having sex with a minor in 1985. He served eighteen months of a three-year sentence.'

Andrea frowned. 'Long time ago. But it does mean he has form.'

Looking up, she saw that they were now in the road where Zoe and Gavin Spears lived. There was a white SOCO forensic van outside their house as well as a uniformed patrol car.

Neighbours in an adjacent garden were chatting and looking over at what was going on.

Parking the car, Andrea unclipped her seatbelt and opened the door. She was still deep in thought about what they had just learned about Gavin Spears.

'We need to talk to him asap,' Charlie said as they made their way towards the house and up the garden path.

North Wales' chief pathologist, Professor Helen Lane, dressed in a full white forensic suit was coming out of the front door.

'DC Jones,' Lane said as she pulled down her mask.

'This is DC Heaton,' Andrea said, introducing Charlie. 'He's only been with us a short while.'

'Nice to meet you,' Helen said.

'Have you got anything for us?' Andrea asked.

'Nothing yet,' Lane admitted. 'We're a bit stretched at the moment with the murder at Tonsgrove.'

'Yes, of course,' Andrea said. 'We now understand that the last time anyone saw Abby she was actually in the summer house in the garden and not inside the house. Have you guys been in there yet?'

'We're working our way through the house. Then we'll go out the back to the shed, garden and bins.' Lane gestured to the front door. 'I'd better get back but thanks for letting me know.'

Andrea spotted Zoe sitting over on the low garden wall. She was vaping and lost in anxious thought. She had a piece of paper in her hand.

'Zoe?' Andrea said as she approached.

Her head whipped round to look at them. 'Have you heard anything?' she asked in nervous anticipation.

'No, I'm sorry,' Andrea said with an apologetic tone. 'We're looking for Gavin. There are a few questions we'd like to ask him.'

'Right,' Zoe said looking distraught. 'He's out there with some neighbours looking for Abby.' She showed them an A4 piece of paper which had a photo of Abby at the centre. Printed on it was:

Help us find Abby White.
We are appealing for the public's help in finding missing teenager Abby White, aged 17 years.
Abby went missing from her home on Monday evening in the Pen-y-garnedd area.

'I see,' Andrea said. 'We do need to speak to him urgently.'

'Why?' Zoe frowned suspiciously. 'Can't you ask me?'

'Can you give Gavin a call and ask him to come back here to talk to us?' Andrea asked.

'Erm, yes. I suppose so,' Zoe said, but she seemed confused.

'Thank you,' Charlie said politely.

'Have you managed to speak to Abby's mother yet?' Andrea asked.

'We keep missing each other,' Zoe explained. 'But she is aware that Abby is missing.'

'I assume that she's going to try to get back,' Charlie said.

'Yes,' Zoe said, but something about this suggested she was hiding something from them.

'We'll need to speak to her as soon as she arrives,' Andrea explained.

'Of course,' Zoe said as she took another long drag of her vape.

Andrea and Charlie walked away.

'What was that about?' Charlie asked.

'I don't know,' Andrea replied. 'Maybe she doesn't get on with her sister.'

Whatever it was, Zoe's manner had definitely been suspicious.

They headed over to the SOCO van where they were given white nitrile forensic suits, boots, masks, and hats.

Making their way up the garden path again, they saw Lane walking towards them holding something in her hand.

'I think we've got something significant,' Lane said gesturing to what looked like a diary. 'One of my officers found this hidden under Abby's mattress in her bedroom. It's her diary.' Lane then opened the diary. 'And this is the entry for last Sunday...'

Andrea peered at the writing:

He was waiting outside the bathroom when I had a shower. He's such a perv. I wish he'd die. He makes me feel sick when he looks at me.

Andrea looked over at Charlie. They needed to talk to Gavin Spears asap.

CHAPTER 20

Meeting Room, Beaumaris Police Station
Wednesday, 19 October 2022
12.58 p.m.

Laura moved her chair forward and settled herself. She was sitting at the large table in the meeting room on the ground floor of Beaumaris nick. Gareth was sitting to her left and Superintendent Warlow to her right.

There was a knock at the door and Gareth went to answer it. It was DS Brooks and DI Carmichael from the NCA. Gareth did all the introductions and poured them two coffees before sitting back down.

DS Brooks, forties, rotund, ginger hair and a short beard, looked over at them. He tapped a folder that he'd put on the table with his forefinger. 'As I explained to Superintendent Warlow, we have been running a surveillance operation for the past six months on Sanam Parveen at HMP Tonsgrove. Some of her family are still based in Lahore in Pakistan.' Brooks then opened the folder and pulled out a photograph of an man in his fifties with a thick black beard. 'This is Sajit Parveen, her uncle. We

105

suspect that Sajit runs a drug gang trafficking heroin from Pakistan to the UK. The Parveen family's UK base is in Blackburn.'

DI Carmichael, fifties, bald, glasses, looked over. 'We had intel from a CHIS that Sanam Parveen was using her position as governor of Tonsgrove as a way of selling heroin for the family.'

A CHIS stood for Covert Human Intelligence Source, which essentially meant an informant or, more colloquially, a grass.

'How reliable is that intel?' Laura asked.

DI Carmichael sat forward on his chair. 'This is usually a very reliable source. But so far, we've been unable to find anything that links Sanam Parveen to trafficking or selling drugs.'

'We've had a tap on her phone and intercepted all her text messages and emails,' DS Brooks explained. 'And we've had surveillance on Sanam when she's not at Tonsgrove. But what we don't have is any reliable way of seeing what she's doing inside the prison.'

'We also don't know if the murder of Sheila Jones is part of some drug turf war within in the prison,' DI Carmichael said. 'But given Sheila Jones' links to Shane Deakins and the Croxteth Boyz OCG in Merseyside, we think it's likely that Jones was dealing inside the prison. The question is whether or not her murder is linked to Sanam Parveen.'

Warlow nodded and then said, 'We do have a suggestion that might help your ongoing investigation into Parveen *and* our investigation into Sheila Jones' murder.'

Laura was feeling a little nervous at the prospect of going undercover. It had been a long time since she'd done anything like that, so to say that it would be taking her out of her comfort zone would be an understatement. But she could also see that having a trained police officer inside the prison would be invaluable in finding out the extent of Parveen's corruption and bringing to justice whoever murdered Sheila Jones.

'We're all ears,' DI Carmichael said with a curious expression.

Gareth shifted on his seat and looked at Laura. 'Our suggestion is to put DI Hart into Tonsgrove undercover as a prisoner.'

DI Carmichael and DS Brooks looked at each other for a second.

'How do you feel about that, DI Hart?' DI Carmichael asked.

'I understand that there are risks in such an operation. Especially as we won't be able to make my identity known to Parveen or any of the prison officers or staff,' Laura said calmly. 'But as far as our investigation into Sheila's murder goes, we've come up against a brick wall. No one will talk to us. Having an experienced officer inside the prison would allow the kind of unique access that would benefit both our investigations.'

DS Brooks frowned. 'If your identity is concealed from everyone, that does make you more vulnerable.'

Laura nodded. 'I understand that.'

'But we would have various strategies in place to keep DI Hart safe and contactable,' Warlow reassured them.

There were a couple of seconds of silence.

'In that case, I think it's an astute move,' DI Carmichael said encouragingly and then looked over at Laura. 'If we can liaise with probation, we could have you in Tonsgrove tomorrow morning. How does that sound to everyone?'

Laura forced a smile. 'Great. The sooner the better,' she said, even though her pulse was now racing at the thought of it.

CHAPTER 21

Rose Cottage
Wednesday, 19 October 2022
01.12 p.m.

As the forensic search continued in Rose Cottage, Andrea and Charlie had made their way to the rear of the property. Becks had told them that the last time she saw Abby was in the garden's summer house listening to music after they'd been smoking weed.

Andrea had just checked her phone and seen that now the news that Abby was missing was out, the social media trolls had started. There were comments trending about Zoe and Gavin Spears. Nothing intelligent. Just the usual toxic stuff about murderers in these cases often being close to home. Gavin Spears had 'the look of a paedo'. There was 'always something weird' about Gavin Spears and how he'd been interested in 'little girls' when he was at school. Andrea knew that she needed to take these comments with a pinch of salt. Social media seemed to attract some very strange and angry people who had an axe to grind about everything and everyone.

The Spears' garden was neat and tidy. Flower beds were well-tended and there was stylish black rattan furniture on the patio.

The grey sky had now been replaced with glowing autumnal sunshine which washed the garden with a lovely primrose hue. Above them, thin, wispy clouds had slowly morphed into what looked like a fish skeleton. High up on a birch tree with golden brown leaves, a crow peered down at them silently.

'Do we think that Gavin Spears has something to do with Abby's disappearance and is just hiding in plain sight?' Charlie asked.

'There's definitely something about his behaviour that's making me feel uneasy,' Andrea admitted.

She also knew there was a long history of killers helping police in the search for their victims. She assumed they got a sick thrill from being in the middle of the chaos and fear they had created. Russell Bishop and his dog helped police scour woodland in the 'Babes in the Woods' case in 1986. Bishop had murdered two nine-year-old girls in the woodland that he helped search. In 2002, Ian Huntley searched for the missing girls in Soham when he had in fact murdered them and hidden their bodies forty miles away the previous day.

At the far end of the large garden, there was a one-storey wooden shed next to a summer house. They stood side by side. It looked like they had interconnecting doors.

Andrea reached out with her gloved hand and tried to open the door to the summer house. It was locked. She then moved left to the shed door. She turned the handle, opened the door and went into the interior of the shed. She was immediately hit by the smell of damp and grass cuttings.

The inside of the shed was cavernous and shadowy.

There were shelving units stacked against the walls, along with workbenches, ladders and old paint pots.

Charlie glanced over as he used his torch to see where he was going as he stepped carefully over some boxes.

'I'm guessing the other one is the summer house that Becks was talking about,' he said.

'Looks like it,' Andrea said.

Moving her torch slowly over the area in front of her, she saw a shape under a grey tarpaulin.

Her heart sank.

'Charlie,' Andrea said in a concerned voice.

Charlie appeared next to her.

The shape under the grey tarpaulin looked like a body.

The colour drained from Charlie's face.

'You okay?' Andrea asked under her breath.

'Yeah, fine,' Charlie reassured her.

Andrea moved forward, crouched down and carefully lifted the tarpaulin, preparing herself for what or who might be underneath.

Then she saw a fringe of dark, green material.

Thank God.

'It's okay,' Andrea said with a sigh of relief. 'It's a carpet.'

Charlie blew out his cheeks. He looked equally relieved.

Andrea gestured to the door that looked like it led into the adjacent summer house. 'Better have a look in there.'

They moved towards the door, opened it and went inside.

Andrea could smell stale weed and tobacco in the air.

There were posters of Billie Eilish, Sam Fender and Tom Grennan on the walls.

There was a dark blue futon that had been folded out onto the floor. There was a duvet spread out, along with some furry blankets and cushions.

On the far side, there was a table with two wine glasses, an empty bottle of wine and a full ashtray.

Andrea was looking around for anything suspicious but nothing struck her as out of the ordinary. As Charlie crouched down and looked at the cushions and blankets, she went over to the table.

There were the remnants of several spliffs in the ashtray and some red wine stains on the wood.

'Andrea,' Charlie said in a concerned tone.

She turned to see what he'd found.

'I think there's a blood stain on this cushion,' Charlie said as he pointed to a dark green cushion that had a Japanese pattern on it.

Andrea came over, crouched down and looked at it. There was a dark stain about the size of a fist and it definitely had the appearance of blood.

Glancing around, Andrea took the edge of the duvet and as she moved it, she saw that the blue material was also stained with a dark patch.

Standing up, she very slowly pulled the duvet back.

Oh my God!

The whole of the futon was stained with a dark patch that measured about six foot by four foot.

She went to its edge and very carefully touched it.

Looking at her forefinger, she saw that it was damp and red with what looked like congealed blood.

Her heart sank as she looked up at Charlie.

'It's blood,' she confirmed.

They were standing in the middle of the scene of a terrible crime.

'Jesus,' Charlie muttered under his breath.

'We need Professor Lane in here right now,' Andrea said with a sense of urgency. Then she looked around. 'There's got to be a door out to the garden in here.'

Charlie went to a long, thick curtain and moved it to one side. Underneath was a wooden door. 'Here we go.' Reaching with his gloved hand, Charlie turned the key and opened the door.

They went outside.

Andrea could see Lane talking to a SOCO to the rear of the house.

'Professor Lane?' she called over loudly.

Lane looked over with a frown. 'Yes?'

'There's something we need you to come and look at,' Andrea explained in a serious tone. 'It's urgent.'

Lane gave a wave of acknowledgement. She then signalled to two SOCOs to follow her and they made their way across the garden to where Andrea and Charlie were standing.

'We've found something significant in the summer house,' Andrea said with a dark expression.

'Right, well you'd better show me,' Lane said calmly as Andrea and Charlie led them inside.

'We found this under the duvet and cushions,' Charlie said.

'Right,' Lane said as she squatted down.

'I nearly missed it as it was completely covered. And there was no sign of a struggle or anything suspicious in here,' Andrea admitted.

'What can you tell us?' Charlie asked.

'Looks like a substantial amount of blood,' she stated and then frowned. 'At first look, I'd suggest that anyone who had lost this amount of blood would certainly be unconscious and possibly even dead.'

Andrea looked around the interior. 'There aren't any other obvious places where there's blood.'

Lane nodded. 'If this is Abby White's blood, where is she now, and how did she leave? Was she taken without her blood leaving any trace elsewhere?'

Charlie looked at them. 'What if her body was wrapped up in something like a rug or carpet and then carried out?'

Lane thought for a second and then agreed, 'Yes, that might explain it.'

Andrea's train of thought was interrupted by some shouting out in the garden. She went outside and saw Zoe marching across the grass towards her.

Andrea put her hand up and stood in her way. 'You can't come in here, Zoe.'

'Have you found her?' Zoe asked, her face twisted in anguish as she tried to look through the door.

Andrea shook her head. 'No. Abby's not in there.'

'Then what is it?' she asked. 'Tell me.'

Andrea thought for a second.

Zoe looked directly at her with pleading eyes. 'Please, tell me what you've found.'

'We've found a substantial amount of blood inside the summer house,' Andrea explained gently.

'No, no... what do you mean?' Zoe asked as she trembled.

'I know this is difficult,' Andrea said trying to manoeuvre Zoe away from the doorway. 'I just need you to let us get on with our job.'

'What's going on?' boomed a male voice.

It was Gavin Spears.

He was in his late fifties with an untidy mop of greying hair, stubble and a bulbous nose. He was wearing a camouflage jacket and work trousers that had patches on the knees.

Andrea looked at him. 'I'm DC Jones from Beaumaris. I assume that you're Gavin?'

'Yes,' he replied as he frowned. 'Have you found something?'

113

'They've found blood in the summer house,' Zoe sobbed.

Spears looked horrified. 'What?'

Zoe grabbed at his arm. 'Something terrible has happened to her, Gav. I know it has.'

Spears put his arm around Zoe as she burst into floods of tears.

'What about Abby?' he asked.

Andrea shook her head. 'I'm afraid not.' Then she looked at him. 'Gavin, I'm going to need you to attend an interview at Beaumaris Police Station at 9 a.m. tomorrow morning.'

Spears looked gobsmacked. 'Interview? I don't understand.'

Zoe wiped her face. 'What has Gav got to go to the police station for?'

'He will be helping us with our enquiries,' Charlie said diplomatically.

'What?' Spears said. 'Am I under arrest or something?'

'No,' Andrea replied. 'But I strongly suggest that you have legal representation when you do attend.'

CHAPTER 22

Wednesday, 19 October 2022
09.26 p.m.

It was dark outside as Laura moved around her bedroom. She retrieved her pyjamas from under her pillow and put them in the small holdall that she was going to take to HMP Tonsgrove the following morning. She had been a police officer long enough to know what she could and couldn't take. She had also heard enough stories to remember what many prisoners said were the essentials. Flip flops because the showers and toilets were usually disgusting. Earplugs in case she was housed with a snorer and to keep the general noise of the prison at bay. Everything else was common sense; underwear, socks, towel, trainers, toiletries and a change of clothes. She also had found a very small reading lamp which an ex-con had told her was essential. However, as it had been agreed that part of her cover story would be that Laura was illiterate, she wouldn't actually be reading anything.

Taking a breath, she could feel that the muscles in her stomach were tight. In her twenty-five years as a copper, she'd worked undercover on basic stuff like sitting in a pub waiting for a suspect to show their face. This was a whole different ball game. But she could see that whatever was going on inside Tonsgrove, it needed to be stopped. Prisoners were vulnerable, especially addicts, so dealers who prayed on them inside played on their desperation. And if Sanam Parveen really was involved, she needed to be brought to justice.

'Mum,' shouted a voice behind her.

It was Jake.

He took a run and dived onto her bed. As he rolled over, he saw the holdall she was packing and frowned. 'What's that?'

'There's something I need to talk to you and your sister about…'

'ROSIE! ROSIE!' Jake bellowed at the top of his voice before she could say any more.

'Bloody hell!' Rosie yelled as she came down the landing. 'Why are you shouting, you bellend.'

'Rosie!' Laura reprimanded her. 'Please don't call your brother that.'

Jake rolled his eyes. 'I know what a bellend is, Mum. I'm not a baby.'

'Right, be quiet the both of you,' Laura said. She could feel herself getting tetchy because of her anxiety and she didn't want to lose her temper with them as she was going to be gone for several days at least.

'Why are you so salty?' Rosie laughed as she bounced on the bed next to Jake.

'Probably her period,' Jake said under his breath.

'It's not her period, you loser,' Rosie sighed. 'If you must know, mine and Mum's periods are in sync and we're not due for another two weeks.'

'Which is all way too much information for your thirteen-year-old brother,' Laura pointed out.

116

Rosie shrugged. 'I think it's good that he knows about stuff like that.' Then she spotted the holdall. 'Where are you going?'

'Right, I need you to listen for a minute, please,' Laura said, trying her best to sound stern. She wasn't very good at doing stern.

'Okay,' Rosie said curiously.

'Are you going on holiday without us?' Jake asked.

'No, I'm not,' Laura replied, struck by the irony of his question. *If only.* 'I've got to go away for work for a few days.'

'Why?' Rosie asked. It was a fair question as Laura hadn't been away on police work since Rosie was so young that she probably couldn't remember.

'I'm going on a residential course for a few days,' she explained calmly.

Rosie's eyes widened. 'A few days.'

'What's *residential* mean?' Jake asked.

'It means you have to stay there,' Rosie said.

'Why? Where is it?' Jake asked.

'It's… in North Wales,' Laura said, realising that she hadn't really thought this through.

Jake frowned. 'So, why can't you come back home?'

'It's a couple of hours' drive,' Laura said. 'And the hours of the course are very long.' She forced a smile. 'And I get some time to myself away from you two nutcases.'

'Oh that's charming,' Rosie joked.

Jake raised an eyebrow. 'Can we get pizza and take-away every night?'

'No!' Rosie and Laura said in unison.

Laura looked at Rosie. 'I want you look after your brother. And make sure that Elvis gets walked properly. And don't let him poo on the neighbours' garden like the last time I went away for a night.'

'That was Rosie's fault,' Jake said. 'She was too busy talking to her boyfriend on the phone and she let the lead go.'

'Callum isn't my boyfriend, thanks,' Rosie said defensively.

Laura let out a sigh. She loved her kids more than anything but having any form of constructive conversation with them was exhausting.

Gareth appeared in the doorway.

'And Gareth will be here most of the time,' Laura said, gesturing in his direction.

Rosie and Jake's faces fell.

'That's not very nice,' Laura snapped.

'No, no,' Rosie protested as she smiled at Gareth. 'We really like Gareth...'

'Thanks,' Gareth said with a wry smile.

'But you just thought you'd have the place to yourselves for a few days and do exactly what you want,' Laura suggested with an arched eyebrow.

'Erm... yes,' Rosie admitted.

Gareth gave them a weary look. 'Well, the way things are going, I'm not going to be here very much anyway.'

Laura gave him a quizzical look.

Gareth gestured that what he wanted to tell her wasn't for Rosie or Jake's ears.

'Okay, back in a second, guys,' Laura said as she went out onto the landing.

They took a few steps away from the open doorway.

'What's happened?' Laura asked under her breath.

'I had a call from Andrea,' Gareth said quietly. 'They've found a substantial amount of blood at the property where Abby White lived.'

'Oh God, no,' Laura said, remembering the lovely smiling face of the seventeen-year-old girl she'd seen up on the scene board.

118

'There's a couple of things that are now pointing towards her uncle,' Gareth explained. 'He's coming in for a voluntary interview in the morning.'

Laura pulled a face. She knew how rare it was for crimes like these to be committed by total strangers. In fact, she remembered that Danielle Jones had been abducted and murdered by her uncle, Stuart Campbell, in Tilbury, London in 2001. The horrible thing about that case was that Campbell had refused to reveal the location of Danielle's body to this day.

'That's horrible... You really have got your work cut out,' she said.

Gareth put his hands onto her shoulders and looked at her. 'I want you to be really careful in there. First sign of trouble or any hint that you've been recognised or your identity has been compromised, we get you out. Okay?'

'Yeah, of course,' Laura said giving him a reassuring nod. However, his words had made her anxiety worse.

CHAPTER 23

Prison Transporter
Thursday, 20 October 2022
07.12 a.m.

The prison transporter – or 'sweatbox' as it was commonly known – was ironically ice-cold inside. Laura had been seated inside it for over an hour as it made its trip over to Holyhead to pick up the final prisoner from a police station holding cell there, before heading back over to HMP Tonsgrove. She had avoided eye contact with the other prisoners inside – everyone seemed to be keeping themselves to themselves. The air smelled of cheap deodorant and sweat.

Laura was holding her bag of possessions. Inside was a spare pair of trainers that had been specially customised by the NCA. The left trainer had a tiny compartment in the heel for her burner phone. It was there for Laura to use in an emergency.

The woman sitting opposite her – forties, tattooed, tough-looking – had been sizing everyone up during the journey. Laura guessed that this wasn't the woman's first time inside; she seemed quite at home in handcuffs.

Laura caught the woman's eye for a millisecond and instantly regretted it.

'What are you in for, Blondie?' she asked with a thick cockney accent. 'Forgetting to pay for your facial?'

The woman to her left had the sides of her head shaved close to her scalp. She frowned. 'Don't you know about her?' she asked.

'No,' the woman asked suspiciously.

'She killed her husband with a kitchen knife,' the shaven-headed woman said with a serious face.

Jesus, what's all this about? Laura thought. They weren't even at the prison yet. *How does she know that?*

'Is that right, Blondie?' the woman asked with a wry smile.

Laura didn't answer.

The viewing grille from the cab at the front of the lorry opened and a male police officer snapped. 'Oi, Dalby. Leave her alone. Just remember your first time inside.'

'I was only nineteen,' Dalby said proudly as she grinned. 'Any chance we can stop for a cuppa somewhere? It's fuckin' freezing in the back here.'

'We'll be there in half an hour or so. You'll have to wait,' the officer said.

'I'll give you a blowie,' Dalby cackled.

'No thanks, Dalby,' the officer said with a wry smile. 'I know where your mouth's been.'

'Fuck off,' Dalby scowled. 'Needle dick,' she muttered under her breath.

'I heard that,' the officer said. 'It's *sir* to you, Dalby.'

'Yeah, well I'm not happy about going to Tonsgrove,' the shaven-headed woman said. 'That woman got murdered two days ago.'

Dalby snorted knowingly. 'Yeah, well, Sheila Jones got everything that was coming to her.'

'You knew her?'

Dalby looked around the lorry. 'I ain't talking about that in here. I don't know who the fuck you are, or any of this lot.'

'Lottie,' the woman said by way of an introduction.

Dalby looked directly at her. 'Whatever.'

Silence.

There was a tense stand-off as they stared at each other, before Lottie looked away.

Oh good, this is going to be fun, Laura thought to herself.

CHAPTER 24

Beaumaris Police Station
Thursday, 20 October 2022
09.30 a.m.

Andrea leaned over and pressed the red recording button on the machine. There was a long electronic beep. Then she said, 'Interview conducted with Gavin Spears, Thursday, twentieth of October, 9.30 a.m. Interview Room 2, Beaumaris Police Station. Present are Gavin Spears, Detective Constable Charlie Heaton, Duty Solicitor Tony Ellis and myself, Detective Constable Andrea Jones.'

Spears, still with an untidy mop of greying hair and stubble, looked annoyed. He had reluctantly agreed to have his mouth swabbed for a DNA sample and have his fingerprints taken when he'd first arrived.

Spears gave Andrea a blank stare with his dark eyes and then leaned in to talk to Ellis, whispering something in his ear.

Laura raised her eyebrow. 'Gavin, do you understand that this is a voluntary interview and that you are here to help us with our enquiries. You are not under arrest but we are recording this interview and anything you do or say can be used in a court of law as evidence.'

Spears looked confused but then nodded. 'Erm, yeah,' he replied with a gruff voice.

Charlie clicked his pen and looked over. 'Just to confirm that Abby White is your niece and you reside at Rose Cottage in Pen-y-Garnedd with your wife Zoe?'

'Yeah, that's right,' Spears said, clearing his throat.

Andrea waited for a few seconds and then asked, 'Can you tell us the last time you saw your niece Abby?'

'It was about eight o'clock on Monday night,' Spears said cautiously as if he'd rehearsed his answer a few times. 'Her friend, Becks, came round to see her and they went up to her bedroom.'

'And that was definitely the last time you saw her?' Andrea asked with a quizzical look.

Spears frowned. 'Yeah,' he said defensively.

Although he was a little confused, Spears seemed strangely calm for someone who was being interviewed about the disappearance of his niece.

'Were you aware that Abby and Becks had gone to the summer house in your back garden on Monday evening?' Andrea enquired.

'No,' he said immediately with a strong shake of his head.

Andrea gave him a sceptical look. 'You're sure about that?'

'Yeah.' Spears shrugged. 'Me and Zoe were watching telly in the living room.'

'Did you see Becks when she left your home that night?' Charlie said as he scribbled notes on an A4 pad.

Spears shook his head. 'No. Zoe saw her leave... Not me. I was taking a shower.'

'Can you tell us what you did once Becks had left your home?' Andrea said.

Spears narrowed his eyes. 'I went up to bed about midnight.'

'You didn't go anywhere else?'

'No.'

'You didn't leave the house?'

Spears glanced over at the Duty Solicitor with an incredulous expression. 'No. I just said that, didn't I?'

Andrea reached over and pulled a folder towards her, allowing a few seconds of silence and the tension to build in the room.

Spears had started to look fidgety.

Andrea then fixed him with a stare. 'How would you describe your relationship with Abby?'

'I dunno.' Spears said with a guarded expression. 'She's my niece.'

Andrea arched an eyebrow. 'Are you close?'

'I suppose so,' Spears said.

'What do you think Abby feels about you and your relationship?' Andrea continued.

'I dunno,' Spears snorted. 'It's just a normal relationship between an uncle and niece, I suppose. I don't understand why you're asking me all this. Shouldn't you be out there, looking for her?'

Charlie stopped writing and looked over at him. 'So, you'd be surprised if Abby was scared of you or found your behaviour inappropriate then?'

'Eh?' Spears snapped angrily. He turned to the Duty Solicitor. 'What the hell does that mean?'

'For the purposes of the tape, I am showing the suspect Item Reference 387H,' Andrea stated as she pulled out a photocopy. Then she turned the photocopy for Spears to look at. 'Can you tell me if you recognise this handwriting?'

Spears now looked very worried. He peered over. 'Looks like Abby's writing to me.'

125

'These are various extracts from a diary that we found hidden under Abby's bed during our search,' Andrea explained. 'This first one is dated the fifth of June from this year. Abby writes: "He burst into my bedroom without knocking again. I was in my bra but luckily I was wearing trackies. I know he does it on purpose. I hate him."' Andrea then took another photocopy from the pile. 'This one is from the eighteenth of August. Abby writes, "He was waiting outside the bathroom while I was having a shower. I could hear him. When I came out he said I had a little scratch on my back and he touched me. Jesus! I felt sick. He's such a perv!"'

There were a few seconds of awkward silence.

Andrea fixed Spears with a glare. 'In fact, Gavin, there are thirty-two separate entries in this diary that reference your inappropriate, predatory behaviour towards Abby. Is there anything you'd like to say about that?'

Spears took a deep breath. He looked furious. 'It doesn't say it's me. I'm not like that…'

'Come on, Gavin,' Charlie said in a withering tone. 'You're the only man that lives in the house. We know it's you that Abby is referring to.'

'Well then, she must be making it up,' Spears said shaking his head. 'It's some weird fantasy she's got or something.'

Andrea glared at him and said loudly. 'You expect us to believe that your seventeen-year-old niece fantasises about you waiting for her outside the bathroom? Hoping that you burst in when she's getting dressed?'

'I dunno, do I?' Spears was now rattled. 'But I've never done any of those things, I swear to you.'

'Come on, Gavin, you need to stop lying to us,' Charlie thundered across the room.

Spears was now visibly shaking. He looked at the floor.

Andrea waited allowing a long silence in the room so

the tension could build. She knew it was time to change tack.

'Gavin, listen to me,' she said in a soft voice. 'You just need to tell us what happened on Monday night. When Becks left to go home, you went out to the summer house, didn't you?'

'No,' Spears whispered as he stared at the floor.

'And Abby was there. She'd been smoking weed,' Andrea continued in a calm voice. 'And maybe things just got a bit out of hand. Is that right?'

Spears put his head in his hands. 'No.'

'You didn't mean to hurt Abby, did you?' Andrea said. 'So, this is your last chance to tell us what really happened before everything comes crashing down around your ears.'

'Nothing happened,' Spears mumbled.

'Gavin, did you go out to the summer house to see Abby on Monday night?' Andrea asked in a stern tone.

Spears nodded.

'For the purposes of the tape, the suspect has nodded to answer yes to the question,' Andrea said.

Then she waited for a moment.

'Gavin,' she said quietly. 'You need to tell us what happened when you went to the summer house and saw Abby on Monday night.'

Spears shook his head. Then looked up at them – his eyes were full of tears.

'Nothing happened, I promise you. Nothing,' Spears sobbed.

Andrea looked over at him. 'Gavin Spears, I'm arresting you on suspicion of the abduction and murder of Abby White.'

CHAPTER 25

HMP Tonsgrove
Thursday, 20 October 2022
09.33 a.m.

Taking a step forward, the prison officer gestured to Laura. He was in his fifties, thin, with a pointy nose and jaw. Laura spotted his name tag – DAVID RICE – and realised he was the prison officer that Gareth and Ben had interviewed the previous day. She was pretty sure that he was responsible for G Wing where Sheila Jones had been murdered. That would make sense as the officers from the NCA confirmed that they could get Laura assigned to G Wing when she arrived. It would make the job of investigating Sheila's murder much easier.

Laura was starting her induction into HMP Tonsgrove.

'Laura Noakes?' Rice asked, gesturing for her to move forward.

'Yes,' Laura said with an uncertain nod. That was going to be her alias while she was in the prison.

A female officer – twenties, long black ponytail, blue eyes – came over.

'Come with me, please,' the female officer said sternly as they walked across the stark room and entered another. It was windowless and looked like a medical examination room.

'I need you to strip,' the female officer said with a stern expression.

Oh God, Laura thought feeling uncomfortable, even though she'd been fully aware that this was going to be part of the induction process.

Taking off her clothes and then her underwear, Laura stood there naked.

Well this is nice, she thought sarcastically.

She consoled herself that at least this was a new, warm prison rather than some draughty, freezing Victorian jail that you found in Britain's major cities.

'Open your mouth,' the female officer snapped in an unfriendly tone.

Laura could see that the female officer was overcompensating. She looked young and inexperienced. The female officer clearly wanted to make sure no one thought she was a soft touch or could be intimidated or manipulated. Laura knew this was sensible.

She opened her mouth and the female officer took a closer than comfortable look inside. In fact, she was so close that Laura could smell her breath – coffee and chewing gum.

'Lift your tongue,' she said.

Laura lifted her tongue. It felt degrading having to do all this while standing completely naked. If she was honest, Laura found it difficult enough to stand naked in front of a mirror at home – let alone in a prison examination room with a stranger.

The female officer then gestured. 'Arms out and legs apart.'

129

Laura nodded and did what she'd been told.

The female officer checked her all over, lifting her breasts for inspection and then said, 'Squat.'

Lowering herself down, Laura felt humiliated but tried to tell herself that this was part of the role of going under-cover.

'Cough,' the female officer said.

Laura coughed while still squatting down. It was to make sure that she was not carrying anything inside her rectum or vagina: drugs, a weapon, a small mobile phone.

The female officer handed Laura the holdall she had brought with her. 'Right, you can get dressed now.'

'Thanks,' Laura said under her breath and then won-dered why she'd thanked the officer for the humiliating search.

When she had dressed, the female officer led Laura out of the room and looked over at Rice.

'All okay?' Rice asked. He seemed to have a permanent smirk on his face as if everything faintly amused him.

'Clean as a whistle,' the female officer said as if refer-ring to a piece of equipment that she'd just checked over.

'Right,' Rice said, holding a clipboard. He took a pen and then looked directly at her with his smug expression. He had tattoos on both wrists which suggested the tattoos stretched up his arms under his shirtsleeves.

'You are Laura Noakes?' he asked, raising his eyebrows.

'Yes,' Laura replied.

'Date of birth?' he asked.

'First of August 1974.'

Rice looked at her. 'And what religion are you, Laura?'

'Erm, I'm not really religious,' she explained.

'I'll put Anglican then,' Rice said as he wrote on the form. 'And have you been in prison before?'

'No.'

Rice looked at her as if this was somehow interesting to him. Then he asked, 'Are you feeling suicidal, Laura?'

She frowned. 'No.'

'Good.'

'Are you currently on medication?'

'No.'

Rice made solid eye contact with her and then asked, 'Have you ever contracted a sexually transmitted infection?'

'No,' she replied but she got the feeling Rice had got a kick from making her feel uncomfortable.

'Any specific dietary requirements?'

'No.'

Rice handed her a piece of paper. 'Here are your pin codes. You get a two-minute phone call today and tomorrow or until you get it topped up.'

'Thanks,' Laura said taking the paper, folding it and putting it in her pocket. However, she wouldn't be using the main prison phone as the calls were monitored.

'Follow me,' he said, curling his finger in a slightly creepy way.

They went out through a door, down a windowless staircase. Their shoes echoed noisily around the stairwell as they walked in silence.

Getting to a steel door, Rice pulled out a bunch of keys and unlocked it. As Laura went to step through the doorway to the outside, Rice stood in her way.

'It's your first time inside, Laura,' Rice said looking directly at her. Then he reached out and put his hand softly on her arm. 'If things get a bit rough or you're getting bullied, just come and see Uncle Dave. I can sort it out for you, if you know what I mean.'

Jesus, he's making my flesh crawl.

'It's okay thanks,' Laura said calmly. 'I'll take my chances.'

He moved his hand away. 'Fair enough,' Rice said with a smirk. 'But you know where I am if you need anything.'

He turned and Laura followed him down a long open walkway that was flanked by high wire fences.

'Hey fish!' shouted a voice from a window. 'Fish?'

Laura glanced up as someone gave a loud wolf-whistle. She knew that new inmates in prison were always referred to as 'fish;. She assumed it was a reference to them being a fish out of water.

'Just ignore them,' Rice advised her as they walked past a large Astroturf pitch that was marked out with various coloured lines.

'You the sporty type, Laura?' Rice asked.

'Sometimes,' she replied.

'There's football and netball on there,' he informed her as they turned left through another steel door within the fence. 'I organise a Park Run every Sunday morning if you fancy that?'

'I'll bear it in mind,' she said flatly. She didn't want to give Rice any hint that she was interested in what he had to say.

As they went inside, Laura could see they were now in G Wing.

The walls were painted cream and all the steel railings, bannisters and plastic seats at the communal tables were green. There were grey doors all the way along both sides of a long building where the wing's 'rooms' were situated.

In the middle, there was a wide staircase that led up to the first floor where there were more 'rooms' with a balcony looking down onto the ground floor.

'You're on the first floor, Laura,' Rice said pointing to the staircase. 'Presidential Suite,' he said, trying to make a joke.

She didn't react.

As they reached the top of the stairs, Laura spotted someone coming the other way.

It was Governor Sanam Parveen.

'New today?' Parveen asked Laura.

'Yes, miss,' Laura replied.

Parveen smiled. 'Actually we use Christian names here. I'm the governor and my name is Sanam.'

Yeah, I'm well aware of that.

Laura gave her a half-smile. 'Laura.'

Parveen frowned. 'I recognise you from somewhere, don't I, Laura?'

Laura gave a nervous swallow as her pulse quickened. 'I don't think so.'

'I'm sure we've met,' Sanam said looking directly at her. 'Manchester?'

Shit!

'Sorry,' Laura said trying to hold her nerve. 'Doesn't ring a bell.'

'Right, well keep your nose clean and stay out of trouble,' Parveen said. 'And you'll find Tonsgrove is a decent place to be. Have a look at some of our educational courses. They're very good.'

Laura nodded. 'I will.'

Parveen gave Rice a knowing smile and walked away.

'Okay, down this way,' Rice said gesturing with a snap of his fingers.

They came to the third door on the left which was wide open. Inside were two single beds with olive green blankets over each. There was a narrow table between the two beds attached to the wall. There were two sets of blue plastic plates, bowls and cutlery. On the far wall was a small television screen.

'Welcome to paradise,' Rice joked as he showed her in.

133

Laura went to the far bed and put down the clear plastic bag that now contained all her possessions.

'Looks like you're getting a new roommate today as well,' Rice observed as he glanced around the room.

Rice stepped out of the room. 'Right, well I'll leave you to it.' As he looked up, he saw someone approaching. 'Looks like your new roommate is here so you can settle in together.'

A large figure appeared at the door.

It was Dalby, the cockney woman from the prison sweatbox.

'For fuck's sake!' Dalby groaned as she looked at Laura and realised they were sharing.

Thanks very much.

'Get on with it, Dalby,' Rice said. 'And be nice. She's new.'

'Yeah, I know. I've met Blondie already,' Dalby said unenthusiastically as she dropped her plastic bag of possessions onto the bed.

There was a tense silence.

'Right, well I'm Laura and I'm going to unpack my stuff,' Laura said for want of something better to say.

Dalby fixed her with a stare. 'Few ground rules, Blondie!'

'Laura,' she corrected her, even though Dalby scared her. She also knew she couldn't let Dalby intimidate her otherwise her time in Tonsgrove was going to be miserable.

'Whatever,' Dalby shrugged. 'I ain't queer for starters. And I ain't gonna put up with you and some other gay sort getting all cosy in here.'

Laura put her spare trainers carefully down on the floor. Then she looked at her. 'I'm not gay.'

'Right.' Dalby pointed to Laura's trainers. 'And hide those away for starters or some fucker will pinch them.'

Laura nodded. 'Thanks.'

'I don't watch Corrie either,' Dalby said pointing to the TV, referring to the UK soap opera *Coronation Street*. 'Can't stand it.'

Laura gave a half-smile. 'Neither can I.'

Dalby laughed. 'Right, you ain't gay and you hate Corrie. Looks like we're gonna get on just fine, *Laura*.' She then lay back on her bed and put her hands behind her head. 'Home sweet home, eh?'

Out of the corner of her eye, Laura spotted something through the door.

Two figures standing over on the first-floor balcony on the opposite side.

Moving as covertly as she could, Laura crossed the room and glanced across, using the door as cover.

Rice and Parveen were in conversation. There was something about the way they were talking that seemed very familiar. Close, even. Then Laura spotted Parveen's hand reach out and brush against Rice's – just for a second.

'What you doing?' Dalby asked with a frown.

'I thought I saw someone,' Laura lied. 'But it's not who I thought it was.'

CHAPTER 26

Rose Cottage
Thursday, 20 October 2022
10.17 a.m.

Andrea and Charlie had driven back to Rose Cottage while Gavin Spears was in a holding cell in the custody suite. Forensics had now confirmed what they suspected. The blood in the summer house was Abby White's. They didn't have enough evidence to charge Spears yet so the clock was now ticking before they had to release him.

As they pulled up, Andrea could see that the SOCO van was still parked outside the house. The whole road was now cordoned off with two marked patrol cars and blue and white police tape. There were half a dozen or so uniformed police officers wearing high-vis jackets with HEDDLU POLICE printed on them.

On the far side of the road, a dozen or so neighbours and locals were gathered in small groups talking or trying to see what was going on at Rose Cottage. They were known as 'rubberneckers' in police slang, although these days that usually referred to people who slowed down to look or even film serious road accidents.

Andrea and Charlie walked up the garden path and saw a young female police officer, twenties, with short blonde hair, standing outside.

Taking out her warrant card, Andrea looked at her. 'Are you the FLO, Constable?'

'Yes, ma'am,' she replied.

'Can you tell me where Zoe Spears is?' Andrea said.

The FLO pointed to the house opposite. 'She's in with the neighbours over there.'

'Thanks,' Andrea said as she and Charlie turned and marched across the road and knocked on the door.

A woman in her sixties in a thick burgundy cardigan opened the door. 'Yes?' she said.

'DC Jones and DC Heaton, Beaumaris CID,' Andrea said. 'We need to speak to Zoe.'

'Of course, come in,' the woman said, opening the door wide. Then she looked at them. 'Have you found her?' she asked in a virtual whisper.

'I'm afraid not,' Charlie replied politely.

'Oh dear,' the woman said pulling a face. 'It's terrible, isn't it?'

Andrea gave her a courteous nod as they came into the neat but slightly old-fashioned hallway. It smelled of lavender and furniture polish.

'She's in there. Poor thing,' the woman said, pointing to the door. 'I'll leave you to it. Would you like a cup of tea?'

Andrea gave her a kind smile. 'We're fine thanks.'

Opening the door, they entered what looked like a sitting room with patterned carpets, a three-piece suite and a small bookshelf with framed photos arranged in height order.

Zoe looked up, her face full of fear.

'Where's Gav?' she asked blinking anxiously.

'Okay if we sit down?' Andrea said gently as she gestured to the sofa.

Zoe nodded but she looked emotionally broken.

Andrea then looked over at her and said gently, 'I'm afraid that we have arrested Gavin on suspicion of Abby's abduction and murder.'

The blood drained from Zoe's face. Her whole body shook as she put her hand to her mouth in shock. 'No,' she gasped.

Andrea leaned forward. 'I know this is a huge shock for you… but there are a few questions we need to ask you.'

Zoe's eyes roamed around the room in horror. She clearly wasn't listening. Then she narrowed her eyes and looked at them in utter confusion. 'Gavin didn't murder Abby. What are you talking about?'

'Although we haven't charged him, we do have enough concerns to have arrested him,' Charlie explained.

'Concerns?' Zoe pulled an alarmed face. 'What do you mean, concerns?'

Andrea waited for a moment and then said in a quiet voice, 'As I said, there are a few questions we'd like to ask you.'

'You don't know that Abby's dead,' Zoe sobbed trying to get her breath. 'Why are you saying that?'

'The chief pathologist believes that due to the amount of Abby's blood that we found in the summer house at your home, it is likely that… Abby is dead. I'm so sorry.'

'But you haven't found her,' Zoe said, her eyes roaming wildly around the room. 'I mean you can't say she's dead if you haven't found her. She could still be out there alive.'

'Although that's highly unlikely, Zoe, it is still possible,' Andrea agreed in a sympathetic tone.

'So, why have you arrested Gav?' Zoe asked, her brow crinkled with utter confusion.

'I'm going to need to ask you a few questions, Zoe,' Andrea said, ignoring her question. 'Is that okay?'

Zoe nodded but didn't say anything.

'How would you characterise Gavin's relationship with Abby?' Andrea asked.

'What?' Zoe said. 'He's her uncle. What does that mean?'

'Would you say that they're close?' Charlie enquired.

'Of course they are. Gav loves Abby as if she was his own,' Zoe insisted.

'While we were searching Abby's room, we found her diary hidden under her mattress,' Andrea stated.

'Okay,' Zoe said with a shrug. 'I didn't know she kept a diary.'

'In her diary, there were multiple entries where she described Gavin's inappropriate behaviour. Waiting outside the bathroom while she showered, bursting into her room while she was getting dressed, inappropriate comments and looks.'

'No, that's not true.' Zoe shook her head and looked horrified. 'I live in that house. I would have noticed. She must be lying.'

Andrea waited as she made direct eye contact with Zoe. 'Can you tell us why you think that Abby would make up that sort of thing about Gavin?'

'I don't know,' Zoe snapped defensively. 'I just know he's not like that.'

Charlie raised an eyebrow. 'You've never noticed anything inappropriate about Gavin's behaviour towards Abby?'

'No, of course not!'

Andrea allowed a few seconds of silence before continuing.

'When we spoke to you on Tuesday,' Andrea said. 'You said that Becks left your home just before midnight and

139

that you and Gavin went to bed just after that. Is that correct?'

Zoe nodded. 'Yes.'

'And you assumed that Abby was in bed asleep?' Charlie asked as he wrote in his notepad.

'Yes.'

Andrea looked at her. 'And Gavin was with you all night?'

Zoe frowned. 'Yes.'

'He didn't go out anywhere or leave the house?' Andrea asked.

'No.' Zoe looked confused. 'Why are you asking me this?'

Charlie stopped writing and looked over. 'Did you know that Abby and Becks had snuck out of her bedroom to go and smoke marijuana in the summer house?'

'They didn't.' Zoe narrowed her eyes. 'Abby doesn't take drugs. She told me.'

'I'm afraid Becks told us that's what they were doing,' Andrea said.

Zoe's eyes filled with tears. 'This doesn't make any sense.'

'Gavin admitted that after Becks had left your home, he went out to the summer house to see Abby,' Andrea informed her.

'What?' Zoe said very quietly. 'No... he didn't.'

There was a long silence.

'I'm assuming that Gavin didn't tell you that he'd been out to see Abby in the summer house after Becks had left?' Charlie asked.

Zoe looked broken and lost. Her breathing was shallow. 'No...'

CHAPTER 27

Gareth stood in line in the canteen, waiting to pay for his white Americano. His head was whirring with having two major crimes running out of Beaumaris CID. It was incredibly unusual. In fact, he couldn't remember a time since he started to work as a copper that two such high-profile crimes had been managed by CID. Part of him wondered if he had enough officers and resources to cope. However, what he didn't want to do was go to Warlow and ask for help. It might have been his pride or ego, but he wanted to prove to Warlow that he was a capable senior investigating officer (SIO).

'Thanks,' Gareth said as he moved his canteen card over the scanning machine to pay and began to make his way towards the double doors.

His mind naturally turned to Laura as he wondered how she would be coping with her first day inside Tonsgrove. He knew how incredibly strong and resourceful she was. In fact, he'd seen it first hand for himself in June 2021 when Laura's son Jake had been kidnapped by a Merseyside drug gang. Despite the incredible stress of that situation, Laura had kept her head.

Still deep in thought, Gareth walked along the corridor as he headed back towards the CID offices.

'Gareth,' said a voice.

He turned to see Warlow heading his way with his usual supercilious expression.

Oh God, what does he want?

'Listen, I've been talking to the Chief Constable,' Warlow said. 'He's concerned that you guys are going to struggle with these two investigations. He thinks that drafting in some CID officers from the mainland might be a good idea.'

Bollocks.

Gareth took a deep breath. 'Actually, we do have a very viable prime suspect for Abby White's abduction and probable murder. And I'd like to give Laura twenty-four hours in Tonsgrove before we go in to see what she's unearthed. So, if you could hold off for a day or two before making that kind of decision, I'd appreciate it.'

Warlow gave him an unconvincing nod and said, 'Of course. Let's have another look at the situation in forty-eight hours. But bringing in other officers isn't a reflection of your ability as an SIO, Gareth, nor of your team.'

'I understand that, sir,' Gareth replied as he bristled. 'I'm just aware that there would be a good deal of disruption. Plus, getting new officers up to speed on both cases would be time not spent on the investigations.'

'Fair enough,' Warlow said. 'As I said, let's reconvene in forty-eight hours. I'm just aware that questions are already being asked of us on social media. And, as you know, it doesn't take long before those misgivings find their way to the local and national mainstream media.'

And there we have it,' Gareth thought to himself. *This is all about Warlow preventing his reputation from being damaged.*

'Yes, sir,' Gareth said as he turned and continued to make his way back to CID. It wasn't that he was controlling, it's just that he didn't want other CID officers from the mainland coming over 'to save the day' and throwing their weight around. He'd seen that sort of thing happen a few years ago and it had been incredibly acrimonious.

Gareth arrived at CID and barged open the stiff double doors rather than risk spilling his coffee by using his hands. He'd made that mistake before.

Ben approached. 'Boss, we've got a DNA forensic match for that hair band and sample that we found in Sheila Jones' cell,' he explained with a sense of urgency.

'Anything interesting?' Gareth asked as he stopped.

'Very,' Ben replied. 'DNA belongs to a Kayleigh Doyle. She's almost midway through serving an eleven-year sentence for possession with intent to supply. Intel on her PNC check says that she has affiliations to an OCG in Birmingham. And that OCG have been setting up county lines in Wrexham and North Wales.'

Gareth nodded and said, 'Which means they were direct rivals to what the Croxteth Boyz were doing in the same area.'

'Yes, boss. And if Kayleigh Doyle and Sheila Jones had affiliations to gangs that were involved in some kind of turf war on the outside,' Gareth said, 'it might well have spilt over into Tonsgrove.'

'It has to be a line of enquiry worth looking at,' Ben said, sounding energised. 'I've arranged for us to interview Doyle at Tonsgrove in an hour, boss.'

'Good work, Ben,' Gareth said as he turned to head back towards his office. It was a significant breakthrough. It also reaffirmed Gareth's confidence that they could handle both cases going forward.

'Boss,' Andrea said looking over from her desk. 'I've just checked. Chris White, Abby's father, has been in Thailand for the past two months. I've confirmed that with passport control, so we can effectively remove him from our investigation.'

'Good... What happened with Gavin Spears?' he asked her, realising that his thoughts for the past hour had been dedicated to what had happened inside Tonsgrove.

'Spears now admits to going to the summer house to see Abby after her friend Becks had left,' Andrea said.

Gareth frowned. 'What for?'

'He can't give us a satisfactory answer to that. But he denies that he attacked her or harmed her in any way,' Andrea stated. 'Zoe Spears claims that she had no knowledge of Gavin's inappropriate behaviour towards her niece.'

'What do you think?' Gareth asked.

'I think that Gavin Spears was sexually attracted to Abby. He'd been trying it on for a while. He knew that she was alone in the summer house and she'd been smoking weed. He went out there, she fought him off and something went horribly wrong.'

Gareth nodded. It sounded like a very feasible hypothesis. 'We just need some forensics now to link him directly to the crime scene.'

Andrea gave him a dark look. 'Or we need to find Abby.'

Gareth took a moment. 'And we've checked the whole house, bins, garden?'

Andrea nodded.

'What about Spears' car?' Gareth asked.

'Forensics have checked it today. Nothing,' Andrea said in a frustrated tone.

Charlie approached. 'Think we have a problem.'

'Go on,' Gareth said.

'Forensics have a partial footprint on the blood stain on the futon,' Charlie explained. 'It's a size seven or eight. I've been down to the holding cell and checked on Gavin Spears. He's a size eleven. And then I checked with Zoe and Abby is a size four.'

'It doesn't mean that Spears didn't attack her,' Gareth said as he processed what Charlie had told them. 'But it does mean that someone other than Abby and Gavin were present during or after the attack.'

'There is something else,' Charlie said as he pointed to a print-out that he was holding. 'A neighbour, Gwyneth Pardour, says that she saw someone sitting in a car outside the Spears' home earlier in the evening. She thinks that her husband wrote down the registration but he was out when police went round to interview neighbours.'

'Okay, why don't you go down there and see if the husband is back and if they remember anything about whoever was sitting in the car?' Gareth said.

Gareth walked back to his office feeling frustrated. He felt that just as the evidence against Gavin Spears had been mounting, the footprint had now weakened the case against him. He knew that was the way it often went with major investigations like this.

It was just a question of two steps forward and one step back until they got the breakthrough they needed. So he needed to be patient despite the pressure that Warlow was putting him under.

CHAPTER 28

HMP Tonsgrove
Thursday, 20 October 2022
11.04 a.m.

Laura sat at a small table in the classroom inside the education block. She had signed up to do a literacy course with Barry McDonald. Barry had been the last person to have any meaningful interaction with Sheila Jones the morning that she was murdered. CID also had intel that Sheila had spent a lot of time in the education block. Laura faking being illiterate was not only a good cover story, it also allowed her to sign up to the literacy course so she could get access to that area of the prison.

'At this stage, I just need a few details from you,' said Barry McDonald, the English teacher. With his goatee beard, scruffy hair, tweed jacket with elbow patches and his broken glasses with a plaster holding the arm to the frame, Barry reminded Laura of a stereotypical teacher from another era. He had that kind of look. 'Just write down what education you've had up to this point and any qualifications that you've got.'

Laura thought of the irony as she left the form blank. She's not meant to be able to read or write. In fact, she had GCSE's, A-levels and a 2.1 degree.

There were about ten other prisoners inside the classroom. Laura recognised a couple from the prison transporter that morning. The walls were covered in posters: of films, art exhibitions, books. Over by the door was a large board where prisoners' work had been pinned up and displayed. In fact, there was nothing inside the classroom to suggest that they were inside a prison.

'Right, are there any questions?' Barry asked.

'I'm dyslexic,' said a young woman with dyed red hair. 'Do I put that down by special needs?'

'Yes, please,' Barry said with a kind smile. 'Okay, once you've filled in those forms, hand them to me and then you can leave. We start tomorrow afternoon at 2 p.m.' Barry had an easy manner as he perched himself on a table. 'I'm looking forward to getting to know you all.' He gave a smirk. 'You never know, you might even enjoy coming here.'

Laura waited until most of the other students had handed in their forms and left. She got up, wondering how she was going to engage Barry in some kind of meaningful conversation.

As her eyes scanned the board of prisoners' work, she spotted a colourful poster exploring the themes of *Romeo and Juliet*. At the bottom was written Sheila Jones.

Laura made a deliberate show of stopping and looking at it.

Barry approached with a quizzical look.

'I'm really sorry but I had to leave the form blank,' Laura said apologetically. 'I'm virtually illiterate.'

'No problem,' Barry said kindly. 'I can go through it with you another time.'

Laura pointed to the poster. 'I went to primary school

with Sheila,' Laura explained sadly. 'Sheila was made up when she knew I was coming in. She was gonna look out for me.'

'Right… It was such a waste what happened to Sheila.' Barry nodded sympathetically. 'I had a lot of time for her. She was bright.'

'Yeah, she was much brighter than me.' Laura looked at him. 'But I know Sheila was no angel.'

'No,' Barry agreed. 'She definitely wasn't an angel.'

Laura shrugged. 'Guess she got mixed up with the wrong people again.'

Barry pointed to Sheila's poster. 'Do you know *Romeo and Juliet*?' he asked.

'A bit.'

'In *Romeo and Juliet*, there are two gangs that run Verona. The Capulets and the Montagues,' Barry explained. 'Well, it's the same in here. Except it's the Scousers and the Brummies. They're the two feuding parties who run things around here. But if someone from one gang should fall in love with someone from the other… As Juliet says: "'Tis but thy name is my enemy… What's in a name? That which we call a rose by any other name would smell as sweet."'

Laura frowned at him. 'Sheila was with someone from…'

'Laura!' snapped a voice.

It was Rice, who glared at her from the doorway.

'I've done a headcount three times!' Rice growled.

'Sorry, my fault,' Barry admitted.

Rice gestured. 'Come on. This isn't a bloody school where you can have a cosy chat with your teacher.'

Barry gave Laura a look to indicate that he didn't have much time for Rice.

'Sorry,' Laura said as she turned to go.

CHAPTER 29

HMP Tonsgrove
Thursday, 20 October 2022
11.47 a.m.

Gareth and Ben were back in the meeting room at HMP Tonsgrove. Opposite them sat Kayleigh Doyle – late forties, red hair, milky skin, well-built, with various face piercings, tattoos and piercing blue eyes.

Kayleigh sat in her chair looking at them with an indifferent sneer.

Gareth pointed to the recording equipment. 'Just so that you're aware, even though this is an informal interview, we will be recording it in case anything you say needs to be used as evidence in court. Do you understand that, Kayleigh?'

'Yeah,' she replied. She had a thick Brummie accent. She gave them a withering look before making a show of yawning and stretching her arms. 'This gonna take long?'

'Depends,' Gareth replied calmly as he leaned over and pressed the red record button. There was a long electronic beep. 'Interview conducted with Kayleigh Doyle.

HMP Tonsgrove. 11.47 a.m., Thursday, twentieth of October 2022. Present are Kayleigh Doyle, Detective Constable Ben Corden, and myself, Detective Inspector Gareth Williams.'

Kayleigh let out an audible sigh and started to look around the room.

Ben took out his pen and started to write on the A4 pad in front of him. Then he looked over at her. 'How long have you been in Tonsgrove, Kayleigh?'

She raised an eyebrow. 'You've got my record. You tell me.'

Gareth and Ben shared a look. This wasn't going to be easy.

Gareth took a breath, sat forward and looked at her. He wasn't going to be intimidated. 'Can you tell us where you were at around 9.20 a.m. on Tuesday morning?'

Green shrugged. 'I was probably in my room finishing off my breakfast.'

Ben frowned. 'Probably?'

'This is a prison,' she said in a derisive voice. 'Every day is exactly the same so it's pretty hard to remember.'

Gareth ran his hand over his scalp for a moment. 'Except Tuesday wasn't the same as every other day, was it?'

Green thought for a second. 'Oh, you mean because someone shanked Sheila Jones?' she said in an ironic tone.

Ben looked over at her. 'Sheila was murdered.'

'Yeah, I heard. It's a shame,' Kayleigh said with more than a hint of sarcasm.

'How would you describe your relationship with Sheila Jones?' Gareth asked.

'Relationship?' Kayleigh snorted. 'There was no relationship. We didn't like each other.'

'You were both affiliated to rival gangs. Is that correct?' Gareth said.

'I ain't commenting on that without having my solicitor here,' Kayleigh said.

Gareth nodded. 'But you've made it clear that there was no love lost between you and Sheila?'

'Correct,' Kayleigh replied.

'And I don't suppose you would have popped in to her room for a cup of tea and a chat then?' Gareth asked.

'No,' Kayleigh snorted. 'I bloody wouldn't.'

Gareth shifted in his chair and then said, 'In fact, it would be a surprise if you'd ever been in that room, wouldn't it?'

Green frowned. 'Yeah, it would.'

Gareth pulled over a folder. 'For the purposes of the tape, I'm showing Kayleigh Item Reference 334G.' He took out a photo and turned it to show her. 'Kayleigh, could you look at this image and tell me what you can see?'

Kayleigh pulled an irritated face, sat forward and peered at the photo. 'Erm, no idea. Looks like a hair band or something.'

'That's right,' Gareth said. 'And we found that hairband in Sheila Jones' room. Would it surprise you if I told you that the hair that we found entangled in that hair band is an exact DNA match for you?'

Kayleigh smirked. 'No, it wouldn't surprise me.'

Gareth was confused by Kayleigh's composure and confidence. He had expected the evidence to rattle her.

'And why's that?' he asked, wondering what she was going to say.

Kayleigh shrugged. 'Sheila Jones isn't the only person who lives in that room, is she?'

Ben frowned. 'Hayley Ross?'

Kayleigh nodded. 'Me and Hayley. We're… you know… together, like. I mean we're not really lesbians. We're just "gay for the stay", if you know what I mean.'

Bullshit!

Gareth narrowed his eyes. 'You and Hayley Ross are in a relationship?' he asked in a suspicious tone.

'Yep,' Kayleigh replied with a cocky grin. 'Why don't you go and ask her?'

'But you just told us that you'd never been in that room,' Ben said incredulously.

Kayleigh shrugged. 'I lied. Force of habit when I'm talking to five-o... This is a voluntary interview, yeah?'

Gareth nodded. 'Yes, that's right.'

'Well, I'm bored now,' Kayleigh said with a huff. 'I ain't gonna answer any more of your questions.'

CHAPTER 30

Pen-y-garnedd
Thursday, 20 October 2022
11.51 a.m.

Andrea and Charlie walked up the neat path of Bwthwyn
Derwen – Oak Cottage – which was two doors down
from where Zoe and Gavin Spears lived in Pen-y-garnedd.

Andrea gave an authoritative knock on the front door
and took a step back. A few seconds later, the door opened
and an elderly woman in her seventies peered out. She had
short, white, slightly spiky hair, glasses and blue inquisitive
eyes. She was wearing cargo trousers and a navy V-neck
sweater.

'DC Jones and DC Heaton,' Andrea explained as they
showed her their warrant cards. 'We're looking for a
Gwyneth Pardour?'

'Yes, that's me,' Gwyneth said with a nod. 'Would you
like to come in?'

'Thank you,' Andrea said with a polite smile as Gwyneth opened the door and gestured for them to come into
the hallway.

They stepped onto the thick burgundy carpet. There was a carved wooden table to one side with an oval mirror above. Coats, hats and umbrellas hung from a series of hooks behind the doors. The air smelled of wet dogs.

'Would you like to come through?' Gwyneth said as she pointed to the door to their left.

'Thanks,' Charlie said.

They entered a large living room with an upright piano in the corner. Jazz was playing on a stereo and the walls were lined with books and records.

'Jack,' Gwyneth said. 'There are police officers here.'

A man, also in his seventies, saw them, got up out of an armchair where he'd been reading a newspaper and approached. He was virtually bald, with ginger eyebrows that were almost invisible and glasses.

'Oh right. Hi,' he said in a confident friendly Scottish accent, gesturing for a handshake. 'I'm Jack. Why don't you sit down?'

'Thank you,' Andrea said as she and Charlie headed for a large, comfortable sofa and sat themselves down.

Gwyneth looked at them. 'I expect you could do with a tea or a coffee?'

Andrea smiled. 'You know what? That would be lovely.' She rarely took people up on such offers but today was going to be the exception. 'Coffee would be great. We both take it white, no sugar, thank you.'

Charlie gave her a friendly smile.

'The kettle's only just boiled so I won't be very long,' Gwyneth said as she left the room.

Andrea looked over at Jack, who had settled himself back down in his armchair.

'It's such terrible news about Zoe and Gavin's daughter being missing. Abby, isn't it?' Jack said shaking his head.

'Abby is actually their niece,' Andrea said. 'But yes, it's a very distressing time for them.'

'Do you know what happened?' Jack asked.

'We're not at liberty to discuss the investigation, I'm afraid, but we're following several lines of enquiry,' Andrea said, trotting out her usual response.

Charlie pulled out his notepad and pen. 'We understand that you or your wife saw a car parked outside their house on Monday evening. Is that correct?'

'Yes,' Jack nodded as he shifted in his armchair and sat forward. 'That's right.'

Gwyneth came in with two mugs of coffee which she handed to them. 'It's only instant I'm afraid.'

'That's lovely,' Andrea said taking the mug.

Charlie smiled. 'Thank you.'

'I was just going to tell them about that car we saw,' Jack said.

'Oh right, yes,' Gwyneth said as she sat in an armchair that matched her husband's. 'It was parked there for ages. I wouldn't have noticed, but it had its headlights on for quite some time.'

'Did you manage to see what kind of car it was?' Charlie asked.

'Oh yes,' Jack nodded. 'It was a white Ford Fiesta.'

'You seem very certain,' Andrea said in a friendly tone.

'We've just helped our granddaughter buy her first car,' Gwyneth explained.

'And she's got exactly that,' Jack said. 'A white Ford Fiesta.'

Charlie looked over. 'And what time do you think the car was parked out the front?'

They both took a moment to think.

'It must have been about 10 p.m. when I first spotted it because the news had just started on the telly,' Gwyneth said.

'Do you know when it left?' Andrea enquired.

'It was gone midnight, wasn't it?' Gwyneth said looking over at Jack.

'Yes,' he nodded. 'To be honest, I think we'd both nodded off in front of the telly, so I can't tell you what time it left. But it was gone midnight when we spotted it had gone.'

Andrea moved a strand of hair from her face and said, 'I understand that you managed to write down the registration number of the car?'

'Yes, that's right.' Jack nodded keenly as he reached over for a small notebook and opened it.

'It was LV12 KJM. It's not that we're a pair of old busybodies.'

'No, of course not,' Andrea reassured him.

Gwyneth narrowed her eyes. 'It was just a bit weird, him sitting there outside their house. And you never know.'

Andrea raised an eyebrow. 'So you saw the driver?'

'Sort of,' Gwyneth replied uncertainly. 'I could see it was a young man.'

Charlie stopped writing and looked at her. 'When you say "young man"…'

'In his twenties, I suppose,' Gwyneth said. 'He was wearing one of those baseball caps.'

Andrea and Charlie shared a look. The last young man they'd seen wearing a baseball cap was Edward Davies.

CHAPTER 31

HMP Tonsgrove
Thursday, 20 October 2022
12.34 p.m.

The prison canteen was a brightly lit room with large windows and rows of long green tables either side. Laura had collected her lunch – a questionable cheese and salad baguette, crips and a tiny yoghurt. She had also been handed a Prison Canteen Order Sheet where she could order everything from phone credit and vapes to snacks, toiletries, batteries and stamps.

Glancing around, Laura found a suitable spot on a relatively empty table, sat down and surveyed the room. On the table next to her were a huddle of loud women who were joking and laughing. Two of the women looked very similar. They were both in their forties, stocky, red hair, fair skin with more than their fair share of tattoos and piercings. One of them had her hair shaved close around the sides and back.

Despite being an experienced copper, Laura had to admit they looked a little scary. She bit into the dry baguette and could also hear that the women had strong Brummie accents.

'I'd stay well clear of those didicoys,' said a voice in a cockney accent.

It was Dalby.

She sat down opposite Laura with her tray of food.

'Why do you say that?' Laura asked quietly.

Dalby nodded towards the women. 'Brummie Paddies. Irish. And nasty fuckers with it. I've seen them kettle girls for a bit of verbal.'

'Kettling' was prison slang for mixing sugar into a boiling kettle and throwing it at a prisoner – face, hands. The sugar becomes a viscous boiling paste that sticks to a person's skin and causes terrible burns.

Dalby surreptitiously gestured to another huddle of women on the far side of the canteen. They were a mixture of mixed-race, black and white women.

'And them are the Scousers,' Dalby explained. 'That's the turf war that's going in here. But someone like you needs to keep well away. Keep your head down and keep out of their way. They'd eat you alive, no offence.'

'None taken,' Laura said, making sure she sounded suitably grateful.

Laura looked up as one of the red-headed women got up from the table.

'Kayleigh,' shouted the shaven-headed woman.

Kayleigh, one of the red-headed women in her forties, turned back to look as the woman launched a yoghurt pot at her head. Everyone laughed as she ducked.

'Fuck off, Niamh,' Kayleigh snapped angrily as she picked up a spoon and launched it at her.

Niamh jumped up and they squared up to each other, their faces only inches apart.

'Here we go,' Dalby groaned.

'You've done enough,' Kayleigh said angrily as she grabbed Niamh's jaw.

Niamh grabbed Kayleigh's hair. 'You brought that on yourself, you stupid bitch.'

Kayleigh went to throw a punch just as a male prison officer approached.

'Calm it down, ladies,' he said in a loud voice.

Niamh and Kayleigh took two steps away from each other while still glaring at each other.

Dalby looked at her. 'Screws usually leave them alone. They did when I was last in here. They're too scared. Some newbie screw decided to make their lives hell for a few days so they torched his car at his home. He kept well away after that.'

'Lovely,' Laura said dryly.

A woman came over with a grin, grabbed Dalby's face and kissed her hard on the mouth. 'Shazza Dalby, you fucking slag,' she laughed as she sat down at their table.

'Fuck me, Ruby. I didn't know you was in here,' Dalby said.

Ruby reached into her pocket, pulled out a fancy yoghurt and slid it across the table to Dalby. 'Here you go.'

'Ta,' Dalby said.

Ruby stared at Laura. 'And who's this?'

'Laura. She's new. First time inside,' Dalby explained. 'I'm trying to show her the ropes and keep her out of trouble.'

'Oh yeah?' Ruby cackled, then stuck out her tongue and grinned at Laura. 'And what's she asking for in return.'

Dalby shook her head. 'She ain't like that, are you?'

Laura shook her head. 'No.'

Ruby pulled out another yoghurt and slid it across the table to Laura. 'Here you go, fish.'

'Thanks,' Laura said gratefully.

'She sounds a bit fancy,' Ruby said to Dalby. 'Bit posh. Is that right, Laura?'

'Nah, she's not really,' Dalby said, shaking her head. 'What d'you know about this Scouser that got shanked on our wing?'

'Drugs, innit,' Ruby replied and then gestured to the group of women behind them. 'Probably that lot.'

Laura watched Kayleigh walking away and wondered if her conversation with Niamh had anything to do with Sheila Jones.

CHAPTER 32

Castellior
Thursday, 20 October 2022
12.53 p.m.

As Andrea and Charlie drove back from Peñ-y-garnedd to Beaumaris, Andrea's phone rang. It was one of the support team at CID.

'DC Jones?' asked a woman's voice with a heavy North Wales accent.

'Speaking,' Andrea replied.

'I've run that licence plate with the DVLA,' the woman explained. 'That car is registered to an Edward Davies. I've got an address in Castellior if you'd like it?'

'I've got it already actually,' Andrea said politely. 'But thanks for calling.'

She ended the call, glanced over at Charlie who was driving and gave him a meaningful look. 'Guess who that white Ford Fiesta is registered to?'

'At a wild stab in the dark, I reckon Edward Davies,' Charlie said dryly.

'Ten points,' Andrea said. 'We'd better turn back and get ourselves over to Castellior.'

Charlie nodded, slowed the car and did a U-turn. 'It's all right, I know a short cut.'

Andrea frowned. 'Did you grow up around here?'

Charlie nodded. 'My parents both worked at Plas Cadnant Estate, so that's where I grew up.'

Plas Cadnant was a stunning estate with holiday cottages and beautiful gardens.

'Yeah, it wasn't as fashionable as it is now,' Charlie admitted. 'But there are worse places to have grown up.'

'Do you have brothers and sisters?' she asked.

'Nope,' Charlie said. 'I'm a classic only child.'

'Bossy, spoiled and selfish?' Andrea joked.

Charlie laughed. 'I was going for mature, resourceful and empathetic.'

'Oh, right,' Andrea said with a grin. She loved that Charlie could make her laugh. It was a very attractive trait.

The conversation had also reminded her of her own childhood.

'You have siblings?' Charlie asked as they turned left onto a main road.

'No,' Andrea said.

There was a short silence as Andrea collected her thoughts.

'My parents died in a car accident when I was six,' she said. Saying it out loud still made her feel uncomfortable and sad.

'God, I'm sorry to hear that,' Charlie said with an empathetic look.

'My grandmother lived in a place called Cedros which is in Trinidad,' Andrea explained. 'But she was elderly and on her own so it was decided that I should go into care. I had a couple of questionable foster parents. Then I ended

162

up with Jenny and Keith. And they were... Well, they were okay.'

'Right,' Charlie said. 'Sounds like you had a pretty tough childhood then?'

'Not really,' Andrea said. 'Not when you think of some of the stuff we see in this job.'

'Yeah, but that's all relative,' Charlie pointed out.

'I suppose so. I try not to get on my pity pot about it,' Andrea said. 'I've got a good job, good friends and a nice life. And that makes me lucky.'

Charlie nodded. 'It's a good way of looking at things.'

As he looked over, their eyes met for a little longer than was comfortable. Then he smiled.

Is it me, or is there a hint of something between us? she wondered with a tiny flicker of excitement.

They drove on in a comfortable silence and after a few minutes, they arrived in Castellior. As they got out of the car, the sky above them was bruised with mauve and black clouds. The air smelled damp with the fallen autumnal leaves and mushroomy odours mixed with the aroma of real fires. Maybe it was their recent conversation but the blazing colours and smells of autumn made Andrea nostalgic for memories of a childhood she'd never had. Maybe they were memories borrowed from old books she'd read as a child. She didn't know. The heat of an open fire, thick knitwear, crumpets toasted over a fire and the promise that Christmas was just around the corner.

As they traipsed along the pathway through the thick blanket of leaves, they spotted Edward Davies arrive at his house in a white Ford Fiesta and park on the driveway.

'Here we go,' Charlie said under his breath.

They stopped walking and watched as Davies got out.

Andrea looked at Charlie. 'We'd better go and nick him.'

163

However, as Davies walked away from the car towards his house, he looked up and spotted them. It's as if he'd sensed their presence.

Shit! He's seen us.

Looking startled, Davies hurried back to his car and got in the driver's side.

'Bollocks,' Charlie said in frustration, 'he's doing a bloody runner.'

Davies reversed at speed off the drive, turned the car and sped off in the opposite direction.

Andrea and Charlie turned, sprinted back to their car and jumped in.

Charlie hit the ignition button and gunned the Astra's two-litre fuel injection engine. He stamped down on the accelerator with such force that the car jolted forward and the tyres squealed under the sudden burst of speed.

Andrea was thrown back in her seat by the force of the acceleration.

'Easy there, tiger,' Andrea said in a cautionary tone. She'd never been in a pursuit with Charlie driving before and she hoped he didn't turn into the kind of reckless maniac she'd experienced with a couple of other male officers.

'What?' Charlie replied in a mock innocent tone.

Grabbing the receiver of the Tetra radio, Andrea clicked the grey talk button. 'Control from five two, are you receiving, over?'

After a few seconds there was a crackle and a male voice. 'Five two, this is Control, we are receiving, go ahead.'

Charlie accelerated up to 50 mph as they sped up the road, and spotted the Fiesta in the distance as it turned left and then disappeared.

'We're in pursuit of a white Ford Fiesta. Registration: Lima, Victor, one, two, Kilo, Juliet, Mike. Registered to an Edward Davies,' Andrea explained as they screamed towards the junction with a main road and then came to a shuddering halt.

Andrea grabbed at her seat to stop herself being flung forward. Then she glanced at the built-in satnav map. 'We're heading north on the A5025. Request back-up, over.'

'Five, two, received, stand by,' the computer-aided dispatch controller said.

'He's going like the clappers,' Charlie said as he pulled out at speed and then stared at road ahead.

'Well you'd better hurry up then,' Andrea said in a jokey tone as she reached over and switched on the siren and the blue lights – known as the blues and twos – that were located in the radiator grille.

'Yes, ma'am,' Charlie said with a grin.

A van tried to pull out of the turning to their right and Charlie stamped on the brake and swerved left to avoid it.

'For fuck's sake,' he growled.

Andrea was thrown hard against her seatbelt and then back by the force of Charlie's braking.

She looked over at him. 'You have done this before, haven't you?' she asked.

'A high-speed pursuit?' Charlie asked.

'Yes.'

'No, not really,' Charlie admitted. 'But I'm a really good driver.'

Andrea gave him a forced smile. *Great! Please don't kill us.*

'Well, at least I am on my PlayStation,' he muttered with a wry smile.

'Very funny,' she said, rolling her eyes.

As Andrea looked at the road ahead, she saw that the Fiesta had made a very tight left-hand turn into a side road.

'Down there,' she said pointing.

Without braking, Charlie turned the steering wheel sharply to follow.

Jesus!

Andrea grabbed the seat again as the tyres screeched on the road beneath them.

The Fiesta was now only twenty yards ahead of them and no match for the powerful two-litre engine of the Astra.

Up ahead, a coach was coming the other way. There wasn't enough room for both vehicles.

The Fiesta's brake lights burned red as Davies skidded towards the coach and hit the front.

'Shit!' Andrea said, although it didn't look like Davies was going to be seriously injured from the impact.

Charlie stamped on the brakes, throwing Andrea forward. The seatbelt cut hard into her shoulder.

In the split second that they stopped, Andrea unclipped her seatbelt, threw open the door, and sprinted down towards the Fiesta.

Davies got out of the car looking shaken. His temple was cut and there was a trickle of blood down his face.

Andrea got to him and saw that he wasn't going to run. Instead, he looked broken and bewildered. She grabbed his jacket and took her cuffs from her belt. 'Edward Davies, I'm arresting you for dangerous driving and on suspicion of the abduction of Abby White.'

CHAPTER 33

'Why did you drive away when you saw us, Edward?' Andrea asked. She was sitting next to Charlie and across from Edward Davies and the Duty Solicitor, Tony Ellis, in Interview Room 1 at Beaumaris nick.

Davies shrugged. His face had now been cleaned and the gash on his temple stitched by the Forensic Medical Examiner (FME), who was essentially the doctor attached to a particular police station.

Charlie shifted forward on his chair and fixed him with a stare. 'You don't know why you drove away?'

'I was scared,' Davies mumbled.

'What were you scared of?' Andrea said.

'You're Feds,' Davies said. 'You looked like you'd come to arrest me so I panicked.'

Feds? Andrea thought. *You twat.*

Charlie frowned. 'What did you think we'd come to arrest you for?'

'I dunno,' he replied as he fidgeted nervously.

'Did you have anything to do with Abby White's disappearance?' Charlie enquired.

'No, of course not,' Davies said, shaking his head. 'I told you that already.'

Charlie arched an eyebrow. 'So, what were you scared of?'

'I dunno. Maybe I'd get falsely accused or something,' he muttered as he shifted uncomfortably in his seat.

Andrea wasn't sure if Davies suffered from something like ADHD, but he didn't seem to be able to sit still. She assumed the nerves from being chased and then interviewed by them didn't help.

She reached over and pulled a folder towards her. 'In the statement you gave us on Tuesday, you said that you were at home all night on Monday and didn't go anywhere.' She pointed to his statement with her forefinger. 'Do you remember telling us that?'

'Yeah,' Davies snorted and then shook his head. 'Of course.'

'For the purposes of the tape, I'm going to show you Item Reference 493J, which is a witness statement that we took today,' Andrea explained as she turned the document to show Davies. 'In this statement, we have an eyewitness who saw a young man sitting in a white Ford Fiesta, registration LV12 KJM outside the house where Abby White lives in Pen-y-garnedd. The car was parked outside for so long that they thought it was suspicious so they wrote down the registration number. Do you recognise that registration, Edward?'

The blood had drained from Davies' face as he looked down at the floor.

Silence.

'Edward,' Andrea said with a slightly raised voice. 'Can

you tell us why you were parked outside Abby White's home for over two hours on Monday night?'

Davies didn't respond. His leg was jigging nervously.

Charlie narrowed his eyes. 'Edward, we need you to answer the question.'

Silence.

'Edward?' Andrea snapped.

He looked up slowly and gave a weak shrug. 'I dunno. I was just sitting out there.'

Andrea furrowed her brow. 'Why were you sitting out there?'

'I dunno.'

'Come on, Edward, you were spotted sitting outside Abby's home the night we believe that she was abducted and murdered,' Andrea said in a severe tone. 'Do you understand how serious that is?'

Davies was clearly shocked by what they'd told him about Abby. He hadn't realised it had changed to a murder investigation. His breathing became quick and shallow.

'I didn't do anything,' Davies whispered, his eyes widening with fear. 'I promise. I didn't touch her.' He took a deep breath to compose himself and then wiped a tear from his eye.

'Then you have to tell us why you were sitting outside Abby's home,' Andrea said forcefully.

'I was just watching,' Davies mumbled. 'I know it's weird. But I thought Abby was with someone else. You know, a bloke. So, I drove over there to watch to see if I could see anything or if anyone arrived or left.'

'Come on, Edward,' Andrea said in a withering tone. 'You just happened to be there when Abby was attacked and taken. But you had nothing to do with it?'

'Yeah,' Davies insisted. 'I did see something.'

Silence.

Andrea looked over at Charlie. *Here we go.*

'What did you see, Edward?' Andrea asked in a sceptical tone.

'A car reversed up behind the house. At the back, there's a track where the garden is,' Davies explained. 'I couldn't see it from the road. But I saw the headlights.'

'But you didn't tell us this before?' Charlie said.

'I didn't want you to know that I was sitting outside the house,' Davies said dejectedly.

Andrea frowned. 'And you expect us to believe that you've now remembered that you saw a vehicle parked at the back of the house where Abby lives?'

'It's the truth, I swear down,' Davies said adamantly. 'I looked at the clock in my car. The car was up there at ten past twelve.'

CHAPTER 34

It was 10.30 p.m. and even though the official lights out at Tonsgrove was at 10 p.m., Laura and Dalby both had the foresight to bring lamps. Since the lights outside had automatically clicked off, Laura had sat silently listening to a podcast that she'd downloaded onto a digital radio. Dalby was thumbing through a magazine. There was the odd shout outside that Laura could hear over her headphones, but other than that it was quiet.

Out of the corner of her eye, Laura saw Dalby put the magazine down and look over at her. Laura didn't react for a few seconds, then she turned.

'What did you do then, Laura?' Dalby asked, raising her voice a little to compensate for the fact that Laura had headphones on.

Laura took off her headphones and shrugged. 'I didn't do anything.'

'Oh yeah?' Dalby smirked. 'Then why are you lying

over there then, in this place?' She picked up her magazine again. 'Don't tell me if you don't wanna,' Dalby sighed with a huff.

Laura waited for a few seconds. She needed to get Dalby on side if she was going to get through the next few days and discover anything about who was responsible for what happened to Sheila Jones.

'I stabbed my husband,' Laura said as she looked over. She, Gareth and the officers from the NCA had discussed the best cover story – which was now typed up in her prison records.

'Right,' Dalby looked interested as she put the magazine down again. 'And why was that?'

'He kept beating me up. The last time he broke my jaw. And he wouldn't let me do anything. Always wanted to know where I was. He put a tracker on my car and my phone,' Laura explained. 'One day I put his dinner on the table and he said it looked like shit and he threw it at me. So, I went over and grabbed a kitchen knife and stabbed him five times. Nearly killed him.' Laura took a breath as though recounting the story was upsetting her. 'And now he's got a colostomy bag.'

'Good. Fuck him,' Dalby said with a half-smile. 'Fair play to you, Laura. Shame you didn't shank him a few years ago, eh?'

Laura smiled. 'Yeah, I wish I had now.'

Dalby laughed. 'Bet you do. How long did you get?'

'Two years. What's it called? "Mitigating circumstances"?' Laura said with a frown.

'Yeah.'

'Brief said I should be out in a year,' Laura explained.

'If you behave yourself.' Dalby gave her a look. 'You got kids?'

'No.' Laura shook her head. 'I can't have kids... You?'

172

'Two boys. Well they ain't boys anymore,' Dalby said. 'They're both in their twenties.' Dalby held up her magazine. 'You can have this when I've finished with it, if you like?'

Laura shrugged but didn't say anything. She was about to reveal another element of her cover story.

Dalby frowned. 'I had you down as the reading type. Thought you'd have your nose in a book as soon as you got here.'

Laura faked an uncomfortable expression. 'No. Reading's not my thing...'

'Oh right,' Dalby said. 'Well, each to their own.'

Laura looked at her. 'Don't tell anyone else...' she said quietly in a conspiratorial tone.

'What's that then?' Dalby asked, looking intrigued.

'I can't really read,' Laura said, trying to sound embarrassed. 'I'm severely dyslexic. And I've got processing issues. I used to get so behind at school that I bunked off most of the time.'

'Right.' Dalby frowned. 'I had you down as someone who'd been to college or uni, or something.'

'I wish,' Laura admitted.

'Well, if there's anything you need to read or forms to fill in, let me know, and I'll give you hand,' Dalby said.

Laura's cover stories had worked. Dalby had mellowed towards her.

'You ain't a grass, are you, Laura?' Dalby asked as she put her hands down her trackies.

What the hell is she doing? Laura wondered.

'No, of course not,' she reassured Dalby.

'Good,' Dalby fixed her with a serious look. 'Cos you know what happens to grasses in a place like this?'

'Yeah,' Laura nodded. 'Or at least I've got a good idea.'

Dalby pulled out a small mobile phone that she'd ob-

173

viously been keeping in one of her orifices. She wiped it clean.

Jesus! Laura thought. *I won't be borrowing that any time soon.*

'Security in this place is shocking!' Dalby joked as she held up the phone to show her. 'Most of the men's prisons in this country now have full body scanners to stop them bringing in drugs and phones.' She grinned. 'In this place, it's just squat and cough. Jesus.' She then gestured to the phone. 'I'm gonna make a call, so whatever you hear in this pad, stays in this pad, okay?'

'Yeah, course.'

'I normally charge five quid for a call in here,' Dalby explained. 'But seeing as you're me pad mate, you can have the first couple on the house.'

'Thanks,' Laura said with a forced smile, remembering where the phone had been hidden. 'I'm gonna listen to my podcast anyway.'

Putting her headphones back into her ears, Laura lay back and pretended to put the podcast back on – but she didn't. She closed her eyes and just listened instead.

'Conor, it's me,' Dalby said. 'Yeah, this place is like a fucking hotel compared to Holloway… Yeah, we've already got a telly in our pad and we've only just arrived… I know. That Mickey-Mouse bitch got shanked in her pad a couple of days ago… Nah, no one's said anything.'

Laura continued to listen to the rest of Dalby's phone call but it was little more than gossip about people she didn't know.

CHAPTER 35

Thursday, 20 October 2022
10.33 p.m.

It was gone 10.30 p.m. by the time Gareth got home. He grabbed a cold beer from the fridge and threw a frozen lasagne into the microwave. He'd try to grab at least six hours sleep before heading back into CID in the morning. He'd arranged with the North Wales Police Media Unit to do a press conference the following morning updating the media on the ongoing investigation into Abby White's abduction and possible murder.

'Hey,' said a voice.

It was Rosie. She wandered into the kitchen, went to the cupboard, got out a box of organic granola and retrieved the soya milk from the fridge.

Whatever happened to Coco Pops? he wondered dryly to himself.

'Hi Rosie,' Gareth said with a friendly smile. When he and Laura had first got together, Rosie had been very hostile. He didn't blame her. Her father had been taken away from her in such horrendous circumstances.

'Microwaved lasagne and beer,' Rosie joked. 'Classic diet of a middle-aged man left to his own devices.'

'Don't tell your mum,' Gareth laughed. 'She's trying to convince me to join her on her intermittent fasting and plant-based regime.'

'I won't,' Rosie said with a smile as she poured the dairy-free milk over her organic cereal. 'Have you heard from her?'

'Just a text,' Gareth replied as he peeled the lid from the steaming lasagne and burned the knuckles on the back of his left hand. 'Bollocks,' he said under his breath.

'She seemed quite nervous about going,' Rosie stated with a frown.

'Really?' Gareth said, trying to sound unsure. 'I think it's quite intense and long days, that's all.'

'Right,' Rosie nodded distractedly as she then laughed at a TikTok video.

The front doorbell rang.

Glancing at his watch, Gareth remembered that Andrea said she was driving past and would quickly update him on the Abby White investigation. He had a meeting with Warlow first thing the next morning, so needed to be up to speed on everything that was going on.

'It's okay,' Gareth reassured Rosie, who had given him a quizzical look. 'It's Andrea. Work stuff.'

Rosie went back to looking at her phone as she munched on her cereal.

Walking down the hallway, Gareth just wanted a hot shower and to crash into bed.

He opened the door and saw Andrea. 'Come in, come in.'

'Thanks, boss.'

Gareth said, 'Do you want to come through for a tea or something stronger?'

'Thanks, but I'd prefer to get home,' Andrea said. 'No offence.'

'None taken,' he said with a smile. 'I think I could sleep standing up at the moment. What happened with Davies?'

'He admitted that he was sitting outside Abby White's home for a couple of hours on Monday night. Reckons he was checking to see what she was up to and if she was with another man.'

'Which isn't creepy at all,' Gareth quipped.

'He maintains that he didn't have anything to do with what happened to Abby,' Andrea explained. 'But he claims he did see a car reverse up behind the back of their garden just after midnight. He didn't mention it before because he didn't want to admit sitting outside her house for hours on end.'

'What did you think?' Gareth asked.

'If I'm honest, I couldn't tell if he was lying through his teeth or if he was telling us the truth,' Andrea admitted. 'But it seems very convenient that now we've caught him sitting outside the house, he's suddenly remembered seeing another car.'

'True. Are there any reports from the house-to-house of a car in that area around midnight?' Gareth enquired.

'Nothing, boss,' Andrea said.

'And Gavin Spears' car was clean when forensics went over it?'

'Yes,' Andrea said. 'And they stressed that the interior of the car hadn't been recently valeted. But we have retrieved Davies' Ford Fiesta and that will now be in the police garage.'

Gareth ran his hand over his scalp in frustration. 'Get forensics to give it a look in the morning.'

'Boss,' Andrea said. 'Any word from Laura?'

'Not yet,' Gareth replied. 'But she would have been in touch if there were any problems.'

'Of course,' Andrea said. 'It's just that she seems so vulnerable in there.'

Gareth gave her a reassuring look. 'She's very resourceful. And she's an experienced officer. Trust me, I wouldn't have allowed her to go in there if I thought she was in real danger.'

'I know,' Andrea said, looking relieved. 'Night, boss.'

'See you bright and early,' Gareth said as he watched Andrea go and then closed the door. He knew how close Laura and Andrea had become since Laura had joined Beaumaris CID.

'Where's Mum?' said a voice in an accusatory way.

Rosie was now standing in the hallway, arms folded and glaring at him.

Oh shit!

Gareth frowned. 'She's on a course over in North Wales. You know that.'

'Bullshit!' Rosie snapped angrily.

'I'm not lying to you,' Gareth said, trying to reassure her.

'You are,' Rosie growled. 'Otherwise why would Andrea think Mum was "vulnerable in there", and why would you use the word "danger"?'

'Were you eavesdropping on our conversation?' Gareth asked indignantly as he wondered how he was going to get out of this. Laura would be mortified if she knew that Rosie had become aware of her undercover operation. But what was he going to say now?

'Yes,' Rosie defiantly. 'I came out of the kitchen, heard Andrea ask about Mum and so I listened. What the hell is going on?'

Gareth looked at her for a moment and took a deep

breath. There was no other way out of this but to tell her the truth. 'Your mum has gone undercover into a prison for a couple of days. She's not in danger but she didn't want you to worry.'

'What?' Rosie's eyes widened in shock. 'Are you actually joking? That sounds dangerous. Jesus. What the hell is she doing that for?'

'There are plenty of people in there looking out for her,' Gareth said, aware that he was lying. 'And she'll be out before you know it.'

'For God's sake,' Rosie huffed. 'What if something happens to her before anyone can help. I've seen *Orange Is the New Black*. They make homemade knives from razor blades in toothbrush handles.'

'That's an American TV series, Rosie.'

'Don't patronise me, Gareth,' she said sternly.

Jake appeared dressed in his pyjamas. 'Are you two arguing?'

'No,' they said in unison.

Jake frowned. 'Are you sure?'

'Yes, it's fine,' Rosie said calmly.

Jake looked confused. 'What were you talking about then?'

'Oh nothing really,' Gareth said and then looked at his watch. 'I think it's time we all went to bed, don't you. I've got a very early start.'

They both nodded but Gareth could see that as Rosie shot him a look, she was not happy.

CHAPTER 36

Beaumaris Police Station
Friday, 21 October 2022
7.00 a.m.

Gareth had arrived at Beaumaris nick at the crack of dawn to have a meeting with Superintendent Warlow and update him on the developments on both cases. The threat of getting extra officers from the mainland was still hanging over his head but he was determined to keep focused. However, Gareth could sense Warlow's anxiety in case Beaumaris CID missed something, made a mistake or lost the public's confidence. Warlow wasn't worried about the victims or getting justice in either of the cases. He was worried in case they reflected badly on him and the decisions he made. But if they came to a satisfactory conclusion, he'd be happy to take the plaudits. It was the typical kind of political bullshit that Gareth knew pervaded every police force.

Abby Wright's disappearance was now featuring regularly on both the local and national news so the morning's press conference was well timed. However, by the time he had walked along the corridor towards the media room, he was aware that someone had leaked the discovery of the blood at the Spears' home and so now social media was awash with theories.

BBC Wales (@BBCWales)
BREAKING NEWS: Sources claim that a significant amount of blood was discovered at Abby Wright's home on Anglesey by forensic officers yesterday.

Gareth was annoyed. He had told the Spears, the forensic team and CID to keep the discovery to themselves until he decided it was prudent to release the information. Yet he knew it could have been any of the SOCOs or uniformed officers who had been at the house yesterday afternoon. The leak could have even originated from the forensic lab. It wouldn't be the first time. Either way, Gareth was angry that the discovery was trending on social media. It should have been information that they had control over.

As Gareth sat down in the media room, he could see from his phone that the case was going viral. He had to admit that a social media explosion often helped a case like this. Abby's face was all over the internet. A Twitter campaign of #FindAbby had gone viral with over a million likes and retweets and a Facebook page had been set up by her school friends.

Looking out at the assembled journalists, Gareth composed himself for a moment. Luke Garrett, the chief corporate communications officer for North Wales Police, who had come up from the main press office in Colwyn Bay, sat next to him. Gareth had met Luke before and had him down as professional but a little cold. Garret came from the new school of thought that believed the media needed to be controlled and even manipulated. He believed in media blackouts and vague press releases. In contrast, Gareth believed this new policy ignored two key reasons why they should keep the media fully informed and up to date. First, the public had a right to know what was happening in their communities, especially if there was any threat to their safety. Second, it was a fact that the police stood a better chance of catching criminals if they used the media to appeal for witnesses.

On the table in front of Gareth were several small tape recorders and microphones. *Here we go,* he thought.

'Good afternoon, I'm Detective Inspector Gareth Williams and I am the senior investigating officer for the investigation into the disappearance of Abby Wright. Beside me is Luke Garrett, our chief corporate communications officer. This press conference is to update you on the case and appeal to the public for any information regarding Abby's disappearance between 12 p.m. midnight on Monday and 6 a.m. on Tuesday morning. Abby's family are understandably very worried, and we are looking for any information that can help us bring Abby back home safely. At this stage in the investigation, we know that Abby was at her home in Pen-y-garnedd on Monday night. Pen-y-garnedd is a very quiet village, so if you saw anything out of the ordinary, however insignificant you think it might be, please contact us so we can come and talk to you. I have a few minutes to take a couple of questions.'

'Can you confirm that a significant amount of blood was found yesterday?' a reporter asked from the front row.

Bloody great! I don't want to have to talk about this now. Nor do I want anyone to think that this is now a confirmed murder case!

'All I am prepared to say is that there has been a thorough forensic examination of Abby's home. If there is anything significant, then we will let you know,' Gareth explained. He wanted to make sure that the media continued to report this as a missing teenager story.

'If a significant amount of blood was found, are you now treating Abby's disappearance as a possible murder?' asked another reporter.

For fuck's sake!

'I can only reiterate what I've already told you. As far as we are concerned, Abby Wright is missing and we are doing everything in our power to find her and bring her home safely,' Gareth said, but he knew he sounded a little irritated.

'From the forensic investigation so far, do you think that Abby is still alive?' a television reporter shouted from the back of the room.

Gareth couldn't help but glare at him for a second. 'Right, thank you, everyone. No more questions.'

As he stood and gathered up his files, he noticed Luke giving him a slightly conceited look.

Oh sod off!

CHAPTER 37

Andrea and Charlie were back at Rose Cottage where the forensic search of the house, garden and surrounding area was drawing to a close. They were still no closer to finding out what had happened to Abby or where she was.

Andrea and Charlie had made their way out to the garden. Above them, the short period of sunshine had been replaced once again by dark, granite-coloured clouds, and the air had become heavy and portentous, filled with the smell of wet earth and dark anticipation. It felt like the darkness was swallowing the sky above them as the wind began to whip around them.

Andrea saw something out of the corner of her eye. A figure was watching them from a window on the first floor. It was Gavin Spears. He had been released pending further investigation as they didn't have enough evidence to charge him.

'He's watching us,' Charlie said under his breath as he saw what Andrea was looking at.

'Yeah, it's creeping me out a bit,' Andrea admitted.

'I agree. There is something very creepy about him,' Charlie said and then turned to look at the summer house. 'For what it's worth, this is what I think happened. Gavin Spears waited for Becks to leave before coming down here. He made some kind of inappropriate advance on Abby. There's a fight and he stabs her. He leaves her here and waits for Zoe to be asleep before carrying out Abby's body and going to dump it somewhere.'

'That's my thinking,' Andrea stated. 'But you've seen the amount of blood. If Spears went back inside the house, he'd be covered in Abby's blood. And Zoe claims that she and Spears went to bed at the same time. So, where are the blood-stained clothes and the murder weapon?'

'Good point. And why have forensics not found any trace of her blood outside of the summer house?' Charlie said, thinking out loud.

'Unless Spears takes off his clothes and shoes, in there,' she said, gesturing to the summer house, '… puts them in bin bags along with the murder weapon. Then he goes inside, straight upstairs and into the shower. When Zoe goes upstairs, she's none the wiser.'

Charlie arched an eyebrow. 'But forensics found no evidence in either Spears' car or Zoe's.'

Andrea scratched her face. It was frustrating that nothing was adding up. She looked over at the dark wooden fence that ran across the back of the garden and behind the summer house. As the sun started to slowly appear from behind the grey clouds, she spotted something in the fence that looked out of place.

Walking across the lawn, she went over to a panel in the fence that was in the far right-hand corner of the garden.

'What is it?' Charlie asked as he followed her.

'I'm not sure yet,' Andrea said as she took out her blue forensic gloves and pulled them on.

As she peered at the fence, she could see that one of the panels didn't quite fit. Then she could see it had small dark hinges on it. Pushing her hand against it, the panel gave a creak but then opened.

It was a gate to a small driveway at the back of the house.

Charlie gave her a quizzical look.

They went out through the gap in the fence.

'Edward Davies said he saw a car pull up at the back of the house around midnight,' Charlie said, thinking out loud.

'Maybe someone took Abby from the summer house and put her directly into a car out here,' Andrea said, looking around. There were several houses and gardens that backed onto the area.

'Yeah, but we've done house-to-house enquiries,' Charlie said. 'And no one's mentioned seeing a car down here. Davies could be lying to us.'

'Maybe,' Andrea said as she scoured the weed strewn ground. 'I don't think forensics came out this way though.'

Charlie went to the fencing panel that had been opened and looked at something. He pulled a clear plastic evidence bag from his pocket.

'You seen something?' Andrea asked as she went over.

Charlie nodded as he very carefully pulled something that seemed to have become trapped in the wood.

'Looks like a woollen thread to me,' Charlie said as he narrowed his eyes.

'It's a long shot, but maybe it's from a rug,' Andrea said as she peered at it. 'Let's get forensics down here.'

A figure appeared.

It was Zoe. She looked like she hadn't slept in days.

The FLO was standing further up the garden.

'Is there anything?' Zoe asked desperately. 'Where is she? Where's Abby?'

'I'm sorry. We will tell you as soon as we hear anything, I promise,' Andrea said. 'Have you spoken to Abby's mother yet?'

'We keep missing each other.' Zoe shook her head. 'I assume that she'll fly home as soon as she can though.' She then gestured to the garden. 'You found the gate then?' she observed.

'It's very well hidden,' Andrea said.

'Yeah,' Zoe said with a sad expression. 'We used to say it was our "secret entrance" and think it was funny.'

Charlie looked at her. 'Neither you nor your husband told us it was there?'

'No,' Zoe said. 'I didn't think it was important.'

Andrea's eyes were drawn up to a different window on the first floor where Spears continued to watch them from.

'He didn't do anything,' Zoe said as she looked up at the window too. 'I know there was all that stuff that Abby wrote. But Gav would never harm her. I promise you.'

Before Andrea could respond, her phone rang. It was a number with the Beaumaris Police Station prefix.

'I'm sorry but I've got to take this,' Andrea said to Zoe as she turned and walked away to take the call. 'DC Jones.'

'It's Stephen Fletcher from Digital Forensics,' a male voice explained. 'We've got something for you.'

'Okay, what is it?'

'We've managed to triangulate the signal from Abby White's mobile phone,' Fletcher said. 'We've narrowed it down to a patch of land in the Pentraeth Forest, close to the Llwydiarth lake. I'll text you the co-ordinates. They're not exact, but they're the best we can do, given the remote location.'

'Right, thank you,' Andrea said as she ended the phone call and then looked over at Charlie.

Zoe was walking back down the garden towards the house.

'We need to go,' Andrea said under her breath. 'We've got a location for Abby's mobile phone.'

CHAPTER 38

Bangor Hospital
Friday, 21 October 2022
10.05 a.m.

Gareth's head was whirring as he pushed the button in the lift for the basement of Bangor Hospital. Having done a press conference appealing for witnesses to Abby White's abduction, he was now trying to get his head back into the investigation into Sheila Jones' murder. It was taking a lot of focus to keep juggling both cases.

Ben was on his phone trying to chase the forensic team for anything they'd found in Sheila Jones' room. He had also just spoken to Shane Deakins, Sheila's partner, who lived over in Wrexham. Deakins was well-known to North Wales Police, so Gareth assumed they were going to get very little from him.

After his conversation with Rosie the previous evening, he thought he should text her to reassure her that Laura was okay. He'd used a couple of contacts to establish that there had been no incidents overnight at Tonsgrove.

Taking his phone, he began to type:

Hi Rosie
Just to let you know that I've checked and your mum is
fine. You really don't need to worry, I promise you.
I'll see you later at home.
Love Gareth xx

He hoped that would allay Rosie's fears for a while. The lift clunked to a stop and the doors opened.

'You've got rugby training tonight, haven't you?' Gareth asked as they made their way down the windowless corridor.

'Should have,' Ben replied. 'If I've got time.' Then he pointed to his knee. 'Plus this knee is really playing up.'

Gareth knew that Ben had been struggling all year with the injury. He'd been living vicariously through Ben's love of playing rugby ever since he'd joined CID. Ben played for the Beaumaris Rugby Club first XV as a nifty fly half. For a moment, Gareth was taken back to his time at the University of Aberystwyth where it was his love of rugby and beer that put paid to his degree in psychology.

'You ever think of still playing, boss?' Ben said. 'You know there's a veterans team at the club.'

Gareth gave him a wry smile, stopped and bent forward. He pointed to a six-inch scar that ran horizontally across his scalp. 'You see that?'

Ben peered over and nodded. 'Yeah.'

'Twelve stitches I had in my head,' Gareth laughed. 'So, that was the one and only time I ever played for Beaumaris Veterans.'

'Fair enough,' Ben said with a smile.

Gareth reached the large black double doors to the mortuary, opened the right-hand one and went inside.

The drop in temperature was marked, as was the instant waft of disinfectants and other chemicals. There were two large mortuary examination tables nearby, with a third on the far side of the room. The walls were tiled to about head height in pale blue tiles, and workbenches and an assortment of luminous coloured chemicals ran the full length of the room.

Looking around, Gareth spotted a figure working over at the third mortuary table. He was taking photographs of a body, using a small white plastic ruler to give an indication of scale, while he mumbled his findings into a microphone attached to his scrubs.

'Good morning, William,' Gareth said in a slightly too chirpy voice, given the circumstances.

Professor William Lovell was one of the foremost forensic pathologists in Wales. His mind was as sharp as his dress sense. He was respected by everyone and he showed a genuine passion for his profession.

'Gareth,' Lovell said with a friendly nod. 'And it's Ben, isn't it?' His voice was deep and sounded like a mixture of public school and North Wales.

Ben nodded. 'That's right.'

The underlying buzz of fans and the air conditioning added to the unnatural atmosphere. The pungent smell of cleaning fluids masked the odour of the gases and the beginnings of rot and decay.

Lovell, who was dressed in pastel green scrubs and a rubber apron, turned off his microphone and looked at them. Pulling down his mask, he revealed a boyish smile on his clean-shaven face.

Gareth's eyes were drawn down to Sheila Jones' body laid out like a white mannequin doll on the metal gurney. Her torso had been cut and opened so that her ribcage and all her internal organs were now on show. However many times Gareth went to a post-mortem, he didn't think he'd ever get used to seeing a human being like that. He didn't really want to.

'What can you tell us, William?' Gareth asked, eager to get on with it.

'Your victim died from multiple stab wounds,' Lovell explained as he went over to the body. He then pointed to a wound in the white flesh about six inches under the right armpit. 'But this is the one that did the real damage. The knife would have severed the axilla artery under here, causing huge blood loss and physiological shock. Your victim would have been incapacitated in seconds and dead in under two minutes.'

'And it was definitely a knife?' Ben asked.

Lovell nodded. 'Yes. Smooth edge, about six inches. If I were to guess, it was a kitchen knife.'

'Anything else that might help us?' Gareth asked.

Lovell walked over to a tiny beaker. He took some tweezers, took something from inside and turned to show them. 'I found this embedded in your victim's right forearm.'

Ben frowned. 'What is it?'

'A piece of glass,' Lovell explained. 'I'm going to test it, but it looks like it happened when she was attacked.'

CHAPTER 39

Andrea and Charlie pulled up in a small car park close to Llyn Llwydiarth, the largest natural lake on Anglesey at the heart of the Pentraeth Forest. With thick undergrowth on its banks, and a dark forest to the south, it felt like it was completely cut off from anywhere. It was actually only six miles west of Beaumaris.

At the southern end of the lake were a pair of Neolithic tombs that were only seven feet apart. The tombs' alignment allowed for a shared passage entrance. The southern tomb had a large capstone that stood on four uprights.

Getting out of the car, Andrea looked down through the wooded area towards the lake. The distant trees were veiled in mist, their trunks covered in dark, bottle green bark from the endless rash of lichen. At points, the bark was gnarled and cracked.

A uniform patrol car had parked next to them and two constables in high-vis jackets got out.

'Jesus, we're in the middle of nowhere,' Charlie muttered under his breath.

'I'm surprised they could get any kind of signal,' Andrea said and then waved at the officers. 'We'll go down this way.'

They started to make their way towards the lake. The further Andrea peered down the shoreline, the more the trees became colourless silhouettes against the blanket of white mist.

This place is seriously spooky, she thought.

Underneath her feet, the ground was covered in spongy moss and decaying leaves from the withered, skeletal branches above. The static mist seemed to have weaved itself around the tree trunks like candyfloss.

A few minutes later, they reached a clearing close to the bank that had been identified by the forensic team as being the location of Abby White's mobile phone. Scouring the area, Andrea couldn't see anything except undergrowth and mud.

'Over there,' Charlie said as he pointed. They could see fresh footprints on the muddy shoreline.

The air was musty and damp. Andrea placed her shoe onto the ground and manoeuvred herself down the bank towards the shoreline.

Above them, a cawing of two crows, who flapped their inky wings, broke the eerie silence. It was as if they were laughing at her struggling down the incline.

Andrea edged down the bank again and eventually got to some level ground.

Charlie was a few yards ahead of her.

'This is going to be like looking for a needle in a haystack, isn't it?' Andrea sighed.

'Not really,' Charlie said as he crouched down and pointed to something lying flat on top of the mud.

It was an iPhone.

CHAPTER 40

Rhosllanerchrugog, Wrexham
Friday, 21 October 2022
11.51 a.m.

Gareth and Ben had made their way from Bangor along the North Wales Expressway and had now arrived in Rhos, a suburb of Wrexham. Its full name was Rhosllanerchrugog. Outside there was relentless drizzle. The sky was covered with low colourless cloud. Everything was muted green and grey. No colours and no hard edges.

'Welcome the land of the Jackos,' Ben said as they passed a brown road sign that read RHOSLLANERCHRU-GOG – PLEASE DRIVE CAREFULLY GYRRWCH YN OFALUS.

Gareth frowned. 'I don't know what that means.'

'The landowner who owned this whole area was a Jacobite,' Ben explained. 'You know, in the 1700s. My taid came from Ruabon which is just up the road. He told me that the miners from Rhos marched into Wrexham when George I was crowned to protest and there were riots. It was part of the Jacobite Rebellion. So, people from Rhos are called Jackos.'

'Thank you for the history lesson, Benjamin,' Gareth said with a smile.

Ben pulled a face. 'Although I think people from Wrexham use 'Jacko' as a term of abuse for anyone from Rhos. It sort of means they're inbred and a bit thick.'

'Right. Well I'll bear that in mind,' Gareth said as they turned right and headed for the address they'd been given for Shane Deakins.

A few minutes later, they pulled into a cul-de-sac of detached new-build houses. From the looks of the cars, Gareth deduced that the people who lived there were relatively affluent.

As they pulled up outside the house, they saw an imposing-looking man with a shaved head cleaning a gleaming white Cherokee Jeep. He was muscular and both his arms were covered in tattoos.

Gareth looked over at Ben as they got out of the car. 'Looks like we've found Shane Deakins.'

Taking a sponge, the man dropped it into a bucket of soapy water before looking over at them. His face twisted with contempt.

Gareth and Ben pulled out their warrant cards to show him. 'Shane Deakins.'

'I got nothing to say to you,' Deakins sneered with a very strong Liverpudlian accent as he tried to ignore them.

'We'd like to talk to you about Sheila,' Gareth said calmly.

'There's nothing to say is there,' Deakins said angrily. 'She's gone. What more is there to say?'

'We're very sorry for your loss,' Ben said.

'Are you fuck!' Deakins snapped as he closed the car door that he'd been cleaning.

'We're investigating Sheila's murder,' Gareth explained. 'I wonder if you'd mind answering a few questions for us?'

'Yeah, I would,' Deakins said. He made a deliberate attempt to ignore them as he took a cloth and began to clean a wing mirror.

'It'll only take a few minutes of your time,' Gareth said calmly.

Deakins stood up tall and glared at Gareth. 'You don't need to investigate what happened to Sheila. Everyone knows what happened to her and why.'

Gareth narrowed his eyes. 'It would be useful if you could pass your suspicions to us.'

'Jesus.' Deakins shook his head. 'If you don't know, I'm not gonna tell you, am I? In my world, that's not how things work.'

Ben arched an eyebrow. 'Don't you want to get justice for Sheila and her family?'

Gareth inwardly cringed at Ben's question as it sounded a little naive, given they were talking to a man like Deakins.

'Justice?' Deakins virtually spat out the word. 'I'm gonna get justice for Sheila, all right. Don't you worry about that.'

Gareth didn't like the sound of Deakins' comment. 'Hope you're not going to do anything stupid, Shane?'

'No. I'm not going to do anything stupid.' Shane shrugged calmly. 'But I will be taking a little trip down to Birmingham and there's nothing you can do about that.'

'Actually, we can arrest you right now if we believe that you are going to carry out a criminal act,' Ben said.

'Go on then,' Deakins scoffed as he put down the cloth and held out his hands as if they were going to be cuffed. 'Actually, under the Police and Criminal Evidence Act of 1984, you need reasonable grounds to arrest me on the suspicion that I'm going to commit a crime sometime in the future. And I'm pretty sure that my brief will run rings around you,' Deakins smirked at them. 'But if you want to look like idiots, do all that paperwork and waste your time, knock yourself out, pal.'

Gareth gave a frustrated look at Ben. However, what it did confirm was that Deakin was convinced that Sheila's murder was connected to the ongoing turf war between the drugs gangs that originated in both Birmingham and Liverpool.

CHAPTER 41

Llyn Llwydiarth, Pentraeth Forest
Friday, 21 October 2022
12.02 p.m.

It had been an hour and a half since Charlie had found what they believed was Abby White's mobile phone on the bank of Llyn Llwydiarth. A dark blue van that had NORTH WALES USMU – which stood for Underwater Search and Marine Unit – printed on the side was now parked up along with a white SOCO forensics van. Further out on the water was a black police RIB (rigid inflatable boat). Several police divers in black drysuits, masks, and breathing apparatus were bobbing around in the water. Others were sitting in the boat, using the two-way radios and maintaining the orange-coloured safety lines.

Andrea had checked with Gareth that it was okay to proceed with searching the lake for Abby White's body. It was a very costly operation but given that Abby White was missing and her phone had been found on the lake's shore, it was logical to think that she might be somewhere in the water. And that someone had put her there.

'There isn't enough money in the world that would persuade me to do that,' Andrea said as she shivered and looked at the police divers in the water.

'Searching for bodies in freezing water definitely isn't on my bucket list,' Charlie joked darkly.

Professor Helen Lane, dressed in full white forensic suit, was down on the shoreline with two other SOCOs checking the ground in the area where the phone was found.

A SOCO approached and handed her and Charlie two light blue coloured Tyvek forensic suits.

Charlie gave her a dry look. 'What happened to the old days where coppers would just trample all over a crime scene in their boots and dropping ash from their cigarettes?'

'Ah, yes. And then back to the station to beat a confession out of a suspect,' Andrea joked.

Charlie shook his head. 'The good old days, eh?'

Dark, gallows humour was sometimes just part and parcel of surviving the grim nature of police work.

Pulling the elastic around her freezing ears to secure her surgical face mask, Andrea got a waft of rubber from the purple gloves she had just snapped on.

Charlie gestured for her to go down the muddy bank towards the water. 'After you.'

'Thanks,' she replied sarcastically as a couple of SOCOs made their way from the bank carrying evidence bags back to the forensic van.

The air was musty and damp as Andrea placed her shoe, now enveloped in a forensic shoe cover, onto the earth and manoeuvred herself down.

'Do you want to take my hand?' Charlie joked.

'No, piss off,' Andrea said as her foot suddenly slid a few inches on the muddy soil, and she nearly lost her footing. 'For fuck's sake!'

Andrea edged down the bank and eventually got to some level ground.

'Good morning,' Lane said as she gave them both a half wave from the water. She was wearing black wellies over her forensic suit, and the water was up to her shins.

Suddenly, there was a shout from one of the police divers.

Andrea looked over and saw the diver gesturing to something in the water about fifty yards from where they were standing on the shore.

Her heart sank for a moment.

The police RIB gunned its engine and moved slowly across the lake to where the diver was treading water.

Another USMU officer reached into the water with gloved hands and retrieved something.

Andrea squinted. It looked like an item of clothing but it was hard to tell from that distance. It looked like it might be red.

'I thought they'd found Abby,' Charlie muttered under his breath.

'Me too,' Andrea admitted.

The RIB turned and headed slowly to where they were standing.

A few seconds later, the boat reduced its speed and drifted to the bank.

The diver on the boat hopped out into the water, which only came up to his knees. He was holding a clear plastic bag which contained whatever they'd found floating in the lake.

'DC Jones?' he asked as he approached.

'I'm here,' Andrea said, raising her hand. Now that they were wearing forensic hats, masks and suits, it was difficult to identify anyone.

'We've found this,' the diver said as he handed her the bag. 'I wasn't sure if it's relevant.'

Andrea peered at the bag. Inside there was an item of pinky-red clothing which was sodden.

She carefully moved it within the bag to see if there were any clues as to what it might be.

Then she saw something that made her catch her breath.

A white logo on the front of what looked like a sweat-shirt. As the logo became more visible, she could see what she feared it was.

She looked at Charlie, who had also spotted what it was.

A pink Adidas hoodie.

It was the one that Abby had been wearing in the photograph that Zoe had given them.

And now it was floating in the lake.

CHAPTER 42

HMP Tonsgrove, Anglesey
Friday, 21 October 2022
2.10 p.m.

Gareth and Ben had been sitting in the meeting room at HMP Tonsgrove for ten minutes. They were there to have a secret briefing with Laura with the cover story that she was helping CID officers with their enquiries for an ongoing investigation.

Even though Gareth knew that Laura was safe, he had still been concerned for her welfare since she left. And he was looking forward to seeing her despite the incredibly bizarre circumstances.

The door opened and Laura came in with Rice, the prison officer they'd seen the day before.

'Go and sit down,' Rice said to her in a hostile voice.

Gareth looked at Rice, sensing his hostility. 'Thank you, we can take it from here.'

Rice nodded, turned and left.

Gareth left a few seconds before looking over at Laura and smiling. 'Hey. You okay?'

Laura smiled back. 'Yeah. It's like being in a spa. Only better,' she said sardonically.

'What's his problem?' Gareth asked gesturing to the door to indicate he was talking about Rice.

'He's pissed off that I turned down his proposition of help in return for sexual favours,' Laura said with a shrug. 'Which was difficult. I mean, you've seen him,' she said with a wry smile.

'Yeah, must have been a tough one,' Ben joked.

'I'm pretty sure that the prison service will be delighted to hear that he's offering that service,' Gareth said.

'Well he and the governor are more than just good friends,' Laura explained. 'I guess that's why he walks around like he owns the place. He thinks he's untouchable.' She looked at Gareth. 'Are the kids okay?'

'Yeah, they're fine,' he reassured her.

Silence.

'We spoke to Shane Deakins earlier,' Ben said. 'Delightful chap.'

Gareth looked over at Laura. 'Deakins seemed convinced that Sheila had been killed as part of this turf war between the Croxteth Boyz and this gang from Birmingham. In fact, he told us he was going to pay "a little visit" to Birmingham, presumably to avenge Sheila's death.'

'Jesus,' Laura said. 'Can't you stop him?'

'We've informed West Midlands Police to be on the lookout for him,' Ben replied.

'According to Barry McDonald...' Laura said.

'The prison tutor?' Ben asked to clarify.

'That's the one.'

'McDonald implied that Sheila was having some kind of relationship with a member of the Birmingham gang. He made some terrible *Romeo and Juliet* comparison,' Laura explained. 'He seemed to think that's why she was killed.'

Gareth processed the information for a moment. 'We've interviewed Kayleigh Doyle. It was her hair bobble and hair that we found in Sheila's cell. She claimed she was having a relationship with Sheila's cellmate, Hayley Ross.'

Ben raised an eyebrow. 'I guess Kayleigh wouldn't admit that her and Sheila were together.'

'No,' Laura agreed. 'But it would definitely antagonise the others in that gang if anyone knew that. In fact, I saw Kayleigh and a woman called Niamh having an altercation in the canteen. Although what they said wasn't explicit, it was enough for Niamh to tell Kayleigh that whatever she was angry about, she had brought it upon herself.'

Gareth looked at Laura. 'Seems that we should be having a look at Niamh Mullan as soon as possible.'

CHAPTER 43

Llyn Llwydiarth, Pentraeth Forest
Friday, 21 October 2022
4.43 p.m.

The North Wales Underwater Search and Marine Unit had been searching Llyn Llwydiarth for nearly six hours by the time Andrea and Charlie returned from Beaumaris where they had dropped off evidence to the forensic lab and caught up on paperwork. As they turned the corner to the lake, Charlie had to apply the brakes as they were met with an impenetrable blanket of fog.

'Jesus. I can't see a bloody thing,' Andrea muttered.

Now crawling at around 5 mph, they drove along the road that surrounded the lake, heading for where they knew there was a car park.

They parked and got out of the car. The orange flash of the indicators coloured the thick mist for a second. Andrea became aware of bright lights coming from down by the shoreline, close to where they had talked to Lane earlier.

It was so quiet that all Andrea could hear was the

sound of her own breathing. She and Charlie walked carefully towards where the arc lighting was coming from. The sound of their footsteps on the stony footpath seemed loud in the silence. Then suddenly, a grating, piercing noise.

It sounded like a woman screaming.

What the bloody hell is that? she thought, now startled.

Glancing up to the sky, Andrea squinted and realised it was the squawk of an enormous bird flying above her towards the fog-strewn treetops.

'Jesus, that made me jump out of my bloody skin,' Andrea admitted.

Charlie pulled a face. 'It's a bit spooky now there's all this fog.'

They started to walk gingerly down the steep bank towards the water.

'Hello?' she shouted.

The fog had become damp and musty. It hung around the trees like thick cobwebs and had a distinct, watery smell.

'We're down this way!' came the shout of a male voice.

Yeah, that doesn't bloody help me! she thought, getting frustrated.

She was now unnerved and disorientated. *If I'm not careful, I'm going to walk straight into that sodding lake.*

A male DS, in a black drysuit, was standing at the water's edge as he took off his gloves. Andrea remembered that he was the senior officer for the USMU.

The DS looked at her. His balding scalp was wet and his face ruddy.

'You're the SIO on this case, aren't you?' he asked.

'Yes,' she replied, wondering why he sounded so fed up.

She guessed searching for a body in the dirty, icy water wasn't something that would fill anyone with joy. 'How are we doing?'

'Nothing so far, I'm afraid.' The sergeant gave a loud sniff, shook his head, and gestured out to the water. 'It might look calm and steady out there. But it's incredibly deep, and the currents underneath are very strong.'

Charlie pulled a face. 'Does that mean you can't narrow down your search area?'

'Not really,' the sergeant replied. 'If I'm honest, if your victim is in here, they could be anywhere now.' He then gestured to the fog. 'This weather isn't helping. It's very dark at the bottom so visibility is very low. And it won't be long until the sun goes down now. But if you really do think there's someone in there, we'll keep going until we find them.'

'Okay. At this stage, I think we should keep going,' Andrea said with a nod. 'Thank you.'

Before she could process what he'd said, Professor Lane approached.

'We've found this down on the shoreline,' Lane said, holding up a clear evidence bag. She handed it to Andrea to look at.

Inside the bag was a gold necklace with an ornate black pendant that had an intricate gold pattern.

'Can you tell how long it's been there?' Charlie asked.

'Not exactly, but not long,' Lane explained. 'It was lying on the top of some mud so it can't have been there more than a couple of days, given the weather this week.'

'Doesn't look like the sort of thing a teenage girl would wear,' Charlie observed.

'Let's see if Zoe Spears can identify it,' Andrea said as she took the bag.

'We also have a series of relatively fresh footprints,'

Lane explained, pointing to an area of the shore. 'At first look, I'd say they were a size 7 or 8.'

'So possibly the same as the footprint we found in the summer house?' Andrea asked.

'Yes,' Lane replied. 'I'll get forensics to take a cast. We might even be able to narrow down the type of shoe, if we're lucky.'

CHAPTER 44

Gareth sat back on the sofa, sipped his cold San Miguel beer and let out a sigh. He was shattered. Andrea had debriefed him two hours ago about the developments in the Abby White investigation. It was almost certain that she had been attacked, taken from her home and that her body had been dumped in Llyn Llwydiarth. Though they had a couple of suspects, they had no overwhelming evidence on anyone.

Sitting forward, Gareth decided that he needed a total distraction. He grabbed his laptop and turned it on. It was now eight weeks until he was due to marry Laura on a tiny island called Cribinau, off the coast of Anglesey at Aberffraw. They had booked the church called *Eglwys Bach y Mor* which was Welsh for 'the church in the sea'. Gareth was excited as it was arguably the most notable and recognised church on Anglesey and dated back to the twelfth century. It was thought to have been the first church on the island and dedicated to St Kevin. The church had been rebuilt at different times in the fourteenth, sixteenth and nineteenth centuries. In 2006, the outer walls were white-washed so that the church now gleamed in the sunlight and looked almost magical.

Jake wandered in with an uncertain expression.

'You okay, Jake?' Gareth asked. Jake clearly wanted to ask him something but was reluctant.

'Yeah,' Jake shrugged unconvincingly.

Since being with Laura, Gareth had tried to bond with both Jake and Rosie with varying degrees of success. He knew he was never going to come close to replacing their late father, Sam, and he had no intention of trying. He also knew that after what had happened to their 'Uncle Pete', he just needed to be patient and supportive.

'You sure?' Gareth asked and saw that Jake was looking at the television.

'Is it okay if I watch the end of the Real Madrid game?' Jake asked. 'They're playing AC Milan in the Champions League.'

Grabbing the remote, Gareth immediately turned the television on then tossed the remote to Jake who caught it.

'Of course,' Gareth reassured him. 'Who's that player you like?'

'Vinícius Júnior,' Jake replied as he put on the game. He was Real Madrid's twenty-three-year-old Brazilian winger who had electric pace and astounding skills. They had recently bought Jake a Real Madrid shirt with VINI JR and the number 7 printed on the back.

Gareth pointed to the laptop. 'I'm looking for suits for us for the wedding,' he explained. They'd decided that Gareth and Jake would have matching suits.

'Okay,' Jake said, completely distracted by watching the game.

Gareth spent the next few minutes trawling through various websites, looking at suits.

'We've definitely got to have waistcoats, haven't we?' Gareth said looking over to Jake.

Jake thought about it for a second. Then his face brightened. 'Like in *Peaky Blinders*?'

'Exactly like that,' Gareth said with a smile but wondering if it was appropriate that a thirteen-year-old was familiar with a TV series like *Peaky Blinders*.

'Cool,' Jake said with a nod.

Rosie came into the living room with her phone in her hand.

'Hi, Rosie,' Gareth said, but noticed she looked very distracted.

Rosie gave him a look, turned and walked out of the living room.

Gareth got up and followed her out into the hallway.

'I saw your mum today,' he said gently as she walked away.

Rosie turned and looked at him. 'Is she okay?' she asked, sounding angry.

'Yes,' Gareth reassured her.

'Right,' Rosie said as she bristled.

'She's going to be fine,' Gareth said. 'And she's doing important work.'

'Clearly more important than being here,' Rosie snapped but Gareth could see that she was getting upset.

'Come on, Rosie,' he said. 'You know that you and Jake are the most important things in the world to her.'

Rosie raised an eyebrow as she took a deep breath. 'Are we?'

Gareth looked at her. 'Of course you are. And I know how proud you are of the work your mum does. She makes a difference to people's lives just at the moment when they need help the most… And she's incredibly good at what she does.'

His words seemed to have struck an emotional chord with Rosie. He saw her eyes fill with tears.

'It's just that I feel really scared and lost when she's not here,' Rosie said as she was overwhelmed by emotion.

'Hey,' Gareth said taking a step forward and giving her a hug. 'Of course you do. You've been through a lot recently.' Then he stepped back, put his hands on her shoulders and looked directly at her. 'She'll be back here in a couple of days. I promise you. And she's safe where she is. Okay? Trust me.'

Rosie nodded as she wiped her face. 'Thank you,' she whispered.

'How are you getting on looking for that bridesmaid dress?' Gareth asked in an upbeat tone.

'I haven't really started,' Rosie admitted.

'Why don't you start to look tonight so when your mum gets back, you've got something to show her?' he suggested.

Rosie nodded as her face brightened with his suggestion. 'Yeah. That's a good idea.'

Gareth watched Rosie as she walked away and went upstairs.

CHAPTER 45

Laura and Dalby were locked in their cell until the following morning at 7.30 a.m. 'Bang up' had been at 8 p.m. so they'd been in their cell for three hours, mainly watching a trashy reality show on the television.

Laura glanced over and saw that Dalby was filling out another 'canteen form' with its assorted items. Laura's mind turned to Rosie and Jake. She wondered how they were getting on without her. As far as she could remember, she hadn't been apart from her children since they moved back to Anglesey. It also grated on her that she'd had to lie to them about where she was going.

'You not filling that out?' Dalby asked as she gestured over to Laura's canteen form that sat on the cabinet beside her bed.

Laura nodded. 'Maybe later,' she said quietly.

'If you can't read or write properly,' Dalby said with a frown, '...how are you gonna fill the bloody thing out?'

Laura shrugged but didn't say anything.

'Christ, Laura!' Dalby exclaimed. 'Why didn't you say something? I can fill it out for you, you daft bugger.'

'I was too embarrassed to ask,' Laura admitted in a soft voice.

'Give it here,' Dalby said in frustration as she came over and took the form. 'I'll run through this for you and you can tell me what you want, yeah?'

Laura gave her a grateful smile. 'Thanks, I owe you one.'

'Yeah,' Dalby laughed. 'We've gotta look for each other in here. There are some right psychos about.'

'If I'm honest, those Brummie women scare the life out of me,' Laura admitted.

'Yeah,' Dalby said with a knowing look. 'Well they should do.'

Silence as Dalby read through the canteen form.

'Why's that?' Laura asked eventually.

'You do know who they are, don't you?' Dalby said as she went back to her bed with Laura's list.

'No.' Laura shook her head, now intrigued.

'You know who Kayleigh Doyle is?' Dalby asked.

Laura nodded. 'I think so.'

'Her dad is Gary Doyle,' Dalby explained as though Laura should know who that was. 'The Doyles?'

Laura shook her head. The name Gary Doyle did ring a bell but to keep her cover story it was best that she feign complete ignorance. 'Sorry, no,' Laura said shaking her head.

'Jesus, Laura, you really are from a different world, eh?' Dalby scoffed. 'The Doyles are the biggest Irish gang in Birmingham. Gary Doyle and his brother Michael ran drugs and guns through their haulage firm for years. They had cousins over in Dublin who had the docks over there completely sewn up. Gary got nicked with fifteen kilos of flake and 200 kilos of weed coming out of Wolverhampton. He got twenty years. But Michael still runs things.'

Dalby looked over and gave Laura a meaningful look. 'I assume you've heard the latest gossip?' she asked in a conspiratorial tone.

'No,' Laura replied, curious as to what she was going to tell her.

'Rumour has it that there's a copper undercover in this place,' Dalby said, raising an eyebrow.

Laura's stomach lurched as she took a breath.

'What?' Laura said, trying to look both surprised and innocent.

Laura could feel her heart hammering against her chest. *Jesus, I feel sick.*

Dalby looked at Laura. 'Of course, everyone is assuming it was someone who came in the sweatbox with us the other morning.'

There was an awkward silence.

Does she think it's me? Keep it nice and steady, Laura.

Laura feigned a confused frown.

Dalby got off her bed and Laura braced herself.

Shit. This is not good.

'Yeah, some of the girls reckoned it must be you,' Dalby said as she approached.

Laura froze. Her pulse was racing.

'Me?' she scoffed as her anxiety went through the roof.

Clenching her fist, she prepared to defend herself if Dalby launched an attack.

Dalby loomed over and smiled at her. 'Yeah, I know.'

Laura held her breath.

'Then I told them that you could hardly read or write,' Dalby snorted as she sat down on the bed and took Laura's canteen sheet to look at. 'I mean, you could hardly be a bloody copper if you're virtually illiterate. No offence.'

'None taken,' Laura said, trying to hide the incredible relief she was now feeling inside.

'Yeah, well, God help any undercover copper if they get found in a place like this,' Dalby said with a dark look.

Her words made Laura shiver.

CHAPTER 46

Beaumaris Police Station, CID
Saturday, 22 October 2022
8.00 a.m.

Gareth stretched and yawned audibly at his desk. He checked his watch and saw it was 8 a.m. The CID team were gathering outside for the morning briefing, moving chairs to face the front of the office where the scene boards were located. Gareth had already had a quick meeting with Warlow at 7 a.m. where Gareth reassured him that they were making good progress in both investigations. Of course, that was a lie. And if they didn't make some significant breakthroughs in both cases in the next few days, officers from the mainland would be dispatched to 'help out'. Gareth knew that essentially they would be drafted in to take over because he'd failed to get results quickly enough. That's just how that bullshit worked.

'Boss, we're ready,' Ben said, knocking on his open door and breaking his train of thought.

'Right you are,' Gareth said, getting to his feet and hearing his knees crack.

Jesus, I'm getting old, he thought wearily.

Walking out into the CID office, Gareth sipped from his water bottle as he'd already had three strong coffees. 'Morning, everyone,' he said attempting an upbeat tone. 'Thanks for coming in early. I know you guys are working around the clock on these investigations and it's much appreciated.' Gareth went to the scene board on the right and pointed to a photograph. 'Abby White. Can you bring us up to speed, Andrea?'

Andrea got up and approached. 'Okay. Yesterday Digital Forensics narrowed down Abby's mobile phone to Llyn Llwydiarth, which is a lake in the Pentraeth Forest. Charlie and I found the phone on the shoreline close to the lake. The North Wales Underwater Search and Marine Unit were brought in' – Andrea pointed to another photo – 'and this pink Adidas hoodie was found floating in the lake. It's the same hoodie that Zoe Spears told us Abby was wearing on Monday night. We also found this necklace on the shoreline close to where we found her phone. Unfortunately, the USMU divers couldn't find any sign of Abby in the lake, although given the lake's depth and the conditions, visibility was very poor.'

'I think we have to make the assumption that Abby is now dead,' Gareth said with a suitably dark expression. 'She was murdered at her home and she was taken to Llyn Llwydiarth where her body was disposed of. But until we have her body, we cannot confirm that she's been murdered to anyone outside this room.' He looked at Andrea. 'Who are our frontrunners in this investigation?'

'My instinct has always been Gavin Spears,' Andrea admitted. 'His behaviour around Abby had been inappropriate and predatory. But we don't have anything concrete to link him to the attack or to Llyn Llwydiarth.'

219

Ben frowned. 'What about his car? Does it have a GPS tracker?'

'Forensics couldn't find anything in his car,' Andrea replied as she shook her head. 'It's too old for a GPS tracker. Plus we have a partial footprint in the blood in the summer house and at the lake, both of which suggest a size seven or eight. Gavin Spears is a size eleven.'

'But Edward Davies *is* an 8,' Charlie pointed out. 'And he admits to sitting outside Abby's home for two hours on Monday night, effectively stalking her.'

Andrea pulled a face. 'The only thing is that forensics went over Davies' car and didn't find a thing. You saw the blood in the summer house. There's no way that Davies could have put Abby's body in his car and then driven her to the lake without leaving some forensic trace in the car.'

Charlie nodded. 'Fair point.'

Something had occurred to Gareth as they were talking. 'What about Zoe Spears? Have we taken a good look at her?'

'Not really. And my instinct is that she's devastated by what's happened.' Andrea narrowed her eyes. 'And does Zoe have a motive?' she asked sceptically.

'Maybe Zoe knows that Gavin's behaviour around Abby is inappropriate but she's turning a blind eye to it,' Gareth suggested. 'We know that around midnight Gavin went down to the summer house. And maybe things got out of hand. Gavin tells Zoe what he's done and she helps him clear up. She puts Abby's body in her car and drives over to Llyn Llwydiarth.'

There was a moment of quiet in the room. No one had looked at this as a theory yet.

'Yes, that is possible.' Andrea nodded thoughtfully. 'In that case, I'll take the stuff we found at the lake to Becks Maddison to look at, rather than Zoe.'

'Good idea,' Gareth agreed. 'We're going to need to get hold of Zoe Spears' phone and car. Forensics didn't find anything in the house, so I'm assuming that Gavin and Zoe would have already destroyed any clothing and the murder weapon… What about Abby's phone?'

'Digital Forensics have got it, boss,' Charlie replied.

'Okay.' Gareth moved over to the other scene board and pointed to another photograph. 'Sheila Jones… Just to keep you up to speed, Ben and I met with Laura inside HMP Tonsgrove yesterday. We still think that Sheila Jones was murdered as part of a turf war between the Croxteth Boyz, the gang that Sheila is affiliated with, and this woman, Kayleigh Doyle, who is affiliated to a gang in Birmingham.'

Ben looked over. 'I've got intel on that, boss. Kayleigh Doyle is part of an Irish criminal family in Birmingham. Her father, Gary Doyle, is serving twenty years for drug trafficking. Apparently it's her Uncle Michael that now runs things there.'

'Thanks, Ben,' Gareth said. 'According to Barry McDonald, one of the prison tutors, Sheila Jones might have been having an affair with someone from the Birmingham gang. And given that we found a bobble of Kayleigh Doyle's hair in Sheila's cell, and she told us that she was in a relationship with Sheila's cellmate, Hayley Ross, it's a fair bet that it was Kayleigh Doyle who was having this affair with Sheila.'

Andrea raised an eyebrow. 'And if someone from the Birmingham gang found this out, there would be even more motive to kill Sheila?'

'Exactly,' Gareth said as he pointed to another photograph. 'This is Niamh Mullan. She's serving three years for GBH and aggravated assault. Laura saw Niamh and Kayleigh having an almighty row in the prison canteen.

Ben and I will be interviewing Niamh today but we need as much intel as we can get on her.' Gareth looked out at the CID team. 'That's it, everyone. Let's keep doing our best work out there. Thank you.'

Gareth turned and went back towards his office.

CHAPTER 47

HMP Tonsgrove, Anglesey
Saturday, 22 October 2022
9.55 a.m.

Laura checked her watch. It was time to head over to the education block for her first literacy session with Barry McDonald. Coming out of her cell, Laura made her way down the corridor towards the stairwell. She had been told to congregate downstairs with the others from G Wing who were due at the education block and they would then be taken across by a prison officer.

Laura was preoccupied with thoughts of how she was going to find any evidence against Niamh Mullan. If Sheila really had been murdered for having a relationship with Kayleigh Doyle, how were they going to get anything to prove it?

Suddenly a figure appeared in front of her, blocking the corridor.

It was Niamh Mullan.

Jesus, talk of the devil.

Laura's stomach tightened. Mullan wasn't on G Wing,

so what was she doing there? And why was she looking directly at Laura?

Shit. This is not good.

'You Laura Noakes?' Mullan asked with a thick Brummie accent.

Laura slowed and frowned. 'Yeah,' she said hesitantly.

'Right,' Mullan growled. 'In here.'

Before Laura had time to protest, someone grabbed her from behind and they both bundled her into a nearby cell and slammed the door.

Still feeling disorientated, Laura was dragged over to a sink. Her heart was hammering against her chest.

What the hell is going on?

Laura caught sight of the woman behind her. She had a shaved black haircut, a neck tattoo and belonged to the gang of Brummie women she'd seen in the canteen.

'What do you want?' Laura cried as Mullan grabbed Laura by both wrists and put her hands into the sink. Her grip was incredibly powerful.

For a second, Laura spotted two fresh cuts across the palm of Mullan's right hand. Were they caused by Sheila Jones when Mullan attacked and killed her in the cell?

The woman with the neck tattoo yanked violently at Laura's hair and then put her in a powerful neck lock. 'We know you're a copper, bitch!'

'What?' Laura gasped, but she was now struggling to breathe. She was terrified.

Kayleigh Doyle appeared at Laura's side. She was holding a kettle that was steaming. She and Mullan had clearly put their differences to one side for now.

'Just admit it,' Kayleigh sneered at her, coming close to her face.

'I'm not a copper,' Laura gasped. 'What the hell are you talking about?'

224

'Yeah, she even smells like a copper,' the woman behind her said.

Kayleigh gestured to the kettle. 'This is boiling water and sugar.' She then gestured to Laura's hands that were still being forcibly held in the sink by Mullan. 'And I'm going to pour it all over your hands. And by the time they get you over to the medical wing, the skin on your hands will have burned off and you'll never use them properly again. So, just tell us the truth, you skank.'

Laura could feel her whole body trembling as she tried to suck in breath. 'I'm not a copper. I promise you. I fucking hate coppers.'

Kayleigh looked over at Mullan for a moment.

'Nice try,' Kayleigh snorted. 'You would say that.'

'I'm telling you the truth,' Laura pleaded.

'Just fucking burn her,' the woman with the neck tattoo growled as she tightened the grip on her throat.

Laura braced herself. She knew the pain of the boiling water and sugar was going to be unbearable.

Mullan looked at Kayleigh and nodded. 'Yeah, just do it.'

'Have this, you copper bitch,' Kayleigh said with a smile as she tilted the kettle.

Laura held her breath and closed her eyes.

Please God, don't let them do this to me!

'Oi, what the fuck do you think you're doing,' bellowed a cockney voice from out in the corridor.

It was Dalby.

'None of your business,' Kayleigh shouted.

'Leave her alone,' Dalby snapped as she kicked open the door and came in.

'She's a copper,' Mullan said. 'She's getting what she fucking deserves so get out.'

'She's not a bloody copper, you daft twats,' Dalby

scoffed. 'Poor sod can't read or write. I had to fill in her canteen form last night.'

There was a tense silence.

Kayleigh frowned and looked over at Mullan.

Laura winced, praying that Dalby's words had the desired effect.

'She wouldn't make much of a copper now, would she?' Dalby said in an almost jovial tone. 'She's my pad mate and she's all right.'

Silence.

Laura felt Mullan loosen her grip on her wrists.

Thank God.

'Yeah, all right,' Kayleigh said as she looked at Laura. 'You're one lucky fucker. Go on, fuck off.'

Laura let out an audible gasp as she was grabbed and pushed out of the cell and into the corridor.

'Jesus, Laura,' Dalby looked at her with a smile. 'You owe me big time.'

Laura took in a long deep breath to steady herself. 'Yeah, I do.'

CHAPTER 48

The Coffee Shop, Menai
Saturday, 22 October 2022
10.30 a.m.

Andrea and Charlie arrived at The Coffee Shop in Menai where Becks Maddison, Abby White's friend, worked. They spotted Becks taking a tray of coffees over to some elderly women at a table by the window.

Becks turned, spotted them and instantly looked anxious. She approached them with a worried expression. 'Have you found her?' she asked in a soft voice.

'I'm afraid not,' Andrea replied gently.

'Right,' Becks said. She looked relieved.

'I'm sorry to come to your workplace,' Andrea explained. 'I did try to call you.'

Becks gave a nod of realisation. 'I saw I had a missed call this morning. Sorry.'

'There are a couple more questions we'd like to ask you,' Charlie said. 'But we could come to your home later, if it's not convenient.'

'I'm just about to start my break so we could go and sit

over there,' Becks suggested as she gestured to an empty table over in the far corner.

'Yes, that would be good,' Andrea said as they followed her across the café and sat down.

'Sorry, do you want something. Coffee, tea?' Becks asked them.

'We're fine, but thank you,' Charlie replied.

Andrea looked at Becks who was blinking nervously. 'There are a couple of things we need to show you,' Andrea explained in a serious tone as she took her phone out of her pocket.

'Okay,' Becks said quietly. She was clearly feeling apprehensive.

'Do you know Llyn Llwydiarth?' Andrea asked.

Becks frowned and shook her head. 'No.'

'It's a lake in the Pentraeth Forest,' Charlie explained.

'Oh, yes. I think I've heard of it,' Becks replied vaguely.

Tapping on her phone's camera roll, Andrea got the photograph of the pink Adidas hoodie that had been found floating in the lake. 'Do you recognise this hoodie?'

The colour drained from Becks' face as she saw the image. She gave a little nod and looked upset. 'It's... the hoodie that Abby was wearing on Monday.' Narrowing her eyes, she looked perplexed. 'Where did you find it?'

Andrea gave her an empathetic look. 'I'm afraid we found it floating in the lake.'

'Oh God,' Becks gasped as her eyes filled with tears and she put her hand to her face. 'You think she's in there?'

Andrea nodded. 'I'm sorry, but we do think it's very likely that Abby is somewhere in Llyn Llwydiarth.'

'Oh no...' Wiping the tears from her face, Becks blew out her cheeks. 'Did... did someone take her there?'

Charlie looked at her. 'That's what we think.'

Andrea tapped her phone and showed her another

photograph. 'We also found this necklace close to the lake... Do you recognise it?'

Becks wiped more tears from her eyes and sniffed as she peered closely at the phone. Then she shook her head. 'No. Sorry. It's not Abby's necklace. She has a silver chain with a cross on it.'

Andrea nodded but felt frustrated as she put the phone away. They'd hoped that the necklace might provide a clue as to what had happened to Abby.

Then Becks' eyes roamed around the room as if something had occurred to her. 'Can I have another look?' she asked.

Andrea nodded, took out her phone and showed her the image again.

After a few seconds, Becks gave her a dark look. 'I thought I recognised it from somewhere... That's Zoe's necklace.'

'Zoe Spears?' Charlie asked to clarify.

'Yeah,' Becks said. 'I remember her showing it to me last Christmas.'

CHAPTER 49

Pen-y-garnedd
Saturday, 22 October 2022
11.15 a.m.

Andrea and Charlie had driven over to Rose Cottage to interview Zoe. As they parked, Andrea could see that the road was now clear of police vehicles, although there was still blue-and-white police tape cordoning off the pavement outside the house.

Andrea and Charlie walked up the garden path and knocked on the door. The young blonde female police officer, who was the Spears' Family Liaison Officer, answered the door.

'Hello, Constable,' Andrea said as she and Charlie went inside and stood in the hallway. 'We're looking for Zoe.'

'She's sitting out on the patio, ma'am,' the FLO replied and then pulled a face. 'She's been drinking quite a lot,' the FLO said under her breath.

'Okay,' Andrea said. 'Where's Gavin?'

'He's gone out for a walk,' the FLO explained.

'Thanks,' Andrea said as they walked down the hallway,

heading for the kitchen which had double doors out to the patio. She wondered if Andrea's drinking was her way of coping with what had happened to Abby or a sign of her guilt and that she knew more than she was letting on.

Sensing that Charlie was no longer behind her, Andrea stopped, turned and saw that Charlie was peering at the family photographs that she had seen attached by magnets to the front of the fridge.

He glanced over at her. 'I think you need to come and see this,' he said ominously.

Andrea walked over to see what he was looking at.

Charlie pointed to a photograph of Zoe and Abby sitting together in a smart restaurant.

Zoe was clearly wearing the gold necklace with the pendant that they had found at the lake.

Jesus.

'Right,' Andrea said quietly as she met Charlie's frown. 'We'd better go and see what she has to say for herself.'

They made their way across the kitchen and out through the patio doors.

Zoe was wrapped in a blanket, smoking a cigarette. There was an empty bottle of red wine on the table and another open.

She turned as she heard them come out of the house. 'What is it?' she asked anxiously. 'Is it Abby?'

Andrea gave a slight shake of her head as she and Charlie sat down on the iron garden chairs opposite her. 'I'm afraid not.'

Zoe blew out a plume of smoke that was whipped away by the breeze.

'But there has been a significant development,' Andrea informed her. 'We've discovered several items that we think belong to Abby at Llyn Llwydiarth.'

'The lake?' Zoe asked in a whisper.

'Yes,' Charlie replied.

'Oh God.' Zoe put her hand to her face as she took a deep breath and sat forward. 'What have you found?'

Andrea took out her phone and showed her the photograph of the pink Adidas hoodie.

'No...' Zoe gasped as soon as she registered what it was. Her face twisted in pain as her hand which was holding a cigarette began to shake.

'I'm really sorry,' Andrea said gently.

Silence.

'Where did you find it?' she asked in a voice that was barely audible.

Charlie looked at her. 'I'm afraid it was found floating in the lake.'

'Oh God, no,' Zoe cried as she dissolved into floods of tears. 'No.'

Andrea showed her the phone again. 'And we also found this.'

Zoe wiped her eyes and then peered at the phone and then looked completely baffled.

'Do you recognise this necklace?' Andrea asked.

'Yes,' Zoe replied with a deep frown. Then she looked at them. 'I don't understand.'

'Is this your necklace, Zoe?' Andrea asked gently.

'Yes, but...' She looked baffled.

Andrea looked directly at her. 'Can you tell me what your shoe size is?'

'What?'

'Your shoe size?'

'It's a seven. Why?'

'I'm going to need you to come to the station for a formal interview,' Andrea said.

'What?' Zoe asked in bewilderment. 'I don't know why my necklace was there. I lost it a few days ago.'

'We can talk about all that at the station,' Charlie said.

'Am I under arrest?' Zoe asked as her eyes widened.

'Not at the moment,' Andrea said. 'But I'm going to need your phone and your car keys right now.'

CHAPTER 50

Beaumaris Police Station
Saturday, 22 October 2022
11.40 a.m.

Andrea leaned forward and pressed the red button on the recording equipment. 'Interview conducted with Zoe Spears, Saturday, twenty-second of October, 11.40 a.m., Interview Room 2, Beaumaris Police Station. Present are Zoe Spears, Detective Constable Charlie, and myself, Detective Constable Andrea Jones.'

Andrea waited for a few seconds and then looked over at her. 'Zoe, just to remind you that you are still under caution and that this interview is being recorded. Do you understand?'

Zoe looked broken. She nodded vacantly.

'For the purposes of the tape, Zoe Spears has nodded her head to confirm that she understands that she is currently under caution,' Charlie said.

'But I don't understand why I'm here,' Zoe said in a shaky voice.

Andrea shifted her chair forward. 'Zoe, I want to take

you back to Monday night. In your statement, you told us that Becks Maddison came over to see Abby and that she left your home just before midnight. And that you and Gavin went to bed shortly after that?'

'Yes,' Zoe replied with a furrowed brow. 'That's what happened.'

'And even though Gavin has told us that he went down to the summer house to talk to Abby,' Andrea continued, '... you had no idea that she was there or that they'd spoken. Is that correct?'

Zoe looked lost. 'Yes.'

Charlie pulled over a folder and took out a photograph. 'For the purposes of the tape, I'm showing Zoe Item References 346H, 421H and 484H. The first item is a photograph of a partial footprint in Abby's blood that we found in your summer house.' Charlie took the photograph and turned it around. 'Could you take a look at the photograph for us, Zoe?'

Zoe peered at the image and then looked upset.

'Would it surprise you that our forensic team have told us that this footprint is a size seven or eight?' Charlie said.

'I don't understand why you're telling me that,' Zoe protested. 'I wasn't there.'

Charlie took another photograph and turned it for Zoe to look at. 'Can you tell me what you can see in this photograph please?'

Zoe peered over cautiously. 'It's a footprint in mud.'

'This footprint was found on the shore at Llyn Llwydiarth,' Charlie said. 'And that footprint is a size seven.'

There were a few seconds of silence.

'Can you tell us what size your feet are, Zoe?' Charlie asked very calmly.

'I've already told you. I'm a size seven,' she replied. 'But I haven't been to Llyn Llwydiarth since I was a child.'

Charlie took a third photograph which he again turned for her to look at.

'Would it surprise you to know that close to this footprint, we also found this necklace?' Charlie asked. 'A necklace that you have already confirmed belonged to you.'

'But I told you I lost it last week.' Zoe shook her head in disbelief. 'Why do you think I'm lying to you?'

Silence.

'Come on, Zoe,' Andrea said as she leaned over the table. 'Don't you think it's an amazing coincidence that size seven footprints with an almost identical tread pattern were found in the summer house and beside the lake where we believe Abby is, along with your necklace? How do you explain that?'

'I can't, can I?' she said sounding desperate. 'I just know I wasn't there.'

'Our forensic team is currently looking at your car and its GPS tracker,' Andrea said. 'And they're also looking at your phone which also has GPS. If you drove out to Llyn Llwydiarth on Monday, we're going to find that out.'

'I didn't. I don't know why you're saying all this!' Zoe started to sob. 'I wouldn't hurt Abby. She's my niece. I love her.'

Silence.

Andrea looked directly at her. She was finding it hard to work out if Zoe really was involved in her niece's disappearance and probable murder.

'Zoe,' Andrea said in a gentle voice. 'This is your chance to tell us what really happened on Monday night. Maybe you noticed that Gavin had gone outside. So, you went out to the garden to see where he was and noticed that the lights in the summer house were on. You went in there. Maybe Gavin and Abby had had a row and it had got out of hand. Or maybe you and Abby got into a terrible row.'

Zoe was shaking her head. 'No,' she whispered.

'You just need to tell us the truth about what happened on Monday,' Andrea said.

Wiping a tear from her face, Zoe looked at her with puffy, watery eyes. 'I don't know what to tell you. I've told you what happened but you don't believe me.'

There was a knock at the door. It opened and Ben poked his head in and looked at Andrea.

'Can I have a quick word?' he said with a serious expression.

'Of course,' Andrea replied getting up from the table. 'For the purposes of the tape, DC Jones is leaving the interview room.'

She went over to the door and out into the corridor.

'What's up?' she asked Ben.

'Digital Forensics have accessed Abby White's phone,' Ben explained and then looked directly at her. 'In the past month, Abby made or received fifteen phone calls from HMP Tonsgrove.'

'What?' Andrea said, trying to process what Ben was telling her. 'I don't understand.'

'I've done a full PNC and HOLMES check on Abby White,' Ben explained. 'Her mother is Kayleigh Doyle.'

What the...?

Andrea narrowed her eyes. 'Are you joking?'

'I know.' Ben shook his head. 'I'm wondering if there's some kind of link between Sheila Jones' murder and Abby White being attacked and disappearing.'

'The two events happened within hours of each other,' Andrea said, thinking out loud. 'I can't believe it's a total coincidence, can you?'

'It seems highly unlikely that the two aren't connected,' Ben admitted. 'We just need to work out how.'

Andrea nodded and then gestured back to the interview room. 'I'll go and see what Zoe has to say.'

Opening the door, Andrea went back in.

'For the purposes of the tape, DC Jones is re-entering the room,' Charlie said.

Andrea sat down and gave Zoe a quizzical look. 'Why didn't you tell us that your sister and Abby's mother is Kayleigh Doyle?'

'I dunno.' Zoe visibly swallowed as she took a deep breath. 'We don't have anything to do with Kayleigh or any of my family. Abby's been with us since she was twelve.'

Andrea gave her a suspicious look. 'Abby has made or received fifteen phone calls from HMP Tonsgrove in the past month.'

'What? That's not possible.' Zoe looked confused and then shook her head. 'Abby hasn't spoken to Kayleigh in years.'

'Well, clearly she has, Zoe,' Andrea said sharply. 'How could you think this wasn't relevant to what's happened to Abby?'

'I don't know. I'm sorry,' Zoe mumbled. 'Kayleigh isn't part of our lives.'

'But Kayleigh is involved with the criminal part of your family in Birmingham,' Charlie pointed out. 'And if someone wanted to get to her, they could have targeted Abby.'

Andrea looked at Zoe. Was she still their prime suspect? There was no explanation of why her necklace was at the lake. But finding out that Kayleigh Doyle was Abby's mother had certainly muddied the waters a little.

CHAPTER 51

Clicking open her pen, Laura knew that she needed to contact Gareth and let him know that there were growing suspicions about an undercover officer in the prison. She just needed to find the right opportunity to use her concealed phone. Laura looked at the page of the exercise book in front of her and the simple sentences that Barry McDonald had written up on the wall which she had copied down. Niamh Mullan was sitting towards the back of the literacy class but Laura could feel her stare. She got the feeling that despite Dalby vouching for her, Mullan still had it in for her.

Laura was feeling frustrated. Although she had managed to obtain some useful intel regarding Sheila Jones' murder, the rumours of an undercover police officer had made her job a hundred times more difficult. Even a casual question about Sheila might be perceived as a sign of being a copper – and that, as she'd already found out, was incredibly dangerous.

239

'This is what we call a "simple sentence",' Barry said as he pointed to the board. 'It's made up from one clause, with two nouns and a verb.' Barry looked out at the class. 'The dog runs in the street. The boy eats some food... Now who can tell me what an adjective is?'

Silence.

Laura looked around. She certainly wasn't going to put her hand up and attract any attention.

'Okay,' Barry said patiently. 'Can anyone give me an example of an adjective?'

Mullan put up her hand.

'Okay, thank you, Niamh,' Barry said encouragingly.

'Bitch,' Mullan said. Laura was pretty sure the comment was aimed at her but she wasn't about to turn around.

Barry frowned. 'Actually that's another noun. Have another go.'

'Rat?' Mullan suggested.

God, give me strength, Laura thought to herself.

'Rat is still a noun,' Barry explained. 'So, remember an adjective is a describing word, Niamh. Think of a word to describing word for rat.'

'Filthy rat?' Mullan said.

'Good,' Barry said encouragingly. Then he looked over. 'Laura, could you go to the shelf next to you and hand out the red literacy text books, please?'

'Of course,' Laura said politely as she stood up. She could see Mullan looking her way but she wasn't going to give her the satisfaction of looking over.

Going to the shelves that were attached to the wall, Laura glanced out of the window.

On the far side of the exercise yard, there was an external staircase coming down from the first floor.

Underneath the staircase, and therefore tucked away

from the view of most of the prison, there were two figures having a very animated conversation.

Laura squinted and instantly recognised them both.

Kayleigh Doyle and Governor Sanam Parveen.

What the hell are they doing? she wondered.

To say it looked suspicious would be an understatement.

As Laura continued to watch, she could see they were arguing aggressively. It definitely didn't look like the kind of argument a prison governor would have with a prisoner.

'Shall I give you a hand with those, rat?' whispered a voice in her ear.

Laura jumped out of her skin as she turned to see Mullan standing behind her.

'I'm fine thanks,' Laura said calmly, hoping that Mullan wouldn't look out of the window and see what she'd been looking at.

'It's all right,' Mullan said loudly as she barged Laura with her shoulder. 'I've got these ones.'

Mullan knocked Laura again and this time put her leg out. Laura tumbled over Mullan's leg and crashed to the floor.

'Jesus,' Laura groaned.

'Oh God, are you all right?' Mullan asked in a highly sarcastic voice.

'It's okay, Niamh,' Barry said, sounding flustered. 'Go and sit down.'

As Laura tried to get to her feet, she noticed that the false heel to her trainer had been knocked open.

And now the tiny burner phone was lying on the floor.

'What's that?' Barry asked as he looked down at it.

Laura got to her feet and reached down to pick up the phone.

Barry looked at her with a disappointed expression. 'I'm going to have to report this, Laura. And you're going to have to talk to the governor.'

'Oh dear,' Niamh laughed. 'You are in deep shit now, rat.'

CHAPTER 52

HMP Tonsgrove, Anglesey
Saturday, 22 October 2022
1.45 p.m.

The door to the meeting room opened and the male prison officer, Rice, brought Kayleigh Doyle into the room. It had been an hour since Andrea had informed Gareth about what she and Charlie had discovered.

Gareth got up from his seat. 'Come and sit down, Kayleigh.'

Rice gestured to the door. 'I'll be back in a bit.'

Kayleigh didn't say anything as Rice left the room. Her body language and face showed that she was angry.

Gareth pointed to the recording equipment. 'Just so that you're aware, even though this is an informal interview, we will be recording it in case anything you say needs to be used as evidence in court. Do you understand that, Kayleigh?'

'Yeah,' she replied with a sneer as though it was a stupid question.

'Okay,' Gareth said as he leaned over and pressed the

red record button. There was a long electronic beep. 'Interview conducted with Kayleigh Doyle. HMP Tonsgrove. Saturday, twenty-second of October. Present are Kayleigh Doyle, Detective Constable Ben Corden, and myself, Detective Inspector Gareth Williams.'

Gareth then shifted in his chair and looked across the table. 'We've been looking at your records, Kayleigh. You have a daughter, Abby, is that correct?'

Kayleigh frowned suspiciously. 'Yeah, so what?' she replied uneasily.

'Are you aware that Abby is currently missing and that we suspect that she has been seriously attacked?' Gareth asked.

'No,' Kayleigh said, looking perturbed. 'Why hasn't anyone told me about this?'

'We've been dealing with your sister Zoe,' Ben explained.

'Stupid bitch,' Kayleigh said getting up from her chair in panic. 'I need to talk to the governor about this and find out why no one's told me.'

'Sit down please, Kayleigh,' Gareth said firmly. 'Zoe told us that you're not in contact with Abby, is that correct?'

'Yeah.' Kayleigh shrugged angrily as she headed for the door. 'So what? She's still my daughter. I have a right to find out what's going on.'

'The door is locked, Kayleigh,' Gareth said. 'I need you to come and sit down. This will only take a few minutes and then you can go.'

Kayleigh glared at him and then muttered, 'For fuck's sake,' as she came back and sat down with a groan.

Silence.

'Can you tell us when you last spoke to Abby?' Ben asked.

They were essentially setting a trap for Kayleigh as

they knew she and Abby had been talking regularly on the phone in the past month.

'I dunno,' Kayleigh sighed angrily. 'Five, six years ago. Something like that.'

Gareth frowned and gave Ben a quizzical look. Then he reached over to the folder. 'For the purposes of the tape, I am going to show Kayleigh Item Reference 478K.' Gareth turned the document for Kayleigh to look at. 'These are the phone records for Abby's mobile phone. And you see these phone calls highlighted in green here?' Gareth said, pointing to the document. 'These are all phone calls made between you and Abby in the past month. Fifteen calls, to be precise. Can you tell us why you've just lied to us about that?'

Kayleigh sat back with a defiant look. 'No comment.'

'Come on, Kayleigh,' Gareth said in frustration. 'We think that something very serious has happened to your daughter. We need to know what you were talking about in the last few weeks and if that's relevant to what's happened to her.'

'No comment,' Kayleigh said as she inspected her nails.

Gareth looked at her in disbelief. 'Don't you want to find out what's happened to her?'

Kayleigh stared back directly at him in defiance. 'No comment.'

'We'd like to ask you about your relationship with Sheila Jones,' Gareth said. 'We understand that you and Sheila were in a romantic relationship in this prison. Is there anything you'd like to tell us about that?'

'No comment.'

Gareth let out an audible sigh and looked at Ben. They were getting nowhere.

CHAPTER 53

Beaumaris Police Station
Saturday, 22 October 2022
3.45 p.m.

It was two hours later and Gareth and Ben were in the meeting room on the ground floor of Beaumaris nick. DS Brooks and DI Carmichael from the NCA had requested a meeting as they had something to show them.

'What have we got from DI Hart?' Brooks asked looking over at them as they got straight down to business.

'We do have a couple of significant developments in the murder investigation inside the prison,' Gareth explained.

'Anything on Sanam Parveen?' Carmichael enquired.

'DI Hart is certain that Parveen is having a relationship with a prison officer, David Rice,' Ben stated.

'Right. Makes sense. We think that's Parveen's MO,' Brooks said nodding. 'She formed a relationship with the Chief Prison Officer at her last prison. We believe she manipulated him to keep control of the sale of drugs. I assume she's doing the same with Rice.'

Carmichael took out a small laptop, turned it on and

then looked over at them. 'We followed Parveen last night when she left Tonsgrove. She drove to this service station on the M6.' Carmichael clicked an MPEG file and CCTV footage appeared on the laptop screen. 'And she met her uncle, Sajit Parveen. We've checked immigration records and Sajit Parveen flew in from Lahore two days ago.' Carmichael pointed to a black Range Rover. 'They then drove in his car down the M6 to Birmingham.'

Gareth's ears pricked up with the mention of Birmingham.

'They then met this man,' Carmichael said as he showed them more CCTV, '...in a retail park in Solihull. We've checked the registration of the man's car and it's registered to a Michael Doyle.'

Gareth and Ben exchanged a look.

Brooks picked up on it. 'You know who Michael Doyle is?'

'Yes.' Gareth nodded. 'His niece, Kayleigh Doyle, is serving a sentence in Tonsgrove for possession and intent to supply. We believe that Kayleigh and several other women, who are connected to the Doyle family, are in a turf war with women affiliated with the Croxteth Boyz in Liverpool. Sheila Jones was one of them, so we assume that her murder is connected somehow to that turf war.'

Brooks gave Carmichael a look.

'We hadn't made that connection yet,' Carmichael admitted. 'But that does seem to be the missing piece in our jigsaw.'

'If Parveen is working with the Doyle family,' Gareth said, thinking out loud, '...then maybe she sanctioned or even organised Sheila Jones' murder.'

'That's definitely a possibility,' Brooks agreed.

Ben looked at them. 'DI Hart had intel that Kayleigh Doyle and Sheila Jones were secretly in a relationship.'

Brooks raised an eyebrow. 'What?'

Gareth nodded. 'We think that one of the other women in that gang, possibly Niamh Mullan, found out about the relationship and killed Sheila.'

'Sounds like there were several motives for Sheila's murder,' Carmichael said. 'When are you due to meet with DI Hart again?'

'Later today,' Gareth replied. 'We've also had another significant development. I assume you've seen that a teenage girl has gone missing? Abby White?'

'Of course,' Brooks replied.

'We actually believe that Abby was attacked and murdered at her home and that her body is now somewhere in a lake about six miles from here,' Gareth explained.

'Oh right, that's horrible,' Carmichael said.

Gareth looked at them both. '*And* Abby White is Kayleigh Doyle's daughter,' Gareth said.

Brooks' eyes widened. 'What?'

'Abby and Kayleigh have been in contact in recent weeks,' Ben said. 'We think that what happened to Abby might even be connected to what was going on inside Tonsgrove.'

Brooks shook his head. 'Poor girl.'

CHAPTER 54

Laura was now sitting in Governor Parveen's office on the ground floor of HMP Tonsgrove. It felt like she was a child again and had been summoned to the headmaster's office at school. Obviously the ramifications of what had happened and her hidden identity were far more serious.

Parveen's office was smaller than Laura had imagined it would be. There was a desk with a computer on the far side and an oval table with six chairs in the middle of the room which she now sat at. Parveen was over at the computer looking at something on her screen.

Gazing around the room, there were photos of Parveen being given various awards or taking part in several fun raising events for charity. One of the photos showed her abseiling down a clock tower with a bright red helmet on. Next to that, a newspaper clipping of a photo of Parveen, still in a her climbing gear, holding a large cheque. Then Laura saw the name of the paper: *Grimsby Evening Telegraph*.

It sparked something in her memory as Laura now remembered where she had encountered Parveen before. Laura had been working for the MMP on a two-year operation in 2015 and 2016. Eight members of a Manchester-based drugs gang had been involved in county lines drug-dealing, trying to flood Grimsby with heroin and crack cocaine. Parveen, who had been working at HMP Lindholme in Doncaster, had been called as a witness for the prosecution of one of the defendants who had been on remand there. Laura was also at Hull Crown Court that day, giving evidence of the surveillance operation that MMP had been running in conjunction with the Greater Manchester Anti-Gang Unit.

Shit, Laura thought as her stomach tightened. *What if she recognises me?*

Getting up from her office chair, Parveen came over and sat opposite Laura and gave her a quizzical look.

Then Parveen put the small burner phone and Laura's trainer that had the secret compartment hollowed out in the heel down on the table and looked at her suspiciously.

'You understand how serious this is, Laura?' Parveen asked.

Laura nodded. 'Yes.'

'Do you?' Parveen said in a doubtful tone.

Silence.

'You're only serving a two-year sentence,' Parveen said narrowing her eyes. 'You'll be out of here in a year with good behaviour. So, why take the risk?'

Laura shrugged. 'I don't know.'

'Technically, this is in violation of Section 40D of the Prison Act and could see you with two years added to your sentence.'

'I know,' Laura said quietly. 'I'm sorry.'

Parveen looked at her. 'I'm sure I've met you before.'

Laura pulled a face. 'It doesn't seem likely,' Laura replied.

'Maybe it'll come to me,' Parveen said with a frown.

I bloody hope it doesn't, Laura thought to herself.

Parveen gestured over at her computer. 'I've seen your file. You're not a career criminal. Your husband abused you to the point where you stabbed him. What's the desperate need for a mobile phone?'

'I just wanted to be able to make phone calls whenever I wanted,' Laura said, but realised this didn't really explain why she had taken such a risk.

'Really?' Parveen sighed and then pulled a face. 'This just doesn't add up, Laura.' She pointed to the phone and trainer. 'Where did you get these from?'

Laura took a breath. She knew that Parveen sensed that something wasn't right.

'A friend helped me,' Laura explained.

Parveen frowned. 'The only people I see with this sort of thing are in drug gangs... Are you part of a drug gang, Laura?'

'No,' Laura replied, now feeling anxious that Parveen was becoming increasingly suspicious.

'But a friend helped you get a burner phone and create a secret compartment in the heel of your trainer?' Parveen said.

'Yes,' Laura said innocently.

'Come on, Laura,' Parveen snorted. 'What's really going on?'

Laura could feel the tension as her pulse quickened.

'I don't understand what you mean?' she said quietly.

Parveen then fixed her with a stare. 'There are rumours that there's an undercover copper in Tonsgrove. I guess you've heard them?'

251

Where the hell is she going with this? Laura wondered nervously.

'Yes, I've heard them,' Laura replied. 'Everyone has.'

'The thing is, if there was a police officer in here under-cover,' Parveen said, her eyes still locked on her, 'I'd know about it, wouldn't I?'

Laura shrugged. 'I suppose so.'

'Unless, of course, there was some reason for me not to know,' Parveen said. 'If you get what I'm saying?'

Laura did her best to look utterly confused. 'Not really.'

There were a few seconds of silence.

'It's just that a police officer who was undercover in a prison might well have a burner phone hidden away in a compartment in her trainer,' Parveen said, searching Laura's face for a reaction.

Oh shit, this is not good.

Laura frowned. 'You think I'm a copper?' she snorted as though it was completely ridiculous.

Parveen raised an eyebrow. 'I'm not sure… There is definitely something about you that doesn't fit.'

'Jesus, I've been called a lot of things in my life,' Laura said shaking her head. 'But never an undercover copper.'

'We'll see.' Parveen gave her a look. 'Until then, I'm putting you in the segregation unit for seventy-two hours.'

Laura nodded.

'And I do expect you to continue going to the education unit in that time,' Parveen said sternly.

CHAPTER 55

Beaumaris Police Station
Saturday, 22 October 2022
4.07 p.m.

Gareth swiped his canteen card across the machine to pay for his coffee but he was noticeably lost in thought. As he walked across the canteen, he was vaguely aware of an officer heading his way. He was in his thirties, bearded, with glasses.

'DI Williams?' he said.

Then Gareth remembered that the bearded man was a digital forensics officer who had helped him when they were searching for Callum Newell earlier in the year.

'Hi,' Gareth said stopping close to the doors. 'It's...'

'DC Thomas,' the man explained. 'We've run a check on Zoe Spears' mobile phone. According to her GPS tracker, her mobile phone remained at her home for the whole of Monday evening and night.'

Gareth nodded. Then he said, thinking out loud, 'I guess if she was smart, she might guess that we could track her phone. And if she did drive out to Llyn Llwydiarth, she'd leave it behind.'

'True,' DC Thomas agreed. 'But we have also looked at the GPS tracker in Zoe Spears' car. It shows that the car stayed parked at their home on Monday evening and night.'

'Right, okay. Thanks for letting me know,' Gareth said as he began to process the new information.

'No problem.'

Heading out of the doors, Gareth's mind now worked overtime. The discovery of the necklace, the size seven footprints at the summer house and at the lake, had all pointed towards Zoe Spears being involved. The lack of a GPS signal on her phone and from her car didn't rule her out entirely but it made her less likely as a suspect. If she and Gavin had killed Abby, they didn't use either of their cars to transport her body out to Llyn Llwydiarth. And would they risk getting someone else involved so that they could use another vehicle? That seemed like a huge risk.

As he headed along the corridor, Gareth started to wonder if Abby's disappearance and possible murder was instead a direct result of the drug turf war that was going on at HMP Tonsgrove. Maybe Gavin and Zoe had nothing to do with it and Abby was attacked, killed and dumped because her mother was part of the Doyle family.

Gareth came through the double doors of the CID office. The air was thick with the smells of coffee and food. The whole team was working flat out and no one was stopping for breaks to eat.

Ben approached. 'Boss, good news and bad news.'

Gareth pointed to his office. 'You know what. I might just go and lock myself in there and drink my coffee in peace,' he said with a dry smile.

'Really?' Ben said.

254

'No.' Gareth pulled a face. 'Okay. Bad news first?'

'I spoke to Digital Forensics.'

'Yeah, so did I,' Gareth said trying not to sound weary. 'They told me about Zoey Spears' phone and car GPS.'

'What do you think?' Ben asked.

Gareth frowned. 'Doesn't explain why Zoe's necklace was found at Llyn Llwydiarth. In fact, the only explanation seems to be that she was there.'

'Unless Abby had the necklace for some reason,' Ben suggested. 'If she'd taken it from Zoe to wear, then it might have come off by the lake.'

'That is possible,' Gareth conceded. 'Good news?'

'I don't know if it's technically *good news*,' Ben said. 'But ANPR have picked up that white Cherokee Jeep registered to Shane Deakins crossing the Menai Bridge at 9 p.m. on Monday night.' Ben went over to the map. 'The Jeep was then spotted on ANPR here on the A5025 at 9.15 p.m.'

Gareth frowned. 'Which is the road going north to Pen-y-garnedd, where the Spears' home is.'

'Exactly,' Ben said.

'Do we have a time when the car went back over the Menai Bridge to the mainland?' Gareth asked, wondering how significant this was.

'Yes.' Ben gave him a meaningful look. 'Deakins didn't cross back over the bridge until 1.20 a.m. on Tuesday morning.'

Gareth processed this for a moment. 'Well, he wasn't visiting Sheila Jones because visiting hours stop at 4 p.m. So, what the hell was he doing for more than four hours?'

'Gets better,' Ben said as he went over to his desk. 'I've looked through some of the house to house statements that were taken in Pen-y-garnedd. We asked neighbours if they'd seen anything or anyone suspicious on Monday night.' Ben opened a folder. 'Mr and Mrs Arthur Roberts who live at number 8 reported to one of the uniformed officers that they hadn't seen anything suspicious on Monday night. *But* they had seen a large white car parked up in the road a few times in the past week at night.'

'Deakins might have been watching Abby's home to get an idea of the family's routine during the evening,' Gareth suggested.

'When he saw Becks Maddison leaving just before midnight on Monday, he decided to make his move,' Ben suggested.

'Have we got any ANPR or CCTV on the road from Pen-y-garnedd up to Llyn Llwydiarth?'

'No, boss,' Ben replied. 'Pretty remote up there.'

Gareth thought for a few seconds then he looked at Ben. 'Deakins was cleaning his car when we arrived. Maybe that's not a coincidence.'

'Forensics also took some tyre tracks from the car park at Llyn Llwydiarth,' Ben said. 'If we can match any of those to Deakins' car...'

Gareth nodded. Even though he hadn't ruled out either Zoe or Gavin Spears' involvement, he was starting to think that both murders were more likely to be linked to the drug war inside HMP Tonsgrove.

CHAPTER 56

Rhosllanerchrugog, Wrexham
Saturday, 22 October 2022
5.54 p.m.

Gareth and Ben had driven the seventy miles from Beaumaris to Rhos in Wrexham in deep discussion about both investigations. With the exception of the necklace, there was no physical or forensic evidence to link either Gavin or Zoe Spears to either the summer house or Llyn Llwydiarth. Deakins on the other hand was a career criminal and part of a vicious, violent Merseyside drug gang. It was no coincidence that Kayleigh and Abby had started to communicate in recent weeks. Maybe Kayleigh knew that her daughter was in great danger and had made contact to warn her to be careful.

They parked their car outside Deakins' home and got out. The temperature dropped as the clouds became hooded in greys and blacks. The faintest hint of drizzle misted Gareth's face. The deep cawing of crows perched high in the trees to their left broke the light chatter of birdsong.

y went up the drive and Ben stopped to look at the Cherokee Jeep's wheels and tyres.

'They're clean as a whistle,' Ben remarked as he peered at them.

'Admiring my car again?' said a voice.

It was Deakins.

He was dressed in a black Adidas tracksuit and white trainers.

Gareth looked at Deakins, thinking that he couldn't look more like an archetypal member of a gang if he tried. He supposed that Deakins was one of those men who thought they were untouchable.

'Just a couple of routine questions, Shane,' Gareth explained with a half-smile. 'If you've got a few minutes. Won't take long.'

'I'm a very busy man,' Deakins said with a smirk.

'We can take you down to the station, if you like,' Ben said calmly.

Deakins fixed Ben with a stare for a few seconds, trying to intimidate him. 'I don't think so,' he snorted. 'Yeah, well I'll talk to you here. I'm not having coppers in my house, contaminating the place and leaving a stench. If you know what I mean?'

Gareth wasn't going to rise to Deakins. He'd dealt with blokes like him before.

'Can you tell us where you were on Monday night, Shane?' Gareth asked casually.

Deakins frowned. 'Erm, I'm pretty sure I was here all night.'

Ben raised an eyebrow. 'That's strange. Because we've got CCTV footage of you driving over the Menai Bridge at 9 p.m. on Monday night.'

Deakins glared at him and then smirked. 'Have you? I guess I must have been visiting my uncle in Rhosneigr then.'

258

Gareth narrowed his eyes. 'You've got an uncle in Rhos-neigr?' he asked in a dubious tone.

'Are you calling me a liar?' Deakins grinned. 'I'm offended. Me Uncle Neville lives in Rhosneigr. He's got a lovely bungalow that looks over the beach there.'

'We're going to need his address,' Gareth said.

Deakins shook his head. 'No chance. He's eighty-three. I'm not having you lot harassing him.'

Gareth gave him a forced smile. 'That's all right. We'll find him.'

'We've got CCTV of you driving up the A5025 at 9.15 p.m.,' Ben said with a quizzical expression. 'That's completely the wrong direction for Rhosneigr.'

'I got lost.' Deakins smirked. 'I don't spend a lot of time on Anglesey.'

'Ever been to a little place called Pen-y-garnedd?' Gareth said.

'Pen-y what?' Deakins snorted.

Gareth looked at him. 'It's a small village just up from the Menai Bridge.'

'Why would I go there?'

'Does the name Abby White mean anything to you?' Gareth asked.

Deakins didn't react to the sound of her name. 'No. Never heard of her,' he replied.

'What about Llyn Llwydiarth?' Ben enquired. 'It's a lake up in the Pentraeth Forest.'

Deakins shook his head slowly. 'No idea what you're talking about. And whatever you think I did, you're way off.'

Gareth went to the Cherokee Jeep and pointed to the tyres. 'Did you know that every tyre has a distinct pattern of wear on its tread?'

'Fascinating,' Deakins said in a withering tone.

'And we've got some very clear tyre prints from several locations on Anglesey,' Gareth continued. 'Our forensic team will be here any minute now to take a look at your tyres to see if we can make a match.'

'I assume you've got a warrant to do that?' Deakins asked.

Gareth took the warrant from his pocket and unfolded it. 'Want to have a read?'

'No.' Deakins shrugged, trying to look unflustered. 'You can do what you want. I've told you where I was and where I went, so you won't find anything.'

'We'll see,' Ben muttered.

Deakins turned to look at Ben again. After a couple of seconds, Deakins gestured to his house. 'Like I said, I'm a very busy man.'

Deakins turned to leave.

A moment later, the SOCO van drew up outside the house.

Gareth looked at Ben. 'Let's pray that his tyres match our prints so we can nick that bastard.'

CHAPTER 57

Andrea and Charlie were now back at Llyn Llwydiarth and the ongoing search for Abby White's body in the lake. Above them the sky was a metallic grey. The jagged shoreline was again covered in a thin veil of mist. The thick undergrowth and trees swept up and away to the darkness of Pentraeth Forest. Having been only planted in the fifties, the forest was known for its red squirrels.

As they made their way through wild grasses from the car park and headed for the lake, they could hear the rhythmic rumble of the North Wales USMU boat's diesel engine. Llyn Llwydiarth came into view. Blazing halogen lights had been erected and now shone over the lake's surface to try and compensate for the lack of daylight.

The sky blackened overhead and Andrea felt the first few specks of rain on her nose and cheeks. As she gazed out towards the boat and the divers, she could see the soft rain swirling in the vanilla halogen beams. There were three divers bobbing around on the water's surface using guide ropes that were attached to the black RIB. Inside the boat, two other members of the USMU were looking at a tiny sonar screen and directing them.

Andrea looked at Charlie. 'I'm starting to wonder if she's even in there.'

Charlie pulled a face. 'Where else would she be?'

'Maybe whoever took her buried her somewhere near the lake rather than putting her body in there,' Andrea said, thinking out loud.

'But the SOCOs checked the whole shoreline,' Charlie said, gesturing out to the lake.

Before they could continue, there was a shout and wave from one of the divers in the water. The sound of the boat's engine grew louder as it moved forward through to the water towards him.

The diver handed over something that he'd found in the lake to be taken on board the boat.

'Every time I hear a shout or any activity, I think they've found her,' Andrea said quietly.

'Me too,' Charlie admitted.

'If Abby really is dead, then of course I want us to find her so she can be laid to rest properly,' Andrea said. 'But all the time we don't find her body, there is still the remotest chance that she's still alive.'

Charlie raised an eyebrow. 'You really think she could be alive?' he asked dubiously.

'My head says no,' Andrea said. 'But my heart is holding on to the last shred of hope.'

Now that the diver had clambered aboard, the boat turned towards the shoreline and chugged slowly to where they were standing. Once it was in the shallowest part of the water, a diver jumped out and waded towards them.

Whatever he had found was now in a clear plastic evidence bag.

'What is it?' Andrea asked as he got closer.

'Shoes,' the diver who had ginger hair and a beard replied. 'Well, trainers. Laces must have got tangled because they were lying together on the lake bed.'

Andrea looked at the navy coloured Converse All Stars. They were Abby's shoes. Then something occurred to her – something that didn't add up.

'This doesn't make any sense,' Andrea said as she looked at the bag. 'If Abby was wearing those laced up, they'd come over the ankle. How would they have fallen off her feet in the water?'

Charlie frowned. 'They wouldn't.'

Andrea looked over at the diver. 'I'm guessing you've done your fair share of retrieving bodies from the water?'

The diver gave her a dark look. 'Yeah, you could say that.'

'I assume that they're normally wearing the clothes that they go into the water in?' Andrea said.

'Usually,' the diver agreed. 'Like you say, if she had been wearing some kind of slip-on shoe, we might have expected those to float off.' He then pointed to the Converse. 'But not those.'

'What about the hoodie you found,' Charlie asked.

The diver shook his head. 'It would be unusual for something like that to come off a body, I agree.'

Andrea narrowed her eyes as she looked at them both. 'It's almost like someone's thrown the jumper and shoes into the lake to make it look as if Abby is in there.'

Charlie gave her a dark look. 'Question is, if she's not in the lake, where the hell is she?'

CHAPTER 58

HMP Tonsgrove, Anglesey
Sunday, 23 October 2023
10.13 a.m.

Laura had been escorted over to the education block from the segregation unit for her literacy lesson with Barry McDonald. She turned to see that Kayleigh Doyle was sitting at the back a few desks along from Niamh Mullan.

'Simile,' Barry said in his usual cheerful tone. 'Anyone tell me what a simile is?'

'It's like when you compare something,' said a girl with a South Wales accent.

'Yes, that's great,' Barry said with a nod. 'It's a comparison where you use the words 'as' or 'like'. Can anyone give me an example of a simile?'

Silence.

Out of the corner of her eye, Laura watched Kayleigh. Normally she'd be joking or messing around with the others that she sat with. However, she was unusually quiet and still, clearly preoccupied by something.

'As cold as ice?' the girl from South Wales suggested.

'Brilliant!' Barry said with an excited pump of his fist. Then his eyes were drawn to something through the window.

Laura looked outside and saw that a van with *D&L Deliveries* printed on the side had pulled up at the back of the education block.

'Ah,' Barry said as he looked at the class. 'I'm going to need two strong volunteers to help me. We've got our delivery of books and stationery for the month.'

Kayleigh shot her hand up immediately. 'I'll help.'

Laura followed. 'Yeah, I don't mind helping out.'

As Laura got up she saw Kayleigh glare at her. She didn't care.

They followed Barry out of the classroom and headed along the corridor towards a set of a glass double doors.

They stopped for a moment by a small office where Rice and two other prison officers were drinking tea and laughing.

'Okay if these two give me a hand with the delivery?' Barry asked obsequiously.

'I'm certainly not helping you lug boxes around, Barry, so go for it,' Rice snorted to the amusement of the others.

Laura could sense that Kayleigh was up to something. Instead of her usual cocky self, she was preoccupied and anxious. She wondered if the delivery van had anything to do with it.

'Come on, keep up,' Barry said in a light tone as he got to the double doors, unlocked them with a big bunch of keys and pushed them wide open so that they stayed that way.

A huge man with black hair and a beard had opened the shutter to the back of the van. Laura noticed a shamrock tattoo on his right hand.

Kayleigh gave Laura yet another filthy look as they were passed heavy cardboard boxes.

'If you follow me,' Barry said, 'I'll open the stationery cupboard.'

Jesus this is heavy, Laura thought.

They followed Barry away from the van, back through open doors and into a small room on the right. Its walls were lined floor to ceiling with shelves with assorted books, paper, files and general stationery.

'Just pop them down over there,' Barry said, pointing to the far corner.

Laura placed the box down as Kayleigh barged past her and hissed, 'Bitch.'

They made three more journeys to and from the van with the boxes.

Laura watched as the dark bearded man pulled down the shutter.

'Right, that's your lot,' he said with a strong Brummie accent.

What the hell is going on? Laura thought as her pulse quickened. There was no doubt in her mind now that the driver was there to help Kayleigh escape.

As they walked back towards the doors, Laura spotted something out of the corner of her eye.

The driver ran past her and grabbed Barry in a neck lock while putting a strip of black gaffer tape over his mouth. The driver and Kayleigh then dragged Barry through the double doors, flung him into the stationery cupboard and then closed and locked the door.

Shit!

Laura held her breath as they both turned to look at her.

'What about her?' the driver asked.

'Fuck her,' Kayleigh sneered. 'She can't do anything.'

The driver ran over to the shutter at the back of the van, pulled it up and helped Kayleigh as she darted inside.

What the hell do I do now?

He then closed the shutter and secured a padlock on it.

Giving Laura a sarcastic grin, the driver jogged around the van, got inside and started the engine.

Laura took a few steps towards the van, looking intently at the back. There was a small platform where the shutter met the body of the van. Above that there was a handrail.

Fuck it. Just do it, Laura thought to herself.

As the van began to move forward slowly, Laura sprinted towards the back.

Jumping onto the raised platform, she grabbed the handrail and pulled herself up. Her daily swimming meant that her arms and shoulders were strong.

Getting her foot up onto the top of the handrail, she pushed herself up and grabbed the edge of the roof of the van where there was a metal lip.

She pulled herself up with everything she had as her arms began to shake with the effort.

Throwing her right leg over, she crawled onto the roof of the van.

Bloody hell!

However, without her phone, Laura had no way of alerting anyone to what was going on.

The van pulled away at speed.

CHAPTER 59

Andrea and Charlie were back in Pen-y-garnedd. Walking up the neat garden path that led to a bungalow located on the street behind the Spears' home, Andrea noticed that the garden was immaculate. The owners, Mr and Mrs Pugh, clearly spent a lot of time and effort maintaining it. There were two beautiful hanging baskets either side of the front door. Andrea hoped that one day she would have the time and inclination to spend her time like that. It felt like such a long time away. But then again, she couldn't believe that she was already thirty-two years old. She remembered waking on the morning of her thirtieth birthday with utter bewilderment that she was thirty. One of her colleagues had reminded her that once she was thirty, she could never be classed as a young person ever again.

Charlie rang the doorbell and took a step back.

'You ever think you'll have a garden like this?' Andrea said, gesturing to the square-cut borders.

Charlie shrugged. 'I like gardening already,' he admitted. Then he frowned. 'Does that make me a bit of a geek?'

'Yes,' Andrea laughed but Charlie's lack of dick-swinging masculinity actually made him more attractive. 'I suppose you like baking too?'

Charlie held up his hands. 'Guilty.'

Andrea shook her head. 'And yet you're actually in your twenties,' she joked.

'I know,' Charlie said with a grin. 'If I had a pipe, then I'd smoke it.'

Andrea chuckled but pulled a straight face as the door opened.

Charlie showed his warrant card. 'DC Heaton and DC Jones, Beaumaris CID.'

An elderly woman in her late seventies in a cardigan and dark slacks opened the door and peered out at them. She seemed pleased to see them.

'Oh yes,' she said nodding. 'That nice young policeman said that you would be calling. Beaumaris, did you say?' she asked as she opened the door and beckoned them inside.

The hallway was dark and old-fashioned. The house smelled of lavender polish and tea.

'That's right,' Andrea replied with a kind smile.

'My brother David lives in Beaumaris,' she said as she closed the front door. 'I don't like it. Too many tourists in the summer for my liking.' Then she pointed to a door. 'Do you want to come in here?'

'Yes, thank you,' Andrea said. 'It's Mrs Pugh, isn't it?'

'Oh gosh, it's Carol, dear,' she said. 'The only person who calls me Mrs Pugh is my local GP and she's about twelve.'

Andrea gave Charlie a look of amusement as they went into a neat, tidy living room.

A man in his late seventies was sitting reading the newspaper. He looked up.

'Ah, hello,' he said removing his reading glasses and going to stand.

'Please don't get up on our account,' Andrea reassured him.

'Would you like some tea?' Carol asked.

'We're fine, thanks,' Charlie said as he and Andrea sat down on a large, patterned sofa.

A small white terrier came scuttling into the room and began to sniff around their feet.

'Angus! Angus!' Carol said, clicking her fingers and pointing. 'Get into your bed.'

The terrier turned, scampered away and settled into a small padded bed.

Andrea raised an eyebrow. 'You've got him well trained.'

Carol gave her a wry smile. 'I've got all the men in this house well-trained, dear.' She looked at her husband. 'That's right isn't it, Frank?'

'Sorry?' Frank asked, shaking his head.

'He's as deaf as a post,' Carol explained.

'We understand that you might have seen a white car in the area in the past few weeks that you thought was suspicious?' Andrea asked. 'Is that right?'

'Well it was Frank who noticed it first,' Carol admitted.

Charlie reached into his pocket, tapped on his phone and showed her a photograph of a white Cherokee Jeep.

Carol squinted as she peered at the image. Then she nodded. 'Yes, that's it.' She looked at them. 'We don't really get cars like that around here. That's why I noticed it.' Then she looked at her husband. 'Frank?' she said loudly as she pointed to the phone.

Charlie leaned forward to show him.

Frank put his reading glasses back on and examined the

image. 'Yes, that's it. Nice-looking car, that. Must have cost a few pennies.'

Andrea knew that it was very significant if Shane Deakins' car had been spotted in the road. He had no reason to be there that they knew of – except for the connection between Kayleigh Doyle and Sheila Jones in HMP Tonsgrove.

'Do you happen to know if you saw that car parked out there on Monday night?' Andrea asked as she gestured in the direction of the road.

Carol thought for a second and then shook her head. 'I don't think we did, did we, Frank?'

Frank shook his head. 'Don't think so.'

'No, sorry,' Carol said apologetically. 'As I told the nice policeman who came here, we saw it four or five times in the last couple of weeks parked out there. But not Monday, I don't think.'

Andrea felt frustrated. An eyewitness to Deakins' car would have been very useful.

'No problem,' Andrea reassured her.

'Terrible thing, what's happened to that girl, Abby,' Carol said with a sombre expression.

Frank looked at Carol. 'Have you told them about Celia and Reg?'

'Oh yes. No, I haven't,' Carol admitted.

They gave her a quizzical look.

'Celia and Reg live over at number 7,' Carol explained. 'Reg is ex-army and… well he's a bit of a busybody, if you know what I mean. But he's got one of those cameras at the back of his house. He's paranoid about people parking in that back lane and blocking him in. Poor Celia is disabled now. Parkinson's. So, he put it in so he can report people who park across the back.'

Andrea gave Charlie a look.

'No, I don't think anyone's asked them about it,' Charlie replied. 'But thank you.'

'I hope you don't think I'm being nosey or anything,' Carol said, pulling a face. 'I just thought if there's anything that might help you find that poor girl.'

Andrea gave her a smile. 'No, it's very useful. Thank you.'

CHAPTER 60

The prison van was now weaving its way through the middle of the prison site and heading for the security checks at the exit. Laura had spread herself flat across the roof but there was nothing for her to cling onto.

As they came around a bend, the hair from her fringe blew into her face and the force of the turn meant that she had to use her right hand and leg to prevent her from rolling over.

Once they were out of the prison, Laura would wait for the van to stop somewhere so she could safely come down off the roof. Then she could raise the alarm about Kayleigh's escape.

However, as the van slowed down at the prison's exit, she knew that the first hurdle was to get out undetected. She knew that vehicles coming in and out of any prison were subjected to rigorous checks. And if they decided to look on the roof, or if anyone had checked the CCTV cameras as they had travelled from the education block to the exit, they would have seen her lying there.

The van came to a stop and she could hear voices talking. She had no idea how Kayleigh was going to hide herself away in the back of the van. The only thing Laura could think of was that some kind of secret, 'invisible' hiding place had been created that wasn't obvious during a routine inspection.

Laura remembered a case that she had worked about ten years earlier. She and another officer had pulled over a Renault van that they had followed from Liverpool docks. They believed that the van was being driven by members of a Manchester OCG and that there were drugs inside. When the van was searched, they found that a false panel had been created behind the driver and passenger seats to create a void. Inside that void was not only £200,000 of cocaine, but also Wayne Finch. Finch was wanted in connection to a murder in Salford but had fled the country. The gang had been using the secret compartment to get Finch in and out of the country undetected.

Suddenly, Laura saw something out of the corner of her eye.

At first, she didn't recognise what it was. Then she realised it was a circular mirror on a long pole that the prison security officers were using to check the roof.

Shit!

The mirror moved slowly across the edges of the van's roof.

Then it headed towards where Laura was lying flat in the middle.

She held her breath.

Pushing her hands, she managed to inch back down the roof and then over to where the mirror had already been.

The edges of her trainers squeaked loudly on the steel roof.

Bugger. Someone must have heard that!

She froze.

The mirror moved towards her.

Oh shit, this is it.

Then at the last moment, it veered away and disappeared.

Phew, that was close.

There was more talking and then the van's engine started up again and they pulled away.

After about thirty seconds, Laura gave a sigh of relief as they left the prison and headed out onto the main road.

CHAPTER 61

Andrea and Charlie were making their way across the road to where Reg and Celia Barnett lived at number 7.

As they approached the house, Andrea gazed up and saw a small black circular box attached to the brickwork.

Well, there's the CCTV camera.

She could see how it could have been missed up until now although she did wonder why the Barnetts hadn't mentioned it when uniformed officers had done their house to house enquiries.

Andrea's phone rang. It was Ben.

'Yes, Ben,' she said as she answered the phone.

'Andrea,' Ben said. 'Forensics have identified the tyre tracks they found at Llyn Llwydiarth as belonging to a large 4x4. They are tyres specifically used for Cherokee Jeeps, but they can be found on a Land Rover Discovery as well.'

'But they haven't matched them to the prints taken from Deakins' Jeep yet?' Andrea asked.

'No,' Ben replied. 'Apparently that's going to take the rest of the day.'

'We have a positive ID on a white Cherokee Jeep being parked in the road close to the Spears' home on several occasions in the past few weeks,' Andrea stated. '*But* our eyewitnesses don't remember seeing it on Monday night.'

'Right,' Ben said. 'Sounds like we're closing in on Deakins either way.'

'Hopefully... We might have found someone with CCTV at the back of the Spears' home,' she said. 'It's on that track that leads to their fence and gate in the garden.'

'Sounds promising. I'll see you back at the nick,' Ben said, ending the call.

Andrea put her phone away as Charlie gave her a quizzical look.

'Tracks at Llyn Llwydiarth belong to tyres used specifically for Cherokee Jeeps,' Andrea informed him. 'But we're waiting for a definite match for Deakin's Jeep.'

Charlie pointed up at the circular camera. 'I just hope these guys had that camera turned on on Monday night. And that it shows Deakins backing up his Jeep to that rear fence.'

Andrea nodded as they made their way to the front door of number 7. 'And if we can see the registration, I'm guessing we can arrest Deakins.'

Charlie nodded with a serious expression as he knocked on the door.

A moment later a man in his late sixties – beard, glasses – peered out at them.

'DC Heaton and DC Jones, Beaumaris,' Ben explained, showing his warrant card.

'We're looking for Reg Barnett,' Ben explained.

'That's me,' he said, looking concerned.

'I wonder if we could come in and ask you a couple

of questions. It won't take more than a few minutes,' Ben said.

'Oh, yes,' Reg said and opened the door. 'This to do with that ghastly thing that happened across the road?'

'Yes,' Andrea said as they went into the hallway. 'We're hoping you might be able to help us.'

'Right,' Reg said. 'Of course. Anything I can do to help. I used to be in the Royal Military Police myself. Twenty years. Mainly in West Germany, as it was then.'

Andrea nodded. 'Right. Even better,' she said encouragingly as Reg seemed very proud of that fact. 'We noticed that you have a CCTV camera mounted on the back of your house.' It seemed better not to mention that it had been their neighbours who had advised them of its existence.

'That's right,' Reg said. 'Unfortunately, my wife is very disabled. Despite all the signs, people still park in our designated spot, so I've had to resort to sending CCTV to the council to report them.'

'Right. Sounds frustrating,' Charlie said sympathetically.

'It is. Very,' Reg said, and then the penny dropped. 'You think there might be something on there that might help find out what happened to Abby?'

'We're hoping there might be,' Andrea replied.

'Gosh, well, I hadn't even thought about that,' Reg said, shaking his head. 'I assumed that whatever had happened was in the house and at the front. But of course, they have that panel in their fence that opens up, don't they?'

'That's right,' Charlie said. 'We have a report of a car driving up here just after midnight on Monday.'

'My wife and I would have been fast asleep in bed,' Reg stated and then pointed to the door. 'I've set all the CCTV stuff up in the dining room. We don't really use it for eating anymore.'

278

They followed him out across the hall and into a dining room that had a dark oak dining table and six chairs.

At one end, there was a monitor, a laptop and some recording equipment.

'Given my background, I feel a bit of an idiot that I didn't think of it myself,' Reg admitted as he sat down opposite the small CCTV monitor.

'Don't worry,' Andrea said in a kind voice. 'We've only realised today ourselves.'

'Right, let's see what we've got,' Reg said sounding enthused. 'My son came round and he's linked it to my laptop. He's a bit of a whizz at that sort of thing.' Reg clicked on some files. 'Okay, this is from Monday.'

The monitor burst into life and the CCTV footage from Monday night appeared on the screen.

The timecode read 19.00.

Reg clicked a button to move the footage forward at high speed.

After about thirty seconds, he slowed it down as the timecode read 23.55.

'Just after midnight, is that right?' Reg asked.

'Yes, that's what we think,' Charlie replied.

As he jogged the recording forward, Andrea could see a pair of headlights appear at the top right of the screen.

The timecode read 00.06.

'I think this might be it,' she said quietly.

A car drove past very slowly and then out of shot.

Andrea looked at Charlie quizzically. Whatever car had driven past, it certainly didn't look like a white Cherokee Jeep.

'They can't have gone very far. The track finishes just here,' Reg explained, indicating to a point just off the screen. 'Do you want to see if the car comes back again?'

'Yes, that would be useful,' Charlie said.

Reg played the recording forward a little and then the car appeared coming from the other direction.

The timecode was *00.23*.

'Whatever they were doing, it took seventeen minutes,' Andrea said under her breath. 'Could you freeze the frame to see if we can get a closer look at that car?'

'Yes, of course,' Reg said as he fiddled around with the recording.

He then froze the image so that the car was central.

'Looks like a VW Golf to me,' Charlie said as he peered at the screen.

'Yes, it does,' Reg agreed. 'Maybe grey or silver. Hard to tell in that light.'

Andrea was disappointed as she'd been confident that they were going to see Deakins' Cherokee Jeep on the CCTV.

She pulled out her notebook and pen. 'Right, so it's LV14 HNJ?' she said as she wrote it down.

'Yes,' Reg agreed.

'You don't happen to recognise that car, do you?' Charlie asked.

'I'm afraid not,' Reg admitted. 'Sorry.'

Charlie looked at Andrea. 'Maybe Deakins just used another car. It's less conspicuous than a Jeep.'

'Maybe,' Andrea thought, but she remembered the tyre tracks that had been found at Llyn Llwydiarth. And they didn't belong to a VW Golf. 'We need to run that plate through the DVLA and see who it's registered to.'

CHAPTER 62

Anglesey
Sunday, 23 October 2023
10.31 a.m.

The delivery van hammered along the road as they headed south from HMP Tonsgrove. Looking up, Laura spotted a sign for Britannia Bridge which was nineteen miles away. She had already presumed that they would be heading for the Welsh mainland and then into England. She also assumed that they would be switching vehicles at some point.

With her fingers clinging to the small metal rack on the van's roof, they sped around a right bend. Laura's legs and then her whole body slid left across the metal so that she was now lying horizontal. And every time the van driver used the brakes, she slid forward towards the front of the roof. She was terrified of being thrown over the front and then under the van's wheels or into oncoming traffic.

Now that they were clear of the prison, Laura was looking for an opportunity to climb down the back of the van in the same way that she had climbed up there. All she needed was for the van to stop. She was praying for red traffic lights so that the van would be forced to come to a halt – even if it wasn't for long.

Looking out to the right, Laura could see that they were close to the coastline. Rain was falling steadily into the dark sea in the distance. It looked like it was heading inland.

Just what I need now. A wet slippery surface to try and cling onto, she thought grimly.

The sky seemed to be darkening by the second. The only thing that now distinguished the sea from the sky was a dark line along the horizon. The sky above was a muted, faintly radiant grey.

She could feel the first spits of rain as they landed on the skin on the back of her hands.

Bollocks. I need to get off here soon.

As they pulled around another bend, Laura saw that they were heading into a small town. It looked like Llangefni but she couldn't be sure.

Up ahead she saw a set of traffic lights.

Bingo.

Except they were green.

Change, come on change.

A town like Llangefni would be the perfect place to make her escape from the van and then alert Gareth and the rest of the Anglesey Police Force that Kayleigh Doyle was hidden in the back of a delivery van heading for Britannia Bridge.

Laura stared at the green lights as they approached, willing them to turn red.

And as if she had been suddenly blessed with magical powers, the traffic lights changed from green to red.

Thank you, God, she thought as she looked skyward and then prepared herself to dismount from the van's roof as quickly as she could. Even if the driver did spot her, he wasn't going to get out of the van to pursue her and leave Kayleigh.

However, Laura realised that despite the traffic lights now being red, the van wasn't slowing down at all.

In fact, she heard the van's engine growl as the driver pushed down the accelerator.

Are you joking?

The van hammered across the red lights, swerved to avoid another car and sped through the town and out the other side.

As the heavens opened above her and the rain started to hammer down noisily of the metallic roof, Laura realised that the van wasn't going to stop for anyone or anything.

CHAPTER 63

Gareth stared intently at the scene boards in CID while detectives made phone calls, typed at computers. He looked at the two faces of their victims: Sheila Jones and Abby White.

Ben approached. 'Think we've got something, boss.'

'Go on,' Gareth said as he continued to look at Abby White's photo and wonder where the hell she was.

'Forensics got that partial print from Sheila Jones' cell,' Ben explained. 'They've now managed to create a full fingerprint. It matches prints that were found on the arm and collar of Sheila's jacket and on the skin of her forearm and hands. The chief pathologist is convinced from the positioning of those fingerprints that they belong to her killer.'

Although it was a relatively recent development, and still very difficult, latent fingerprints could be formed when the body's natural oils and sweat on the skin are deposited on any surface.

284

Brilliant, Gareth thought as he processed what Ben had told him.

He turned to look at Ben. If they had a fingerprint of the person who had attacked Sheila, then they would have the murderer. Every convicted prisoner inside HMP Tonsgrove would have their fingerprints and DNA on the national database.

'So, who is it?' he asked Ben expectantly.

Ben pulled a face. 'That's the problem. The fingerprint isn't on any of the databases.'

What?

'That doesn't make any sense.' Gareth frowned. 'Everyone inside Tonsgrove has their fingerprints on the national database.'

Ben gave him a meaningful look. 'Not everyone, boss.'

Gareth took a moment. 'Are we saying that Sheila Jones was killed by someone other than a prisoner?'

Ben shrugged. 'I guess that's what the evidence is telling us.'

Gareth looked back at the scene board. 'I was convinced that either Kayleigh Doyle or Niamh Mullan had killed Sheila.'

Ben pointed to a photo. 'We know that Parveen is working with Michael Doyle. And we're assuming that Parveen is allowing Doyle to bring drugs into Tonsgrove for Kayleigh Doyle, Niamh Mullan and the others to sell.'

Gareth nodded. 'Which makes Sheila Jones and her little gang of Scousers the enemy. Which is why I thought one of them killed her.'

'That also makes Sheila Jones a major nuisance to Parveen as well,' Ben pointed out.

Gareth raised an eyebrow. 'You're not suggesting that Parveen dressed up in a hoodie and balaclava and stabbed Sheila to death in her own prison?'

'No.' Ben shook his head. 'But maybe someone did her dirty work for her?'

Gareth went back to the board again. 'And Laura told us that she suspected that Parveen and David Rice are having some kind of affair.'

'And as a prison officer, David Rice's fingerprints aren't on any national database,' Ben said.

'Rice was nowhere to be seen when Sheila was killed,' Gareth said thinking out loud. 'Even though he's the main prison officer on that part of G Wing.'

'There is something else,' Ben said as he gestured over to his desk.

'What is it,' Gareth asked as he followed him over.

Ben pointed to his computer screen as he sat down. 'I've been looking at the CCTV from Tuesday morning again.'

'Okay.'

Ben played the recording and then froze the CCTV on the screen as Hayley Ross came out of the room she shared with Sheila. 'This is not exactly scientific,' Ben conceded as he pointed to the frozen image. 'But look at the top of Hayley's head as she comes out of the room.'

Gareth peered at the screen.

'The top of her head is level with the viewing hatch on the door,' Ben said. 'Agreed?'

'Yes,' Gareth said, wondering where Ben was going with all this – but he was intrigued.

'Okay,' Ben said as he played the CCTV footage forward. On the screen, the hooded, masked figure made their way up the corridor. As they turned to go into the room, Ben paused the image so that it was frozen on the screen. 'Right, so this is our attacker going into the room. They're roughly the same distance from the door as Hayley was when she came out.'

'Yes, I can see that,' Gareth agreed.

'If you look at the top of our attacker's head,' Ben said. '...it's about four, even five inches above the top of the viewing hatch on the door.'

Ben looked at Gareth with a quizzical expression.

'Yes, about four or five inches,' Gareth said.

Ben looked at him. 'I've checked Hayley Ross' prison records. She's five foot nine inches, so she's pretty tall for a woman.'

'So, whoever attacked Sheila was almost certainly over six foot,' Gareth said.

'Exactly,' Ben said. 'There can't be many people working in that prison who are over six foot tall.'

'Can we get David Rice's personnel record sent over from the prison?' Gareth asked.

'I've already requested it, boss,' Ben said with a confident look. 'They're sending over a PDF copy right now.'

Gareth gave a half-smile and gave him an approving pat on his shoulder. 'That's great work, Ben. We need to get you working towards your sergeant's exams by the end of the year.'

Ben couldn't help but give a proud smile.

The doors to CID opened and Andrea and Charlie strode in.

Gareth went over to them as he knew they'd been over to Pen-y-garnedd.

'Any luck with that eyewitness?' he asked them.

'There's good news and bad news,' Andrea said pulling a face.

'Why do people keep saying that?' Gareth groaned. 'Good news first please.'

'We have multiple sightings of a white Cherokee Jeep in Pen-y-garnedd in the weeks leading up to Abby's disappearance,' Andrea explained.

'Anyone see the reg?' Gareth asked hopefully.

Charlie shook his head. 'I'm afraid not.'

'It's a pretty distinctive car,' Ben said.

'What about Monday night?' Gareth asked, realising they hadn't mentioned it.

'No,' Andrea said.

Gareth could feel his frustration. 'Bollocks... Doesn't mean he wasn't there though.' He looked at them. 'I assume that's the bad news.'

Andrea's expression told him that it wasn't.

'Go on,' Gareth said, trying to hide his annoyance. They just needed a break even though he thought that Shane Deakins was still probably their prime suspect for Abby's abduction.

Charlie pulled out a memory stick. 'There's a house that backs onto that track that leads up to the Spears' back garden. They've got a security camera attached to the outside of their house.'

'How the hell did we miss that?' Gareth asked.

'Easily missed, to be honest, boss,' Andrea said.

'It's a black circular box about six inches in diameter,' Charlie stated. 'And it's about twenty feet up.'

Gareth gave them a quizzical look. 'And this is the bad news because...?'

Charlie slotted his memory stick.

'I'm not sure it's technically bad news,' Andrea admitted.

Charlie gestured to the computer screen. There was footage from the security camera now on the monitor. 'So, at six minutes past midnight, this car drives down the track that goes to the rear of the Spears' home.' Charlie then moved the recording forward. 'And then at twenty-three minutes past midnight, the car comes back the other way, having turned around.' Charlie then froze the image of the car.

'Looks like a Golf for me,' Gareth said, thinking out loud.

'Yeah, that's what we thought,' Andrea said.

'We've got the registration,' Charlie said. 'We're just waiting for the DVLA to check our request and come back to us about who the registered owner is.'

Gareth looked at them. 'It could still be Shane Deakins.'

'Especially if he wanted help in abducting Abby,' Charlie agreed.

'Okay, let me know as soon as you get that information back,' Gareth said, thinking it was a shame that they hadn't seen Deakins' Cherokee Jeep so they could go and arrest him there and then.

Ben signalled across the room to Gareth that he needed to talk to him. He was holding his office phone. 'Boss?'

'What is it?' Gareth asked as he strode over.

'I've got Governor Parveen from HMP Tonsgrove holding on line two,' Ben explained. 'She wants to speak to you and she says it's urgent.'

'Okay, I'll take it in my office,' Gareth said. His stomach tightened as he made his way across the CID office. Even though he knew it might be something to do with Sheila Jones' murder, his thoughts immediately went to Laura. Had her cover been blown or had she become involved in an incident and got hurt?

Coming into his office, he took a breath as he picked up the phone and hit the flashing button for line two. 'DI Williams speaking.'

'Hi, it's Sanam Parveen,' said a voice.

'Hi, how can I help?' Gareth asked.

'We've just done a routine roll check and we've got two missing prisoners,' Parveen explained.

'Right,' Gareth said, trying to process what she'd said.

'We're pretty sure that a prisoner called Kayleigh Doyle

289

has escaped in a delivery van,' Parveen said. 'I can give you the details.'

'Please,' Gareth said. He was immediately suspicious. From the intel and CCTV that the NCA officers had given him, he knew that Parveen and her uncle were working with Michael Doyle, probably to supply and control the drugs inside HMP Tonsgrove. Kayleigh was part of the Doyle crime family so Gareth assumed that Parveen had facilitated Kayleigh's escape.

'It's a blue Ford Transit from a delivery company called PDT Delivery,' Parveen explained. 'Licence plate is KM15 JNH. It left our site about fifteen minutes ago.'

'I'm assuming you did all the usual security checks,' Gareth asked, but clearly there was something very fishy going on.

'Of course,' Parveen said in a defensive tone. 'I've no idea how she got past all those, but that's the only vehicle that has been into the prison and left in that time slot.'

Don't get defensive with me, Gareth thought angrily. *You're a bent prison governor, for God's sake!*

Then something occurred to Gareth.

'You said two prisoners,' he said. 'But you've only mentioned Kayleigh Doyle. Who else is missing on your roll check?'

'A new prisoner who's just arrived called Laura Noakes,' Parveen said. 'But as far as we know she's not affiliated to any gang. We've no idea where she is or why she's gone missing.'

Gareth's stomach tightened with anxiety.

CHAPTER 64

Anglesey
Sunday, 23 October 2022
10.39 a.m.

The rain was now hammering down as Laura clung to the wet van roof. The only positive was that due to the traffic heading for the Britannia Bridge, they had kept to a reasonable speed, especially around corners.

Looking up, Laura saw a sign: BRITANNIA BRIDGE 5 MILES

She glanced at her watch. By her calculations, HMP Tonsgrove would have done a routine roll check about ten minutes earlier and realised that she and Kayleigh Doyle were missing. By now, a call would have been made to North Wales Police. If they'd checked the prison CCTV, they might have spotted Kayleigh getting into the back of the van. They might have also spotted her lying flat on the roof.

The wind picked up and blew the rain into her face. Her hair was now matted to her forehead.

Jesus, why can't I have a normal job where I sit in a

nice warm office in front of a computer and work 9–5, she grumbled to herself.

Maybe they weren't going to switch vehicles until they were across the Britannia Bridge and onto the Welsh mainland.

If the van wasn't going to stop until then, what was she going to do? She didn't fancy her chances of clinging onto the wet metallic roof for another fifteen minutes.

Then she had a thought. What she really needed to do is attract the attention of someone to her presence on top of the van. Hopefully, that person would then report seeing a strange woman on top of a van to the police and that would give their position so they could be tracked.

Crawling closer to the back of the van, Laura peered at the road behind them. They were still traversing country roads, so she needed to keep at least one hand clutching the metallic ridge on the side to stop her sliding off.

Directly behind them was a community ambulance.

Sticking her head up for a few seconds, she waved.

However, the ambulance drivers were in deep conversation and Laura was too high up in their field of vision for them to see her.

Bollocks.

Then she had an idea.

Reaching down, she began to try to untie the laces on one of her trainers. It was easier said than done with one hand, in the pelting rain while on top of a moving van!

The laces eventually untied. Pulling the trainer from her right foot, she took it and then looked down at the ambulance.

Taking aim, she threw the trainer at the front of the ambulance, hoping it would hit the windscreen and alert the driver to her presence.

Just as she threw her trainer, the ambulance slowed a little.

The trainer hit the road and went unnoticed underneath the ambulance instead.

For fuck's sake!

Laura gave an audible growl as she reached down again to untie her left trainer with one hand.

After a few uncomfortable seconds, she pulled it up.

Right, don't mess this up, Laura!

She tossed the trainer as hard as she could down towards the ambulance.

It landed with a THUD on their windscreen.

The driver and his passenger immediately looked up to see where it had come from.

Laura waved at them furiously until they spotted her.

She made animated facial expressions to show that she was in trouble and distressed.

The ambulance driver nodded and signalled that he'd seen her.

Thank God.

CHAPTER 65

Gareth had quickly assembled the whole CID team along with members of the North Wales Tactical Response Unit and the Armed Response Officers. All the police stations on Anglesey had been alerted to the fact that an undercover officer was now missing and might well be on a delivery van heading for the Britannia Bridge.

Parveen had confirmed that Kayleigh and Laura had both escaped while unloading stationery supplies by the prison's education block. Barry McDonald, the prison tutor, had been locked inside a room while they made their escape. Gareth had no idea why Laura hadn't made contact or why she'd decided to escape with Kayleigh and her accomplice. However, she was an incredibly experienced police officer so he had to trust that she had good reason.

'Right, guys,' Gareth said as he pulled on his heavy Kevlar bulletproof vest. His heart now pounding hard against his chest. 'We believe that DI Laura Hart is inside a delivery van with this woman, Kayleigh Doyle, who is part of the Doyle crime family in Birmingham.'

'Do we have any idea which direction they're heading in?' Charlie asked.

'No,' Gareth admitted as he pointed to a map. 'The Doyle family have criminal connections to the Republic of Ireland. So, they could be trying to smuggle Kayleigh out of the country via a ferry from Holyhead to Dublin.'

The Chief of the Armed Response Unit, Sergeant Repton, went to one side to take a phone call on his mobile phone. He spoke in a low tone.

Ben looked over. 'I've spoken to the Border Control and Security Team at the port, put them on high alert and spoken to local plod at Holyhead Police Station.'

'Great, thanks, Ben,' Gareth said. If they were going to Holyhead, Gareth was aware that it was the UK's second busiest ferry port with over two million passengers passing through it every year – so finding someone, even with a description – wasn't going to be easy. It was made even harder by the fact that you didn't need a passport to travel from Holyhead to Dublin.

Andrea looked over. 'They could be going for one of the bridges to get to the mainland and then down to the midlands,' she suggested.

Gareth nodded. 'That's the other possibility.'

Charlie took a phone call and walked slowly over towards his desk.

Gareth then looked out at the assembled officers. 'For those of you who aren't aware, the Doyle family are a very violent OCG based in the Birmingham area. Our intel is that whoever broke Kayleigh out of HMP Tonsgrove was armed with a handgun. Therefore we need to approach with caution as they are very dangerous.'

Sergeant Repton pointed to his phone. 'We've had a

report from an ambulance crew of a woman signalling from the roof of a van about five miles south of Britannia Bridge. She appeared to be in some distress. When the ambulance signalled for the van to pull over, the driver ignored them.'

Gareth nodded. It sounded like a significant development.

'Details of the van,' Gareth asked as he prepared himself to give the go-ahead for everyone to proceed to that location.

'It's a blue delivery van. Ford Transit,' Repton explained.

'That's it.' Gareth nodded as his anxiety went through the roof. *What the hell is Laura doing on the van roof?*

'I'll radio ahead and get the bridge shut down to all traffic,' Repton said as he headed for the CID doors with the Authorised Firearms Officers (AFOs).

'Boss!' Charlie said as he approached and looked at Gareth and Andrea.

'What is it?' Gareth asked as he grabbed his car keys.

'DVLA have come back with the registration of that VW Golf on the CCTV,' Charlie explained.

'Who does it belong to?' Gareth asked.

Charlie raised an eyebrow. 'Rebecca Maddison.'

'Becks? What?' Andrea said sounding surprised.

'Right,' Gareth said, thinking that his head was about to explode with the information he was trying to juggle. 'You and Andrea go and pick her up, bring her here and ask her what the bloody hell she was doing on Monday night. We're going to the Britannia Bridge.'

CHAPTER 66

Anglesey
Sunday, 23 October 2022
10.53 a.m.

Laura's wet clothes were now stuck to her body. She was shivering.

I'm going to get hypothermia at this rate.

Looking up, she spotted a sign.

The sign read: BRITANNIA BRIDGE 3 MILES.

It was about fifteen minutes since she'd managed to signal to the ambulance driver that she was on the van roof and was in trouble.

She assumed that information would have now been relayed to all units of Anglesey Police Force who would be on the lookout for the van. If they'd managed to move quickly, they might have even managed to close off Britannia Bridge.

As she looked to the right-hand side of the road, she noticed a line of blue metal railings.

An enormous steel structure came into view.

Britannia Bridge.

The driver slammed on the brakes.

The bridge was completely blocked and sealed off with police cars. Their blue lights flashed, throwing strobed patterns onto the steel structure.

There was no way they were driving across.

The force of the brakes was too much for Laura to hang on.

She lost her grip on the side of the van and as it lurched to a stop, she felt herself being propelled along the wet surface of the roof towards the front edge.

Oh shit, this isn't good.

Grabbing out frantically with her hands for something to hold onto, she could see, almost in slow motion, that she was going to go over the front of the roof.

A split second, she saw the van's bonnet heading up towards her.

CRASH!

She seemed to bounce slightly off the bonnet and slide down onto the wet road surface below.

Fuck me, that hurts.

She lay looking up at the dark sky and raindrops as she desperately tried to get her breath. The fall had completely winded her.

Then a figure loomed into view.

It was the huge man with black hair and beard who had been driving the van.

He was pointing a Glock 17 handgun in her face.

CHAPTER 67

Menai
Sunday, 23 October 2023
10.55 a.m.

Andrea and Charlie pulled off the Pentraeth Road and into the small town of Menai. They had been trying to get their heads around the fact that the VW Golf they had seen on Reg Barnett's CCTV was registered to Becks Maddison. It just didn't make any sense whatsoever. Why had Becks lied to them? Why had she driven up to the rear entrance of the Spears' home just after midnight and then driven away twenty minutes later? How was she involved in what had happened to Abby White?

They pulled into Dale Street and soon found the property they were looking for. According to the electoral register, Becks lived in the first-floor flat of number 32 which they saw was a pebble-dashed house next to what looked like a fashionable café called Brew.

Andrea pulled up the collar of her coat against the heavy rain.

They jogged across the road and Andrea splashed

299

through a puddle, feeling the cold water against her ankle.

'Bloody hell,' she muttered under her breath.

As they arrived at the front door, there was a loud clap of thunder as the rain intensified.

Charlie looked at the two bells beside the front door and pressed the one marked R MADDISON – FLAT B.

'I just don't get it.' Andrea frowned. 'My instinct is that a girl like Becks Maddison isn't involved in Abby being attacked and abducted.'

Charlie raised an eyebrow. 'Maybe she wasn't on her own that night?'

'Maybe I just got it completely wrong,' Andrea said. 'The CCTV shows that it's her car.'

'And given that she'd already driven over to Abby's home that night,' Charlie said, 'it has to be her driving on that CCTV recording.'

Before they could continue, there was the sound of a key turning in a lock.

Then the door opened.

Becks peered out at them. She was wearing a towel around her head and a pink, fluffy dressing gown.

'Oh hi,' she said with a frown. 'Oh God, have you found Abby or something?'

'I'm afraid not,' Andrea said gently. 'But there are a few more questions that we'd like to ask you if that's okay?'

'Erm,' Becks said hesitantly. 'Really? I mean, of course.'

Andrea looked directly at her. 'There are a few things that don't quite add up about the events on Monday night. We just need to check a couple of things with you.'

She could see that Becks now looked very uneasy.

'Won't take more than a couple of minutes,' Charlie reassured her.

'If we could come in...' Andrea said, gesturing to the door.

'Actually, place is a pigs' stye up there,' Becks babbled nervously as she pointed to the staircase behind her. 'I'll just go and get dressed and then I'll meet you in that café in five minutes,' she said pointing to the trendy café next door.

Before Andrea could say anything, Becks had slammed the door in her face. She could then hear Becks running up the staircase.

Charlie furrowed his brow. 'What the hell was that about?'

'I've no idea,' Andrea said, mystified by Becks' strange behaviour.

'She was keen for us not to come into her flat,' Charlie said.

'Yeah, that was definitely suspicious,' Andrea agreed.

'I assume we're not going to the café?' Charlie said.

'No,' Andrea replied, shaking her head. 'I'm waiting right here for her. And we're going to need to go and take a look around her flat.'

'Yeah,' Charlie said.

After a few seconds, Andrea looked at Charlie. 'That's if she actually opens the door again.'

Charlie took a few steps back from the house. 'I wonder if there's another way out of the flat at the back.'

Taking a few steps to the left, Charlie reacted. 'Shit!'

'What is it?' Andrea said joining him.

A figure climbed over a fence and started to run in the opposite direction.

It was Becks.

'Oi!' Charlie shouted as he broke into a sprint after her.

'Go after her,' Andrea shouted. 'I'm going into the flat.'

Moving back towards the front door, she gave it an almighty kick and the door gave way with a crash and flew open.

CHAPTER 68

Britannia Bridge
Sunday, 23 October 2022
10.59 a.m.

As the rain lashed down, Gareth peered along the approach road towards Britannia Bridge. The uniformed officers reported seeing a woman fall from the van roof when it stopped suddenly. The driver had then taken the woman at gunpoint into the back of the van and closed the rear doors.

Since Gareth and Ben had arrived at the scene, the blue delivery van had remained motionless where it had stopped.

Gareth could feel his stomach tensing with anxiety. Laura was inside the van with an armed man and an escaped prisoner. And she had no idea what they planned to do next.

'What the hell are they doing in there?' Ben asked.

'I wish I knew,' Gareth said feeling overwhelmed with worry.

The raindrops bounced and splashed off the pavement and dripped noisily from a nearby building and roof.

Gareth's radio crackled. 'Oscar Sierra one to Gold Command, are you receiving, over.'

Gold Command was Gareth's radio handle as he was the officer in charge of the operation at the bridge.

Gareth clicked the radio. 'Oscar Sierra one, this is Gold Command, I am receiving, over.'

'I'm going to send two men into an advanced position, over.'

'Received and understood, stand by,' Gareth said.

The shadowy figures of two AROs, with Glock machine guns at the ready, hurried into position about fifty yards from the stationary van, training their weapons on the target vehicle. An ARV had already pulled across to block the road at the side of the bridge. Its rotating blue light illuminated the painted steel barricades and enormous chains that swung in a giant U-shape from the limestone towers, giving the scene an eerie atmosphere.

Suddenly the sky seemed to fill with a thundering noise.

At first, Gareth assumed that it was the distant rumble of thunder from the storm. However, as it got closer, he realised that it had a rhythmic, mechanical quality to it.

Ben looked skyward. 'What the hell is that noise?'

Gareth was now confused. 'It's a helicopter.'

'Air support?' Ben asked.

'No.' Gareth shook his head. 'The North Wales Police chopper is attending a serious road traffic accident on the A55. And there isn't another one available.'

'Eh?' Ben said. 'Well whose helicopter is it?'

Gareth had a sinking feeling as he looked at Ben.

'You're kidding?' Ben said aghast. 'They're getting out of here in a chopper?'

'Maybe,' Gareth said, praying that there was another explanation.

303

Glancing at the dark sky above, Gareth saw a white helicopter hone into view.

Suddenly the whole sky lit up as it put on its huge halogen search light.

'Bloody hell!' Ben said as they squinted up at its powerful beam as it began circling above the bridge with its spotlight cutting through the gloom.

'What are we going to do?' Ben shouted as the noise of the rotor blades got louder and louder.

'I don't know,' Gareth admitted. 'We can't just shoot it down.'

Ben looked at him. 'What if they take Laura with them?'

'I don't know.' Gareth shook his head despondently as he watched the helicopter circle again, its beam swathing the van in a brilliant white light before it descended slowly towards a large piece of flat road at the bridge's entrance.

The back doors to the van opened.

Gareth held his breath.

A man with dark hair and a beard came out of the back of the van. He was holding a figure in front of him at gunpoint.

It was Laura.

Oh God.

A woman with red hair got out behind them.

Kayleigh Doyle.

They backed away from the van and made their way very slowly towards the waiting helicopter.

Gareth clicked his radio. 'All units, this is Gold Command. One of the suspects heading to the helicopter is a police officer. Hold your fire, repeat, hold your fire.'

The door to the helicopter opened and the three figures moved backwards towards it.

There was a flash of lightning that lit up the entire sky, illuminating the Snowdonia mountains in the distance behind. Then, a second or two later, the deep grumble of thunder.

The dark-haired man pulled Laura with him.

Gareth watched helplessly as the woman he loved was bundled towards the door to the helicopter.

Michael Doyle put Laura into a choke hold as they walked backwards towards the helicopter.

The noise of the rotor blades was deafening. The down-wash of wind from the spinning blades battered against Laura's face, flinging her hair across her face.

As they reached the helicopter, Doyle jammed the muzzle of the Glock 17 handgun hard into the side of her head.

'You're strangling me!' Laura gasped as she tried to resist him.

'Shut up,' Doyle snapped over the noise of the engines.

Laura realised that if she got into the helicopter with them, she was as good as dead. They weren't going to land and then let her go.

She needed to think of something – and fast.

Out of the corner of her eye, Laura spotted two dark figures moving on top of the huge stone archway that stood at the centre of the suspension bridge. Then she saw the tell-tale glint of a red laser. They were police marksmen getting into position.

Kayleigh went behind them and clambered through the small door to the helicopter.

A figure approached from the road.

It was Gareth.

He was holding up his hands in a conciliatory fashion.

'Just let her go,' Gareth shouted.

'Get back or I'll blow her brains out,' Doyle shouted.

Gareth was now only about fifteen yards in front of

them. 'Take it nice and easy. Just let her go and you can fly out of here.'

'Oh yeah,' Doyle hissed sarcastically. 'Until you blow us out of the sky. I don't bloody think so. She's coming with us, dickhead.'

Laura felt Doyle put a foot on the step up to the helicopter.

'I promise you!' Gareth yelled. 'Release her and you can go. We're not going to bring a helicopter down. Think about it!'

'No chance,' Doyle yelled as he began to pull Laura inside.

I can't breathe.

Laura's head was starting to swim from lack of oxygen. She tried to pull his forearm away from her throat.

She could hear the helicopter's engine starting to increase power.

In a matter of seconds, she would be pulled inside the helicopter and taken away to an almost certain death.

CHAPTER 69

Menai
Sunday, 23 October 2022
11.00 a.m.

Andrea moved slowly up the staircase towards Becks Maddison's flat. As she reached the landing, she could see it was neat and tidy. Music was playing from somewhere inside the flat. Up on the wall was a poster for the Boardmasters Festival 2022. There were a row of coats and jackets hanging on pegs.

Pushing open the door to her right, Andrea saw the tiny kitchen which was spotless. Freshly made toast sat in the toaster. Presumably Becks had been making herself breakfast when they'd knocked.

Over by the kettle, Andrea saw two mugs, both with tea bags inside and a pint of milk sitting to one side. She touched the kettle. It was still hot.

Two mugs?

Was there someone in the flat? Did Becks have a boyfriend?

'Hello?' Andrea called. 'Is anyone there?'

Silence.

As Andrea went back out onto the landing, she could hear a faint, rhythmic tapping noise. It wasn't clear where it was coming from.

The next door to her left was open. Inside was a double bed, clothes and a dresser strewn with make-up, There were a couple of magazines on the floor beside the bed.

There was also a row of shoes. Andrea crouched down, took one of the shoes and looked at the size.

It was a size seven.

Following the sound of the music, Andrea went into what appeared to the living room. The television was on. The video for Taylor Swift's 'Anti-Hero' was playing.

On the far side, there was a clothes horse with various items of clothing hanging out to dry.

Andrea did a double take.

Hanging at the centre of the clothes horse was a black T-shirt with a colourful logo.

It was a Newcastle Brown Ale Logo with Sam Fender written on it in red lettering.

Andrea felt a shiver go up her spine.

It was the same T-shirt that Abby White had been wearing when she'd gone missing from her home.

What the hell is going on? Andrea wondered. There was, of course, a remote possibility that Abby and Becks both had the same T-shirt. But given what Andrea had seen in the CCTV footage – Becks driving up to the rear entrance of the Spears' home – it made her feel uneasy.

Taking the remote, Andrea turned the television off. The music was making it difficult to think.

Her radio crackled. 'Five zero from three nine, are you receiving me, over?' said a voice.

It was Charlie.

She wondered why he hadn't just called her on her phone. Maybe there wasn't any signal in the flat.

The tapping sound continued, even though Andrea hadn't located its source.

'Three nine, this is five zero. I am receiving, go ahead, over,' she said.

'I have the suspect in custody,' Charlie said. 'I'll meet you by the car, over.'

'Received, three nine, over and out.'

Andrea was relieved that Charlie had apprehended Becks. She had a lot of explaining to do.

Walking along the landing, she could hear the tapping sound to her right.

Opening the door, she saw it was the bathroom.

She looked over at the closed shower curtain.

She turned to go but saw something out of the corner of her eye.

Peering into the bathroom, she realised what she had spotted.

There was a dark figure standing behind the shower.

Shit!

Taking two steps back, Andrea felt her pulse start to race.

'Right,' she said in a stern voice. 'I am a police officer. I can see you standing in the shower. So, I want you to come out, nice and slowly.'

For a second, the figure didn't move.

Andrea held her breath. She had no idea if the person was going to attack her but she needed to prepare herself.

Then a hand took the side of the shower curtain and pulled it back very slowly.

Andrea looked at the figure standing there.

A teenage girl with red hair and blue eyes.

It was Abby White.

CHAPTER 70

Britannia Bridge
Sunday, 23 October 2023
11.02 a.m.

Michael Doyle tried to pull Laura into the helicopter with him. She tried to resist him but he was far too powerful.

At this rate, he's going to break my neck.

Laura looked over. Her eyes met Gareth's. She could see the look of desperation in his face.

'Let her go!' Gareth shouted in desperation.

Doyle shook his head as he took a backward step inside the helicopter.

'I can't do that,' he shouted.

Laura looked at Gareth. Was this the last time she was ever going to see him? The thought of it was overwhelming. There had to be a way out of this. But what?

'Right, bitch,' Doyle growled into her ear. 'Stop resisting and get in the fucking the chopper or I'll break your neck right here and now.'

Then something caught her eye. It was the red laser

sight glimmering from the top of the stone archway. It was trained in their direction.

This is it. Now or never.

FUCK YOU!

Laura managed to loosen Doyle's grip on her neck. She then bit as hard as she could into the flesh of his forearm.

'AARRRGGHH!'

Doyle yelled in pain and released her from the choke hold.

In that moment, she dropped to the ground as fast as she could. Could the same manoeuvre she'd used before really save her life again?

The police marksmen now had a clear shot.

Silence.

What are you bloody waiting for?

Laura held her breath.

CRACK! CRACK!

Two bullets hammered into Doyle's chest and he collapsed forward and onto the ground.

He was dead.

Thank God.

CRACK! CRACK! CRACK!

Laura covered her head as she lay on the ground as bullets hit the rotor blades and the engine.

CRACK! CRACK!

The advancing AFOs were clearly firing bullets to disable the helicopter.

Laura felt a hand grab hers.

'Come on,' said a voice.

It was Gareth.

He pulled her up to her feet and they sprinted away from the helicopter, which was now making a whining noise.

As they got to other side of road, Gareth looked at her.

311

'Are you all right?' he asked in a panic.

Laura rubbed her throat. 'Yeah, now I can breath I'll be fine.'

Black smoke was pouring from the turboshaft engine on the helicopter.

There were six AFOs surrounding the helicopter, pointing their Heckler & Koch machine guns at those inside.

The rotor blades started to slow down.

Kayleigh clambered out of the helicopter with her hands raised.

She was followed by the pilot.

They were both pushed to the ground at gunpoint and put in cuffs.

Laura turned to Gareth with a weary smile. 'Next time I watch *Donnie Brasco*, remind me that it's just a film.'

Gareth smiled back. 'Yeah, I will do.'

CHAPTER 71

Beaumaris Police Station
Sunday, 23 October 2022
11.39 a.m.

Andrea pressed the red button and the electronic noise sounded. 'Interview conducted with Abby White. Interview Room 2, Beaumaris Police Station. Present are Duty Solicitor Cerys Davies, Abby White, Detective Constable Charlie Heaton and myself, Detective Constable Andrea Jones.'

Andrea then took a few seconds. She couldn't quite believe that she was sitting opposite Abby White after the events of the past few days. Obviously there was huge relief that she was alive and well. But to say that she had some explaining to do was an understatement. So far, Abby had been very quiet and virtually said nothing.

'Abby,' Andrea said calmly, 'do you understand that you are being charged under the Criminal Justice and Police Act of 2001 for wasting police time?'

Abby nodded nervously. 'Yes.'

Andrea sat back in her seat, wondering quite where to

start. Then she looked over at Abby. 'Can you tell me exactly what happened last Monday evening, Abby?'

Charlie took out his pen and clicked it, ready to take notes.

Abby took a deep breath, then leaned in to the Duty Solicitor. They talked in low voices for a few seconds.

'I... er...' Abby said hesitantly. 'My friend Becks came round to see me.'

Andrea nodded. 'That's Becks Maddison, isn't it?' she asked.

'Yes.'

Andrea looked at her again. Abby looked totally overwhelmed.

'We've spoken to Becks,' Andrea said softly. 'She told us that you went to the summer house where you listened to music. Is that correct?'

Abby nodded. 'Yes.'

Andrea leaned forward and shifted on her seat. 'And where did Becks go once she had told your aunt that she was leaving?'

'Erm... She just went to her car and then drove it around the back,' Abby explained.

Charlie stopped writing and glanced at her. 'Can you tell us what time that would have been?'

Abby frowned. 'I think it was just before twelve,' she said quietly.

'Okay,' Andrea said. 'And then what happened?'

'My uncle came down to see where I was,' Abby said. 'And then when he was gone, Becks brought the car up to the back gate.' Abby then looked across at Andrea uneasily.

'It's okay,' Andrea reassured her. 'Go on.'

Abby shook her head and then looked down at the floor. 'I can't,' she whispered.

314

'Abby?' Andrea said gently.

Silence.

Abby looked slowly up at her. She now had tears in her eyes. She used her hand to wipe them away.

'I think we can guess what you and Becks did. We found all the blood,' Andrea explained. 'But I'm pretty sure that you had a very good reason for doing it.'

Abby took a deep breath and blew out her cheeks. 'But won't I go to prison?'

'I can't tell you that right now,' Andrea said. 'But if you've acted because you felt that you were in danger, then that will be taken into account.'

Abby nodded as she wiped her face again. 'Me and Becks had seen this film. The woman had collected her blood over a few weeks so she could fake her death. *Gone Girl.* So, me and Becks thought I could do the same. And then we put the blood over the mattress. Then I got into the back of Becks' car to hide and we drove off.'

Silence as Andrea nodded, taking all this in.

Charlie looked over. 'Can you tell us where you went after that?'

Abby didn't say anything. She looked terrified.

'Abby, did you and Becks drive up to Llyn Llwydiarth?' Andrea said.

She nodded her head. 'Yes...'

Andrea raised an eyebrow. 'And why did you do that?'

Abby took a few moments to compose herself again. 'We... wanted to make it look like someone had put me in the lake. We threw my hoodie and shoes in.'

'Okay,' Andrea said. 'And where did you go after that?'

'We went back to Becks' flat,' she said.

'And you've been there ever since?' Charlie asked.

'Yeah.' Abby nodded. 'I haven't been anywhere else.'

315

Andrea waited for a few seconds as she processed what Abby had told her.

'Can you tell me why you and Becks decided to fake your murder?' Andrea said.

'A few weeks ago, a man had come to our house,' Abby said. 'My aunt and uncle were out. And… he…' Abby's breathing had become shallow with anxiety.

'It's all right,' Andrea reassured her. 'Take your time.'

'He said that I needed to give my mum a message,' Abby said.

'Okay,' Andrea said.

Abby's eyes filled with tears again. 'He said that I had to tell her that he was from Croxteth and that it was time for her to retire from her business. He said she'd know what that meant. Then he said… He said that if she didn't, to tell her that he was going to take me away and kill me.'

Andrea gave her an empathetic look. 'It's okay.'

Abby nodded but she was shaking. 'I was so scared. I didn't know what to do.'

'And your mother is Kayleigh Doyle who is currently at HMP Tonsgrove?' Andrea asked, to clarify.

'Yes.'

Charlie stopped writing and looked over at her. 'Do you think you could describe the man?'

Abby nodded. 'Yeah, he was really tall. He had a shaved head and tattoos.'

'Did he have an accent?' Andrea said.

'Yeah.' Abby nodded. 'He was from Liverpool.'

Andrea and Charlie looked at each other. *Shane Deakins*.

'Did you tell your mum what he'd said to you?' Andrea said.

'Yeah,' Abby replied.

'What did she say?' Charlie said.

316

Abby thought for a second. 'She was really worried. But then I came up with a plan…'

'To fake your own abduction and murder?' Andrea asked to clarify.

'Yes,' Abby said. 'We thought that would keep me safe until…'

Andrea frowned and looked at her. 'Until…?'

Abby hesitated. Then she said, 'Mum told me that a few things were going to happen so that me and her could be together. And we could start a new life somewhere else.'

Andrea realised that Kayleigh had escaped from Tonsgrove so she could go and start a new life with Abby somewhere.

Andrea narrowed her eyes. 'When we were searching Llyn Llwydiarth, we found a necklace belonging to your aunt on the banks of the lake. Can you tell us why you took that necklace from your aunt and then deliberately left it there?'

Silence.

Abby looked very uncomfortable. 'I don't know,' she mumbled.

Andrea gave her a quizzical look. 'Come on, Abby. You deliberately left your aunt's necklace at the place where you wanted us to believe your body had been disposed of. You must have had a good reason for doing that?'

Abby's face changed. She looked angry. 'Yeah, I did have a good reason.'

Andrea raised an eyebrow. 'Can you tell us what that is?'

'I did it because I hate her,' Abby hissed under her breath.

Charlie frowned. 'Why do you hate her that much?'

'She knows what my uncle is like. And she knows what he's like around me.' Abby bristled with fury. 'He's a disgusting perv. And I've told her that. But she doesn't want to hear it. She said that I was a liar.'

'Has your uncle ever assaulted you in any way?' Andrea asked in a soft voice.

Abby shook her head. 'No, not really.'

'You were angry with your aunt so you thought you'd make it look like she had been involved in your murder?' Andrea asked to clarify.

'Yeah,' Abby replied. Then she looked at Andrea. 'I'm not going back there. And I've told my mum. She said she's going to sort it out.'

Andrea didn't like the sound of that. 'What did she mean *sort it out*?'

Abby shrugged. 'I dunno.'

Andrea looked over at Charlie and wondered if Gavin Spears was now in some kind of danger.

CHAPTER 72

HMP Tonsgrove, Anglesey
Sunday, 23 October
1.30 p.m.

Gareth and Ben pulled up in the car park of HMP Tonsgrove. Half an hour earlier, he had dropped Laura home
once she'd been checked over by the FME at Beaumaris
nick. She had another suspected cracked rib but nothing
more serious than that. Gareth knew that she was going to
be looked after by Rosie and Jake until he could get back.
She'd been through quite an ordeal and needed to rest.

Gareth was trying to get his head around the fact that
Abby White was alive and had faked her abduction and
murder. It was clear from what Andrea had told him that
Abby had very legitimate reasons to fear for her life. And
of course, he was glad that she was alive and safe. However the cost of their investigation in terms of man hours
and money spent was enormous. He was also trying to
work out how to handle the media furore that would no
doubt ensue, as well dealing with Warlow's reaction, which
would be focused on covering his own arse.

'Good timing,' Ben said as he pointed to a figure coming out of the prison and heading for a car.

It was David Rice: now their prime suspect in the investigation into Sheila Jones' murder.

Getting out of the car, Gareth slammed the car door with deliberate force.

Rice glanced over at the noise and then saw them approaching. His face fell.

'Everything all right?' Rice asked with a quizzical expression.

'We're going to need you to attend a formal interview at Beaumaris Police Station tomorrow morning at 9 a.m.,' Gareth said in a serious tone. 'We will also need to take your DNA and fingerprints at that time.'

Rice shrugged. 'I'll be bringing a lawyer with me,' he said with a slight sneer.

'That's your prerogative,' Gareth said with a raised eyebrow. 'We'll see you tomorrow.' Then Gareth stopped. 'By the way David, how tall are you?'

'Six foot two,' Rice said, looking bemused. 'Why?'

'No reason,' Gareth said as they turned and headed back to their car.

CHAPTER 73

Pen-y-garnedd
Sunday, 23 October
1.35 p.m.

Andrea and Charlie stood on the doorstep of Rose Cottage waiting for someone to answer the door.

The FLO eventually opened it.

'Everything okay?' Andrea asked her.

'Yes, ma'am,' the FLO replied. 'Actually, now that you've found Abby, I've been called back to the station.'

'Of course,' Andrea said.

The FLO shook her head. 'I can't believe what happened,' she said under her breath.

Andrea nodded. 'That's the thing about this job. Just when you think you've seen everything…'

Charlie gestured. 'Is Zoe in?'

'Yes,' the FLO replied. 'She's sitting outside on the patio.' The FLO pulled a face and whispered. 'She's been drinking again and she seems to think that Gavin has disappeared.'

Andrea didn't like the sound of that one bit. 'Disappeared?'

Charlie gave Andrea a dark look.

The FLO shrugged. 'She said that Gavin popped out to the garage to get something about an hour ago and he hasn't come back. She's not really making any sense.'

'Right, okay,' Andrea said, trying to process what the FLO had told them. It wasn't time to try to explain why Gavin's possible disappearance was concerning.

'Bye now,' the FLO said as she turned to go.

'Yes, bye,' Andrea said, feeling a little uneasy.

'We'd better go and talk to Zoe,' Charlie suggested.

They walked down the hallway, through the kitchen and out onto the patio as they had done before.

Zoe was on her second bottle of wine. She looked up as they approached.

'Have you seen her?' Zoe asked frantically.

'Yes,' Andrea said calmly. 'Don't worry, Abby's fine.'

'I've asked but they won't let me see her yet,' Zoe said, her voice slurring. 'When is she coming home?'

Andrea thought for a few seconds. 'I don't think that Abby is coming back here.'

'What?' Zoe looked horrified. 'What are you talking about?'

Andrea gave her a stern look. 'I think you know exactly what I'm talking about, Zoe. Abby is currently talking to social services as she is still a minor but I'm pretty sure they will agree that her living with Gavin is putting her in danger.'

'Don't be ridiculous,' Zoe sneered. 'She made all that stuff up about Gavin. None of it's true.'

Andrea fixed her with a stare. 'Zoe, you keep telling yourself that, but deep down you know exactly what was going on. And you failed to protect your own niece.'

Zoe got up from her chair but she was a little unsteady on her feet. 'Don't you dare talk to me like that!'

322

'Sit down! We don't have time for this,' Andrea said. 'We understand that you think that Gavin has disappeared.'

Zoe nodded. 'He went to the garage to get a step-ladder about an hour ago. I haven't seen him since.'

'Any idea where he might have gone?' Charlie asked.

'Nope.' Zoe shrugged. 'His car is still here so I don't understand it. Or maybe he's just decided to leave me. Who knows?'

Andrea looked at Charlie. 'Let's go and have a look.'

They walked across the patio and around the side of the house where the detached garage was situated.

The main up-and-over door to garage was still closed – and there was no sign of Gavin.

'Boss,' Charlie said as he pointed to something.

A set of keys were hanging in the lock of the garage.

Andrea gave him a dark look. 'This is not good.'

CHAPTER 74

Laura poured herself a third glass of white wine and lay back on the sofa in the living room. She'd had a shower, an hour's nap and was now in her dressing gown. Elvis was lying beside her on the rug as she stroked his head. The television was turned to BBC1 but the volume was turned down. There was some kind of game show on.

Jake and Rosie had been in and out since she got home, watching television, eating snacks and looking at their phones. As far as they were concerned, she'd been away at a residential course in North Wales. However, she got the distinct impression that there was something up with Rosie. She seemed to bristle every time Laura had tried to make any form of conversation.

Jake looked over and pointed to his phone. 'Harvey's online on Xbox. Can I go and play with him?'

'As long as you're not on it for the rest of the evening,' Laura said with a smile.

Jake danced out of the room, singing to himself.

As soon as he was gone, Rosie fixed her with a stare. 'You were in a prison?'

'What?' Laura said, completely thrown by her accusation.

'Don't lie to me, Mum,' Rosie said angrily. 'I know you were in a prison... undercover or something.'

Oh God, how do I get out of this?

'How do you know that?' Laura asked.

'I overheard Andrea talking to Gareth the other night,' Rosie explained. 'And then Gareth told me.'

'Did he? Great,' Laura groaned.

'Why did you lie to me about it?' Rosie demanded.

'I didn't want you to worry,' Laura said, trying to explain. 'And I couldn't tell Jake, could I?'

'I know that,' Rosie snapped. 'But I'm not a baby.' Then she narrowed her eyes. 'And what the hell were you doing in a prison? Was it to do with that woman who was killed a few days ago? I saw it on the news.'

'I can't talk about it, darling,' Laura said. 'But I'm fine aren't I?'

'But it sounded dangerous,' Rosie said.

'I promise you, I wasn't in any danger at all,' Laura said with a smile.

A figure appeared at the doorway.

It was Gareth.

'Hi,' he said, giving her a knowing look. 'You okay?'

Rosie looked between them. 'What's going on? Why wouldn't Mum be okay?'

Laura gave Gareth a forced smile. 'I was just telling Rosie that while I was working undercover, I wasn't in any danger at all. Was I?'

Gareth shook his head. 'No. Of course not. It was fairly routine stuff.'

Laura turned to look at Rosie. 'You see, darling. Nothing to worry about.'

Except that Rosie wasn't listening. Instead she was fixated by something on the television.

Glancing over, Laura realised that the BBC News was now on.

And to her horror, there was CCTV footage of a woman clinging to the roof of a van with the caption: Anglesey police officer tries to foil prison escape…

Oh shit! That's me!

Rosie's eyes widened in horror. Then she glared at Laura. 'Fairly routine! You're clinging to the top of a bloody van. On the news! How is that not dangerous?'

'What are we watching?' asked a voice.

It was Jake.

'NOTHING!' all three of them said in unison as Rosie grabbed the remote control and changed the channel.

CHAPTER 75

Beaumaris Police Station
Monday, 24 October 2022
09.30 a.m.

It was the following morning as Gareth leaned over and pressed the red recording button on the machine. There was a long electronic beep. Then he said, 'Interview conducted with David Rice, Monday, twenty-fourth of October, 9.30 a.m. Interview Room 1, Beaumaris Police Station. Present are David Rice, Detective Constable Ben Corden, Duty Solicitor Tony Ellis and myself, Detective Inspector Gareth Williams.'

Gareth settled himself back in his seat and pulled over a folder so that it was in front of him. He then looked over at Rice. 'Just so that you're aware, David, this is a voluntary interview but we are recording it in case anything you say needs to be used at trial. Do you understand that?'

'Yes,' Rice said with his usual annoying smirk.

'We need to ask you about the events on Monday morning on G wing at HMP Tonsgrove,' Ben explained.

Rice raised an eyebrow. 'We've been through all that already.'

'You claim that you were dealing with a case of minor theft at the time when Sheila Jones was murdered,' Ben said.

'That's right,' Rice said confidently.

Ben frowned. 'I assume there will be paperwork to prove that's what you were doing?'

Rice shook his head. 'No, there won't be. If I had to fill out paperwork every time a prisoner made an accusation of theft, I wouldn't be able to do my job.'

Gareth looked at him. 'Convenient though, isn't it?'

Rice snorted and looked at the Duty Solicitor.

'Do you want to explain to me why you think I had anything to do with Sheila Jones' murder?' Rice said.

'Did you have anything to do with her murder, David?' Gareth asked.

Rice laughed. 'No. Why would I?'

Gareth waited for a few seconds. 'We took your finger-prints this morning—'

'So what?' Rice snapped, interrupting him.

'Our forensic team has a fingerprint that we believe belongs to the person who murdered Sheila,' Gareth explained.

'Good for you,' Rice said with a grin.

'And I'm pretty sure that when we compare that fingerprint with yours, we're going to find a match,' Gareth stated.

'Yeah?' Rice said as he scratched at his nose. 'Well I'm *pretty sure* that they won't match because I wasn't there.'

Ben looked at him. 'You're sure about that?'

Rice furrowed his brow. 'You still haven't told me why I'm supposed to have wanted to murder Sheila Jones. I hardly knew the woman.'

Gareth ignored him and asked, 'How would you describe your relationship with Sanam Parveen?'

'Relationship? She's the governor of the prison where I work,' Rice said, but the question seemed to have rattled him a little.

'We have information that suggests that you and Sanam Parveen are in a romantic relationship,' Ben said. 'Is there anything you'd like to tell us about that?'

Rice stopped in his tracks. He was no longer smirking. 'Who told you that?'

'Are you in a romantic relationship with Sanam Parveen?' Gareth enquired.

'No, of course not,' Rice growled. 'I'm a happily married man.'

Gareth waited for a few seconds for the tension inside the interview room to build.

'What do you know about the Doyle family, David?' Gareth asked looking directly at him.

Rice's eyes roamed around the room for a few seconds. 'I don't know what you're talking about.'

'Come on, David,' Gareth said loudly. 'You know that the sale of drugs in Tonsgrove is partially controlled by the Doyle crime family who are based in Birmingham.'

Rice was visibly rattled. He turned to the Duty Solicitor, Tony Ellis and they talked for about a minute.

Ellis looked across the table. 'I'm advising my client not to answer any more questions in this interview.'

CHAPTER 76

An hour later, Gareth was in his office feeling the growing frustration of not being able to pin Sheila Jones' murder on David Rice. The good news was that Rice had reacted to both questions about his relationship with Sanam Parveen and his knowledge of the Doyle family. As far as Gareth was concerned, Rice's reaction had almost certainly proved his guilt.

As he sat back in his chair, he gave a loud sigh.

'Sounds like you might need some help?' said a familiar voice.

It was Laura and she was standing in the doorway.

He frowned. 'You're meant to be at home resting.'

'I got bored.' She shrugged with a half-smile. 'You know what I'm like.' She came into his office and pointed to a circular bruise on her temple. It was where Michael Doyle had pushed the handgun into her head. 'Look at this,' she said.

330

'Looks nasty,' Gareth said, leaning forward to have a look.

'Actually, it looks far worse than it is,' Laura admitted. 'But I'm happy to get sympathy for it.'

'I've had a call from the CPS,' Gareth said. 'Kayleigh Doyle and the pilot have pleaded not guilty to all charges.'

Laura shrugged. 'Not a big surprise.'

Andrea appeared in the doorway. 'We've got a problem, boss.'

'Right,' Gareth said trying not to sound disgruntled. 'Is it Gavin Spears?'

Andrea had already told him that Spears had gone missing the previous day and despite various enquiries, no one could find him.

Andrea gave him a dark look. 'A uniformed patrol have found a body on the beach on Newborough. Description and the clothes are an exact match for Gavin Spears.'

'Cause of death?' Gareth asked.

'Multiple stab wounds,' Andrea said.

'Christ,' Gareth said sitting back in his chair.

'My guess is that someone from the Doyle family travelled up from Birmingham and killed him in revenge for what he'd been doing to Abby,' Andrea said.

Gareth nodded. 'Sounds about right. You and Charlie had better get down there.'

'Yes, boss.' Andrea turned to go just as Ben arrived.

'Tell me you have some good news, Ben,' Gareth said with a tired smile.

Ben pulled a face. 'Do you want me to come back?' he joked.

'No,' Gareth said, rolling his eyes. 'What is it?'

'David Rice's fingerprints and DNA don't match the samples we found on Sheila Jones' body or in her cell,' Ben said.

'Shit!' Gareth growled, shaking his head. 'How is that possible?'

'Rice was our frontrunner, wasn't he?' Laura asked.

'He was our only runner at the moment.' Gareth groaned. He looked at Ben. 'I want us to run a PNC check on every male member of staff in that prison.'

'Actually, I've already started to do that,' Ben replied. 'There are only nineteen male members of staff there. The first eight PNC checks didn't show up anything.'

'That's great, Ben,' Gareth said, trying to keep his annoyance in check.

'There is something else, boss. Forensics have found something on that glass sample they found on Sheila Jones' body,' Ben explained. 'They want you to go and have a look.'

Gareth looked at Laura. 'Fancy a trip to forensics?'

'It's what I live for,' Laura joked.

CHAPTER 77

Beaumaris Police Station
Monday, 24 October 2022
10.59 a.m.

Laura and Gareth entered the forensic wing of Beaumaris nick and headed for the lab to their left. Laura could see that the investigation was starting to really get to Gareth.

The forensics lab was brightly illuminated with several rows of forensic equipment – microscopes, fume hoods, chromatographs and spectrometers – as well as vials and test tubes of brightly coloured liquids.

A lab technician in a full forensic suit, mask, and gloves approached them at the doorway. 'Can I help?' she asked.

'DI Hart and DI Williams,' Laura explained. 'We've just had a call in CID that you'd found something to do with a glass fragment?'

'Yes.' The lab technician nodded as she handed them forensic gloves and masks to put on. 'I'll take you over.'

They followed her over to see the chief lab technician, Nicola Sterling, whom Laura had met a few times since arriving at Beaumaris nick.

'DI Hart, DI Williams,' Nicola said from behind her mask. She was looking at a computer screen with a coloured graph on it.

'What have you got for us?' Gareth asked.

'We've been running some tests on that glass fragment that was found embedded in Sheila Jones' skin,' Nicola explained and then pointed to the screen. 'It had us stumped for a while, but I think we know what it is.'

'Go on,' Gareth said as he looked over at Laura. 'I need something positive, given the way my day is going.'

'Like that is it?' Nicola said pulling a face and then pointed at the coloured graph on the screen. 'The fragment is a tiny splinter of glass of from a pair of prescription glasses.'

Gareth looked deflated. 'Doesn't really help us that much.'

'Actually, we can tell the type of prescription from the shape and depth of the glass,' Nicola said. 'And the person wearing these glasses suffers from severe hypermetropia.'

Gareth and Laura looked none the wiser.

'In layman's terms, they have extreme long sightedness,' Nicola explained. 'Too extreme to be corrected by laser surgery. And probably characterised by very thick lenses.'

Laura immediately looked at Gareth. 'Barry McDonald.'

'What?'

'Barry McDonald has thick glasses,' she said. 'And his glasses have been broken very recently because he's only repaired them with a sticky plaster.'

Gareth's eyes widened. 'And he was the last person to talk to Sheila on Tuesday morning.'

'Thanks, Nicola,' Laura said as she and Gareth turned, took off their masks and gloves and headed for the doors out of the lab.

Laura frowned. 'We don't have motive though.'

As they looked up, Ben was hurrying down the corridor towards them. Whatever it was, it was urgent.

'Boss, we've got a hit on the PNC searches,' Ben explained, slightly out of breath.

'Barry McDonald?' Gareth asked.

Ben looked confused. 'How do you know that?'

Laura looked at Ben. 'We think that fragment of glass came from his glasses. Sheila must have punched him when he attacked her, broken his glasses and a tiny glass fragment became embedded in her arm.'

'What did you find?' Gareth asked.

'There are notes from the North Wales Substance Misuse Team on the file. McDonald used to live with his sister Lizzie in Wrexham,' Ben explained. 'This was about five years ago. His sister had just come out of rehab for heroin addiction and he was looking after her. One night he left her to go to work. She went out, scored some heroin and had died from an overdose by the time he got home.'

Laura raised an eyebrow. 'And the heroin was supplied by Sheila Jones?'

Ben shrugged. 'It doesn't say on the notes. But it would be a fair bet.'

'Let's get him in,' Gareth said.

CHAPTER 78

Beaumaris Police Station
Monday, 24 October 2022
12.30 p.m.

Gareth leaned over and pressed the red recording button on the machine. There was a long electronic beep. Then he said, 'Interview conducted with Barry McDonald, Monday, twenty-fourth of October, 12.30 p.m. Interview Room 2, Beaumaris Police Station. Present are Barry McDonald, Detective Inspector Laura Hart, Duty Solicitor Tony Ellis and myself, Detective Inspector Gareth Williams.'

Barry sat on his seat looking lost in thought. He hadn't said a word since Gareth had arrested him at HMP Tonsgrove.

'Barry?' Gareth said as he settled himself in his seat. 'Do you understand that you have been charged with Sheila Jones' murder, contrary to common law?'

Barry looked over at them with a deadpan expression. 'Of course.'

Laura pulled over a file. 'For the purposes of the tape, I'm showing the suspect Item Reference 394H.' She pulled out a document and turned it to show Barry. 'This is a police report from Wrexham Police Station from the thirteenth of September 2018. You were arrested for loitering with intent and being in possession of a knife in a public place for which you received a six-month suspended sentence and a fine. Can you tell us what you were doing that night?'

Barry shrugged. 'I was waiting outside Sheila Jones' flat.'

Laura raised an eyebrow. 'And why were you doing that?'

'I think you know why,' Barry said calmly. 'I was waiting to kill her.'

Laura exchanged a look with Gareth. This wasn't how they were expecting the interview to go.

'Why did you want to kill Sheila Jones?' Laura asked.

'She sold my sister the heroin that killed her,' Barry said with no hint of emotion. 'So, I wanted her dead.'

Barry then leaned into to talk to the Duty Solicitor for a few seconds.

The Duty Solicitor nodded and then looked over at them. 'My client has decided that he will be pleading guilty to the murder of Sheila Jones in this interview. And he is willing to fully co-operate in this interview as long as that is taken into consideration when it comes to sentencing.'

Gareth nodded. 'Yes, I will make it clear in my report to the judge that Barry has co-operated, if he can tell us everything we need to know today.'

Gareth then looked over at Laura trying to hide his surprise. They had both assumed that Barry would be pleading not guilty.

Before they could ask another question, Barry leant forward slowly and said in a cold, monotone voice, 'I'm going to make this very easy for you now. Sheila Jones effectively murdered Lizzie that night. It was unforgivable.

And from that day, I swore that I would avenge my sister. Shortly after I was picked up in Wrexham that night, Sheila Jones was arrested for possession and intent to supply Class A drugs. At first I thought that I'd lost my chance to kill her for a long time. But I followed Sheila's case and I eventually secured myself a job teaching English and Humanities at HMP Tonsgrove about a year ago. I spent the next twelve months meticulously planning to kill her.' Barry looked at them with an almost expressionless face. 'And then last Monday, I did just that. And now I'm content that my sister has been avenged.' Barry then sat back in his seat. 'There really isn't anything else to say, is there?'

Gareth found Barry's clinical version of events chilling. He looked over at him. 'You will be held here or in a suitable prison until we can secure a sentencing hearing at the Crown Court at Mold. That shouldn't take more than two to three days. Is there anything else you'd like to tell us today before you're taken away?'

Barry took a deep breath and then nodded. 'Actually I'd like it to go on record that I feel no remorse for what I've done and I hope that Sheila Jones rots in hell.'

CHAPTER 79

12 weeks later

Laura stood in the chilly vestibule of the church. *Eglwys Bach y Mor – the church in the sea.* Her legs felt wobbly and her hands were shaking slightly with nerves.

She looked at her sister, Emma, who, because of her MS, was now walking with a stick, and Rosie, her two beautiful bridesmaids. They had tiny white flowers in their hair.

'God, I'm nervous,' Laura said. 'Why am I so bloody nervous?'

'It's your wedding day,' Emma suggested with a loving smile. 'You are actually meant to be nervous.'

Laura pulled a face. 'But I'm nearly fifty and I've got two kids.'

Rosie reached over to the pew beside her and handed her a small can of gin and tonic. 'Maybe you haven't drunk enough, Mum.'

'Rosie!' Emma said with mock horror. 'We're meant to be looking after her, not getting her hammered.'

'Bollocks,' Laura said with a shrug and took two huge

swigs of G&T. Rosie probably had a point. 'That's better,' she sighed.

Jake appeared from around the corner. He was dressed in a smart dark blue suit with a waistcoat. His hair had been immaculately coiffured back.

'Mum? We're ready,' Jake whispered with an excited grin and then gave her an enthusiastic thumbs up.

Laura looked at Emma and Rosie. 'Aww, he looks so handsome and grown up,' she said, feeling like her heart might melt.

Music started to play. She and Gareth had chosen 'The Lark Ascending' by Vaughan Williams. The soaring notes of the violin seemed to fill the air.

'Right. Better get on with it then,' Laura whispered with a nervous laugh.

Composing herself, she stood upright and walked slowly into the aisle. Rosie and Emma walked behind her.

The whole church had been filled with candles and lanterns. It looked like a magical winter wonderland.

The dozen or so guests stood and looked back down at her as she walked. She felt a little overwhelmed. The aisle seemed to go on forever.

Laura glanced to her right and saw Ben. Looking incredibly smart in his navy blue suit, he gave her a grin.

In the next row, Andrea caught her eye and smiled. She was standing next to Charlie. They had come together and Laura was so incredibly happy that Andrea had found someone she really liked.

As Laura reached the front of the church, Gareth turned to look at her. Their eyes met and he gave her a reassuring smile and then a sexy wink.

Taking a deep breath, Laura felt a tear in the corner of her eye.

Oh come on, Laura, get a grip.

Having refused to wear a traditional dress of any kind, Laura was wearing a cream-coloured fitted jacket with three-quarter-length sleeves and a full lace skirt. She held a simple bouquet of white roses. Her hair was loosely pinned up with the same white flowers that Emma and Rosie were wearing.

As she joined Gareth at the altar, she looked down and saw that her hands were shaking.

'Hey,' Gareth whispered looking into her eyes. 'You look absolutely beautiful.'

Laura smiled. 'You're not so bad yourself.'

They both laughed a little too loudly and it echoed around the church.

Gareth reached over, took her hand and gave it a squeeze.

Then he looked over at Jake and whispered. 'You got the ring, mate?'

Jake's face fell as he frantically patted all his pockets before he eventually found it in his trouser pocket and then held it up triumphantly.

'Got it!' he said loudly.

Laughter rang around the church, followed by a smattering of applause.

The vicar looked out and said 'Dearly beloved...'

AUTHOR NOTE

This book is very much a work of fiction. It's nothing more than a story that is the product of my imagination. It is set in Anglesey, a beautiful island off North Wales that is steeped in history and folklore spanning over two thousand years. It is therefore worth mentioning that I have made liberal use of artistic licence. Some names, places and even myths have been changed or adapted to enhance the pace and substance of the story. There are roads, pubs, garages and other amenities that don't necessarily exist on the real island of Anglesey.

It's important for me to convey how warm, friendly and helpful the inhabitants of Anglesey have always been on my numerous research visits. The island itself is stunning and I hope that my descriptions of its landscape and geography have done it some justice.

ACKNOWLEDGEMENTS

Thank you to everyone who has worked so hard to make this book happen. The incredible team at Avon who are an absolute dream to work with. Sarah Bauer and Helen Huthwaite for their patience, guidance and superb notes. The other lovely people at Avon – Elisha Lundin, Raphaella Demetris, Becky Hunter and Maddy Dunne-Kirby, as well as Toby James in the art team, who produced such a fantastic cover; Katie Buckley in the sales team; and Francesca Tuzzeo in production, without whom this book wouldn't exist.

To my superb agent, Millie Hoskins, at United Agents. Emma and Emma, my fantastic publicists at EDPR. Dave Gaughran and Nick Erick for their ongoing advice and working their magic behind the scenes.

Finally, my mum, Pam, and dad, Dave for their overwhelming enthusiasm. And, of course, my stronger, better half, Nicola, whose initial reaction and notes on my work I trust implicitly.

If you loved *Dead in the Water,*
why not go back to the beginning of the
Anglesey series?

Will there be blood in the water?

The first book in Simon McCleave's gripping
crime thriller series.
Available in all good bookshops now.

Some secrets should stay buried for ever...

The second book in Simon McCleave's pulse-pounding crime thriller series.

Available in all good bookshops now.

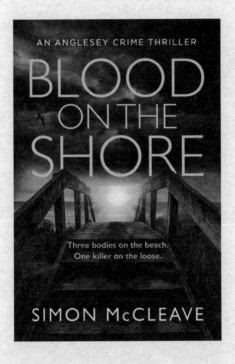

Some secrets will always surface...

The fourth book in Simon McCleave's pulse-pounding crime thriller series.

Available in all good bookshops now.

Your FREE book is waiting for you now!

Get your FREE copy of the prequel to the
DI Ruth Hunter Series NOW!

Visit:
http://www.simonmccleave.com/vip-email-club
and join Simon's VIP Email Club.